LOVE ONE ANOTHER
Stories of Justus and Mercy Part 2

RE Russell

Love One Another, Stories of Justus and Mercy Part 2
Copyright @ 2023 RE Russell

All rights reserved. No part of this publication may be reproduced or transmitted in any form or by any electronic or mechanical means including photo copying, recording, or any information storage and retrieval system now known or to be invented, without permission in writing from the publisher or the author.

Cover illustration:
Author photo: Mary Denman, used by permission

ISBN: 978-1-955309-52-3

Published by EA Books Publishing, a division of
Living Parables of Central Florida, Inc. a 501c3

EABooksPublishing.com

To Janie

Carlisle Divided Stories of Justus and Mercy Part 1
won Best Religious Fiction from
Next Generation Indie Book Awards 2023

Included to promote story continuity from Part 1 to Part 2 of the series.

APRIL

CHAPTER 40

CARLISLE DIVIDED STORIES OF JUSTUS AND MERCY PART 1

José awoke with a start to the vibration of his mobile phone ringing. He shook the cobwebs from his head and made his way to the night table where the phone gyrated.

"Hola."

"José, this is Jackie. Is that you?"

"Si, ah yes, it's me."

"I tried to reach you at the restaurant this morning, but Ramone said you were out. He said you were in a bad place yesterday. I hope you're feeling better."

"Not much better yet. Unless you tell me all I heard yesterday was fake news."

"You know I don't do fake news, my friend."

"So, no, not much better. Any word on Hamsa?"

"He's still being held without bail, in solitary, for his protection. That's what I'm calling for. I want to hear what happened in the interrogation room earlier. I would've done it yesterday but with the whole Wyz deal happening, I didn't have time. Are you well enough to meet me for some lunch in an hour or so?"

José checked the clock and noticed it was after ten. *I must've been exhausted yesterday.* He looked out the window at the sunshine and thought about other sunny days in far more beautiful places.

"Hello, José, you still there? Look, I got you in to see Hamsa, you owe me a story."

"I guess I do. Give me the place and the time and I'll be there. Not Restaurant Tapas please."

"I'll come by and pick you up. We can go someplace downtown."

He remembered the last woman who gave him a ride and thought about turning her down. *Maybe if I accepted Susan's invitation back then my friends would've been spared.*

He did want to see Jackie and he did need some information about what else was happening in town. "Come by around 11:30, so we can beat the crowds."

He gave his address and hung up. He noticed he had other missed calls too from Ramone, Tony, Father Menendez, Amena and Erica Miller. He decided to get cleaned up before he had any further conversations. It took a while to clean things after all the blood. He did the best he could with what he had and made himself presentable. A shower and shave. A new man he mocked himself in the mirror. *Perhaps it's time for some conversation and a different perspective.*

She picked him up in a late model white SUV. She was dressed for spring on camera. "You look very bright and refreshing this morning," he said, when he got in. He was in jeans and a burgundy striped shirt. The car smelled like Jackie's perfume. It had the scent of a friend.

"Thank you, Señor Chef. I wish I could say the same for you. You don't look so good my friend. Have you been sick? Too much spicy food?" She smiled trying to lighten his mood.

He looked into those delightful hazel eyes. They had a turquoise tone today. Even that didn't cheer him. "I'm in a dark place right now. Much I've worked these many months to achieve, has come apart, in just a few short days."

"Wow, you weren't kidding. This is gonna be a barrel of laughs."

Sardonic Jackie. Please be kind. I need a tender ear now. "Where are we going for lunch?"

"It's on the station, but the budget is limited. There is an all you can eat sushi place in the BNS building. Is that OK?"

"Yes, that sounds good."

She parked in the deck, and they walked over. "They validate, if you eat here."

They were seated opposite each other, in a quiet booth, with a dark tabletop and faux candle on one side. Bottles of soy sauce nearby. One each, regular and low sodium. They each ordered various types of sushi along with fried rice. Jackie pulled out her phone and stylus to signal the beginning of the interview.

"This is a question that has bugged me since our Valentine's dinner back in February. How does a chef from Villa Maya speak Syrian?"

"I grew up in the middle east. Semitic languages are similar although dialects do vary."

"So, you're an Arab?"

"No, I'm the other one."

"You're a Jew."

"Yes, that's how I was born. I've been reborn a Christian and try to follow the Master now."

"I think I know this part. He leads you all over to help you do good, etc."

The plates of sushi rolls arrived, and each went through the required ritual of creating a custom soy sauce and wasabi bath to compliment the food.

As he finished with his sauce, he took a bite of his eel roll. He enjoyed the sensation of dining and paused to let it register. Then he continued his explanation. "The Master used to lead me. Now, I'm not so sure. I came here to help clear the hate and stop the killing. To show the Master's love to those who'll listen. Now, I find that nothing I've done has made any difference at all. In fact, I think I made it worse. Jeremiah's dead, who knows what will happen to Carafe Homes now. My young friend, Hamsa, is accused of terrorism. Two boys are dead who were full of hate. Gang members are being killed in a gang war the conversion Da Wyz helped start. My friend Pastor Rich is being removed from his leadership role by a renegade group of haters too. I've caused too much pain in this place. I need to go."

Jackie finished a piece of a tuna roll and pointed at him with her chopsticks.

"So, you're facing some resistance and now you're going to run. You didn't strike me as the type to back down from a fight. I thought that's what you were picking all along."

"I don't run often, but I try to pick fights I can win. This one seems hopeless. Carlisle is lost to me."

At that comment, Jackie's tone changed in a marked way. She cocked her head to one side and moved from sympathetic friend to defender of her city. "Look José, or whatever name you're calling yourself today, this is the real world. If you push powerful people, they're going to push back. What's the old saying, *an eye for an eye*? If you're not ready to play in the adult version of this game you're right, you should go. This place has ugliness no question, but it's not all evil. Right now, there's a boy in jail who needs a friend. His only one is planning on leaving town. There's an initiative that's working for affordable housing, that was your idea. It needs leadership now. Yet, you're planning on leaving town. The Pastor Rich thing is news to me, but if it is so, you have a friend who followed your instructions. Who is now in need. Yet you're leaving town. There's even a news lady who started to believe again in the goodness we all have in us, because of your message of hope." She swallowed hard. "Yet, you have no hope. I guess this was all a foolish dream. Now, it's time for the dreamer to wake up and face reality. Looks like you don't like the alarm call. Time to decide José, Yosef, Joseph, Justus are you going to play or run? I think you need to suck it up, buttercup."

At that, she took another bite of Sushi.

José looked down at his plate, not very hungry. Her comments stung. He didn't speak.

"So, if you're leaving town, I want to know what happened in the interrogation room, before you go."

José spoke about Hamsa's interview for a few minutes. Lunch went on in a distant, professional way for a time. After he could stand it no longer, he said, "I gave you what you asked for. Our business is complete. We're even now. I'll take the bus back to VM, I'm sure you have many stories to chase."

"José, I don't want us to end this way. I spoke harshly but . . ."

He raised his hand to stop her, "Jackie, thank you for lunch, but I must go now. There are no other words we need to speak."

On the journey back to Maria's boarding house, he thought about all she said. He didn't have much fight left in him. His hope drained away. She spoke truth, perhaps not in love, but truth none the less. He realized that today was Good Friday. He didn't want to see any of his *allies*, so he made his way to a Tenebrae service at a Methodist Church Up the Hill. Tenebrae is Latin for *darkness*. That's just what he felt. The service progressed in silence with images of famous paintings of Christ's Passion displayed progressing through the stations of the cross. Paintings by Ciseri, El Greco, Rubens, Caravaggio, Raphael and Velazquez. José remembered when each was unveiled for the first time. The ever-increasing darkness of the service remembering the crucifixion suited his mood well. Remembering the crucifixion and all that led up to it, was just like watching it again. The betrayal, the arrest, the fleeing of friends into the night, the fake trials, the Roman Governor washing his hands. And worst of all, the crowds shouting, "Crucify him!" He wept for Jesus, his Master, for himself, for Carlisle, for so many consumed by the darkness of hate and fear he had known through the ages. A darkness that is tangible tonight.

SUNDAY IS ON THE WAY

I watched as they made you carry your cross,
I know now you would never have put it down.
You provided the way back through your loss,
It was so sadistic to make you wear their crown.

I wept helpless as you struggled by
I didn't understand why it had to be this way.
You were the Christ not a criminal to try,
This showed the worst of us in the light of the day.

Dear Father why must he suffer so?
Surely another way can be found.
I watched as your blood dripped on the road,
Closed my eyes until I heard the cross hit the ground.

The soldiers cleared the path as you stumbled along.
They grabbed another to shoulder the load.
He tried to turn away get lost in the throng,
But with threats they dragged him back in the road.

To Golgotha they led all the long way.
They thought they would kill you but we both know now
You gave your life willingly this day.
Despite my despair, it would be better somehow.

The Darkness upon us
Despite the noon hour,
I could feel it engulf us
Dark ways seem to have so much power.

The crucifixion so cruel, so bloody, so brutal,
Yet your concern was for those nearby,
The ones who believed their hope now futile—
The soldiers, the thieves, your mother and I.

I wanted it to end long before it was finished
This darkest of days.
At the end it sounded like even your hope diminished
But Sunday is on the way.

APRIL

CHAPTER 1

The dawn of a fresh springtime Saturday came with songbirds and a beautiful sunrise. José didn't sleep much last night, but the new day inspired flickers of hope within.

A knock on the door of his one room with bath apartment, interrupted his contemplation. "Señor José," Maria said and then in Spanish. "You have visitors señor. Please come down to the main room."

"Si señora. Un momenta por favor."

José moved away from his window and let the curtain fall as he headed toward the mirror to be sure he was presentable. He shaved quickly, combed his wavy black hair and donned a large tan T-shirt and comfortable jeans. He came down and was delighted to see Reverend Tony and Ms. Roberta smiling at him. At six-foot three-inches, Tony seemed to tower over Roberta's diminutive frame. He still looked like the football lineman he once was. An imposing figure in the AME Zion pulpit no doubt. Roberta, now well in her sixties appeared frail but was anything but.

"Joseph we're very concerned about you," Tony said as he reached out a hand, then pulled him in for a big hug when José reached out to shake it.

Roberta gave him a hug that seemed beyond the physical capacity of that dear lady. Joseph resisted at first then just let it warm him from the inside out.

They moved over to a sitting area for coffee. The room had two wingback chairs Maria must have picked up at a second-hand shop and a sofa that almost matched. A small oval coffee table completed the space. The wood floor creaked as they moved out of the foyer. José and Roberta each took a chair and Tony took the sofa.

"Joseph, I'm not pulling any punches. This is going to be a tough time for us. However, I know you're in a dark place. I've been there myself. The *dark night of the soul*, I heard it called in seminary. You do everything you think is right and it all goes wrong. The Lord doesn't speak to you. You can't tell what happens next. You want to run away. I bet you've been there before this time too."

"Tony, someday I'll tell you more, but these seem to get darker and longer each time I endure them. Not sure I can do this anymore. All I've worked for is undone. Jeremiah was a key. He had the wealth, the story and the desire to make a lasting difference. Without him we're worse than when we started."

"Look at me. I can see you, because you let God work through you. I'm not undone. We've helped to clean-up the area where I live, because of your gift. D is out of the Biz because of you, I'm convinced. Reggie is back in the old neighborhood doing good, just like I've prayed over the years, because of you. Evil isn't the only thing moving here. That's why it's lashing out so strong. You're attacking a stronghold. Evil doesn't surrender a fortress without a fight," Ms. Roberta said.

Tony continued the thought, "Evil triumphed last night, didn't it? But you know the way the old sermon goes—'Sunday's comin'. Joseph we're here to remind you—God works through you. Da Wyz, eh Jeremiah died but thanks to your obedience, he's with Jesus, not the enemy. You know that frosts Satan in a big way. The gangs're fighting, but they did that before you got here. It just shows your work isn't done yet. We need you here. You just got some setbacks. Call your spirit back to us, you're welcome and needed. Come to Jeremiah's funeral Monday, I think you'll be blessed by it. Come to our Sunday service tomorrow.

Be encouraged my friend. It's a dark night. Day will return. Even with Jesus in the grave God was still in control. The enemy thought he won Friday night. He knew he bit off more than he could chew when Jesus showed up to minister to the dead on that Saturday long ago. Evil was about to get the surprise of the ages on Sunday."

Joseph took in a deep breath and let it out slowly. He leaned toward his friends. "Tony, Roberta, your visit means more than you know. Thank you for coming. I have many thoughts to fight through now, but your words and the words of another are bringing me around. The Master and I still must make peace on these matters. I don't want to go on for fear of others being harmed by my actions. I don't want to be responsible."

"You can't take all this on yourself. You're not Superman, are you? This is God's work, we're the vessels, remember. A wise man told me that a few weeks ago. Let God be God, and let man be man. He's not finished with Carlisle yet and he's not finished with you. 'Be strong and courageous, God is with you.' I paraphrase what God said to Joshua before he conquered Canaan. The same phrase you uttered to Pastor Rich in my office a couple of weeks ago."

They enjoyed their coffee and Maria brought over some muffins she baked. They exchanged stories of the past few weeks. Joseph felt some release from his friend's contagious optimism, but deep remorse still haunted him. *Am I sufficient for this task? Am I worthy? Where are you my Lord?*

"You look tired my friend. Be encouraged, we both know God isn't done here yet. Let's pray together and then we'll let you rest," Tony said.

✣ ✣ ✣

Early the next morning José went to a Sunday sunrise service at Iglesia Pentecostal Camino a La Paz. The name, The Road to Peace, caught his attention earlier on his walks around Villa Maya and he wanted to visit when the time was right. Here he praised the God of his salvation and began to feel the night lifting.

Ushers walked the aisles with boxes of tissues for those that needed them. José took a handful when they offered to him. During this service he surrendered himself once more. He kneeled face to his chair in the middle of the service while the new day dawned, he prayed.

"Lord, I know you aren't capricious like the false gods of old. I know you are good and always seek the best for those who love you. I know that no matter how long I live, I'll never be a sinless man. You know the plan, I don't. You are God, and I am not. I vowed a long time ago to follow you wherever you led. I've kept that vow over the years, but you know it hasn't been without missing the mark at times. Master, please forgive me for believing I'm good enough to earn your favor. That I can do enough good to make you do what I want. You love me because you made me and because of who you are, not because I earned it with obedience and good works. Forgive me now. Show me what you would have me do. I can and do trust you because you are God, and I am man."

As he left the service rejoicing in his heart again at the resurrection, he felt led to visit the Church of Carlisle for their eleven o'clock Sunday service. With the holiday bus schedule, he could just make it in time. When he entered, he was greeted by one of the ushers at the door who smiled and stated, "He is risen!"

Justus repeated the customary response with great vigor, "He is risen indeed!"

He found one of the few remaining open seats in the back of the sanctuary to see what the Lord was going to do next in this place.

SUNRISE

What is possible
At a new day's dawn
Night is gone
Though yesterday's trouble is real
Today is fresh

How will I deal
Dwell in the past
Or enjoy the sunrise
What is possible

Is it yesterday again
Will something new begin
We only believe it cannot change
Because we do not let it

We are what must change with the new day
We must not let our pride hold us in place
Our desire to be right in front of us
Yes, change means we were wrong
But to ponder this means we can be better

The world changed around us
We were a part of what was wrong
What is right we can be a part of now

Are you a sunset or a sunrise
You are the one who chooses

Listen or Don't

APRIL

CHAPTER 2

Justus could feel the Spirit moving in the nondenominational congregation of the Church of Carlisle this Easter Sunday as Pastor Rich's sermon stirred their hearts. The Church with well over one thousand members served a congregation Up the Hill in Carlisle. Pastor Richard Taylor led the church for the past couple years after moving from other churches out of state. His resume both long and successful created mixed feelings among the other large churches in the Carlisle area. Some looked upon him with suspicion about his ambition to be a megachurch pastor while others embraced his inclusive style. He loved his family, especially his wife Maryanne. His salt and pepper hair, good looks, welcoming smile and gentle demeanor drew people to him.

Excerpts from today's message Justus found particularly inspirational included the parts where Rich said, "Brothers and Sisters, I have a new appreciation for our Lord when he was betrayed by one of his own this Holy Week. I too felt that when a group of our members confronted me about my March sermons on poverty. They didn't listen to the Kol Yahweh. They listened to their own biases and ambitions. They sought their own glory not the glory of God. I too, listened to them and not the voice of God. I planned to resign and see what God had next for me and my family. After fervent prayer and many days of fasting, it's apparent to me that God wants me right here in Carlisle continuing to shepherd this congregation. While my story does not end in death and resurrection, it does end in resuscitation. My ministry here is alive and well."

Rich went on further to say, "When it comes to those who did betray us, let us not look upon them with harsh judgment, but extend the love and mercy of Christ to them this Easter season."

He closed the service with a challenge Justus praised the Master for.

"I also want us to put our money where our mouth is. I'm announcing that we'll kick off a fund-raising drive to help the poor in Carlisle to obtain affordable housing. We have one hundred thousand dollars we saved from the building as seed money, but I want us to raise over one million dollars to create a rent subsidy endowment. We'll work with the endowment created by the late Jeremiah Michaels, our brother in Christ these last few months, to get more families out of poverty and into housing close to great schools. To show support the elder body has pledged another three hundred thousand to this goal. We're forty percent of the way there and we've just started. Please pray over what God would have you do to help our neighbors at this time."

After the service, Pastor Rich came over. "Justus, I saw you from the pulpit, I had to find you before you got away. Please join me and the kids for lunch. There is so much to share with you."

"Rich, how is it that you're preaching today? What have I missed?" Justus asked.

"Come to lunch, Maryanne had to leave after the early service to visit her mom who's ill, but I have the kids and a few others from church coming to the house. It's a wonderful story to share. Especially if you can stand my Easter lunch without my wife's amazing cooking."

They dined over honey glazed ham, potato salad, deviled eggs, green beans and much more. The group ate around a large dining table with a bright pastel purple tablecloth. The wooden ladder-back chairs had comfortable beige fabric seats. The room painted light gray had lots of family photos dotting the walls.

Justus enjoyed seeing the younger children vying for the last piece of apple pie á la mode. Pastor Rich settled the tussle by giving one the ice cream and the other the pie.

Justus, Pastor Rich, Wes Meisner, his wife Nanette and a couple of other elders who joined them for lunch now moved to the study. Everyone got a refill of iced tea or coffee. The children went outside to play frisbee. They were all seated around a large coffee table with a large Bible in the middle. The chairs all matched with the sofa and love seat. Walls painted light yellow complimenting the green and brown furnishings well. Sunlight streamed into the room from the two floor length windows on the far side.

"Now that everyone is fed, I can tell you the story. Wow, where to start?" Rich focused his attention on Justus.

Wes, who looked to be beyond retirement age with silver hair slicked back with glistening hair gel, said, "No Pastor, let me help you with this story. As you guys know, Randall Pendergraph preached the past two Sundays. He stayed away from any controversial subjects and made sure not to mention poverty. The first Sunday he spoke on the accuracy of Scripture. Last Sunday was Palm Sunday, so, after all the kids marched in waving green paper palm branches and shouting Hosanna, he just had speakers read about the Triumphal Entry from all four Gospels and gave a very short message."

"He did tell us what Hosanna means, but that's all I got out of the message," said Nannette from across the room. She wasn't as lean as Wes but still had a commanding presence and a booming voice. This was a powerful couple dedicated to the Master's kingdom, Justus could tell.

"Randall said he was going to continue the series in Matthew that I interrupted to do the poverty series," Rich said. "Officially I was *on a scheduled leave*."

Nanette, chimed in again, "Rumors flew all over the church. Since Rich hadn't resigned, we all tried to figure out the reason for his absence."

"Monday of Holy Week, the day before those two boys, Stu and Jimmy, died in the bombing. What a horrible thing that was. Anyway, Wes came to see me right here, unannounced," said Pastor Rich.

"I rang the bell at 9 am. Maryanne answered. She looked confused. 'May I see Rich, please?'" Wes said.

"She told me, 'He doesn't want to see anyone from the church right now.'"

"I need to know what's going on. I talk to the staff and get the run around. I want to speak with Rich. Get it from the horse's mouth so to speak. Her confusion cleared and she asked, 'So, you don't know?'"

"No ma'am, I'm in the dark. I've been traveling in Asia and just returned. Rich didn't return any of my calls. The time difference made it very hard to keep up. I'm the chair of the Elder Council. I need to know if I can help. 'Let me check and see,' she said."

"I wasn't sure who to trust at that point but agreed to visit with you," Rich said. "Maryanne brought us some coffee. You still had jet lag from all that travel. She's only been gone a few hours, but boy do I miss her being here today." Rich paused.

"Anyway, I told Wes, the church doesn't want me anymore. I got the message loud and clear from Paul Stanley, Thomas Spratt, Randall and a few others. It hit me like a wrecking ball. I've been holed up here fasting and praying for the Father's direction ever since. I have no clear direction from the Spirit on this now. I overstepped on the poverty series. I hit too many people in the comfort zone. In the name of church unity, I think it best that I resign."

Wes took over the narrative now. "I told Rich that I didn't know about any of this. Paul Stanley and the rest are just power-hungry jerks. I tried to keep my language under control. They didn't speak for the church or the Elder Council. They're part of it but not a majority. What you did took great courage and showed remarkable leadership. I was proud to support you then and am proud to support you now. Let me speak to some of the other elders and see if we can address this. This is wrong and we need to make it right. I'll call a council meeting for this

Wednesday. Please don't resign before then. I have a better idea, work up a wiz bang Easter message. We want to hear from you Easter Sunday and a whole bunch more after that."

"Wow, what an answer to prayer. God showed me I was not as alone as I felt. The Spirit touched me so at that point I could barely speak. I was no longer alone," Pastor Rich said.

"I told him 'Pastor, you know that better than me.' I can assure you there are many who want you in our pulpit," Wes continued.

"When I left, I had to give Maryanne a big hug. She'd been crying I could tell. I told her God's gonna make this right, I know it. They waited until I was gone to pull this stunt. Now I'm back and determined to make this right. No, wait. Maryanne, that's the business executive in me speaking. I'm not going to make it right. Our sweet Lord will make it right. Then it will be made right indeed. Rich did nothing wrong. I hugged her again and she sobbed on my shoulder. I cried too. I'm old school so I still carry a handkerchief. By the time we were done, I didn't know who needed it more." Now Wes paused and took a sip of his iced tea.

"The Elder Council couldn't all meet until yesterday morning at 9. Paul and Thomas tried to delay or cancel it all week but at last, all were present except Pastor Rich. Randall sat in Rich's place," Wes said.

"I told 'em, Ladies and gentlemen, we have a crisis we need to address. There's a small group of church members who call themselves, United for Jesus, that want Pastor Rich to resign over the sermon series he did on poverty in Carlisle. This group of cowards didn't see fit to try to present their case to this entire body, but instead went around us straight to the Pastor. They waited until I was overseas for two weeks to be sure I couldn't intervene. They represented themselves falsely, speaking for the church and tried to bully Pastor Rich out. They even went so far as to tell the Pastor that if he didn't resign with discretion and soon, they'd begin spreading rumors about him, assassinating his character. Elders, this is wrong and must be addressed. I charge Paul Stanley, Thomas Spratt and Randall Pendergraph of this group with the aforementioned charges. Gentlemen, what do you have to say for yourself? How do you answer this?"

Paul spoke for the group, "I don't like being called a coward or a liar. I may bring you up on charges of assassinating my character. What you say has some truth to it, but we presented the views of many in the church to Pastor Rich. Pastor Randall pointed out flaws in his sermons that Rich ignored. We're concerned about the unity of the body and felt it our duty as leaders to present the case to Pastor Rich and not wait for your return. He took it hard and never offered a defense. He left the pulpit empty. We had to scramble to get Randall to fill in for him. He put the church at risk. He put church unity at risk, and he needs to go. We made no threats to Pastor Rich. I don't know what he heard."

Wes said, "I looked at Thomas, 'is that what you recall also?'"

"I stand with Paul," he said.

"Then I looked at Randall. 'Randall, what about you? A man who reads and follows God's Word. A man who wants to lead his own church someday. An ordained minister of God's Word. You preached two Sundays ago about the authority of his word. In it, you know it says you will not bear false witness. What do you say?'

"He told me, 'Wes, I disagreed with Pastor Rich on his poverty sermons and still do. I think he overstepped his bounds as a Pastor and distorted God's word in his sermons to twist us to a radical way of thinking. God's word compels me to speak truth. As much as it pains me to say it, Paul and Thomas are wrong. He didn't leave the pulpit vacant; he was coerced. We did threaten to impugn the Pastor with rumors, if he didn't comply. In fact, and it grieves me to say it, I know they've been spreading rumors these past couple of weeks since he hasn't resigned. I'm not ashamed of my part in this but I am ashamed to be associated with these two who claim to know Christ but have such a deep-seated prejudice that has blinded them to the truth.'

"Paul said some ugly words about Randall's heritage and threatened him with never working in Carlisle again. He couldn't contain himself.

"I looked at the council and said, I think we can accept the resignations of Paul Stanley and Thomas Spratt from the elder body effective immediately. Gentlemen, please leave the room.

"Paul and Thomas both got up, shoving chairs under the table, slamming the door on the way out.

"Then I turned to Randall and thanked him for his honesty but asked for his resignation from this council and from our church also effective immediately. I told him we'll arrange a severance package for you, so your family is cared for. Then said, 'please leave this meeting now.'"

"I then looked around at the remaining eight members of the council. It was scary to see. Some had ashen faces, some had red faces. All were confused and grieved by what they witnessed.

"Let's have a short recess before we consider further business," someone suggested.

"I left the room and called Pastor Rich. My fingers were shaking as I dialed. Please come to the church now if you can."

We waited about twenty minutes for everyone to collect their thoughts and settle down. I saw Rich arrive in the parking lot so decided it was time to reconvene, we began to review what we heard and saw. Most were ashamed. After a prayer for wisdom, I said, "We need to decide if we want Pastor Rich to lead us going forward. It'll be a simple 'yes or no' vote. Write it on a piece of paper and drop it in the offering plate I'll send around. Once we get that answer, we can decide what happens next."

"The vote was unanimous to keep Pastor Rich. I held each one up so all could see eight yes votes. Just then, Pastor Rich knocked on the door.

"The entire council applauded, got up and gave him a big hug. There were tears of joy flowing all over the place as we told him of the vote."

Rich now took up the story, "Brothers and sisters, I told them I was humbled by your love and devotion to me and my family at this time. At Wes's direction, I've been preparing my Easter sermon and look forward to giving it tomorrow. I read a few excerpts, but you all heard the whole thing already. So, I won't repeat it again. Let's just praise Father, Son and Holy Spirit for what He's done for us."

Wes finished the story by saying, "I told the Pastor I think we; the Elder Council would like to pledge to this drive, and you should speak about that pledge on Sunday. Folks, I know you need to talk to your spouse about this, but let's make it a priority to give me a number before the services tomorrow. Rich can announce from the pulpit, that the money will be raised, and he has complete support from us. You heard the result this morning."

Everyone applauded at the conclusion of the story praising God.

"I called you Justus and thanked you for your prayers and encouragement. Did you get it? I told you, God has a strange way of doing things, but we have a holy consensus at my church to help the impoverished in our city. I stand in awe of how he works."

"I didn't get the message until the bus ride to church this morning. It shined hope in my soul as did your sermon and the details of this story. It helped me see how God was working all along," Justus said.

As they broke up to go home, Rich pulled Justus aside. "Will you join the Pastor's lunch in May? More people than Father Menendez and Reverend Tony need to hear the Master's message from you. I know he's been working on you too, my friend. I saw the text traffic. I was silent, but I was praying for you."

"Sounds like we both had a dark night of the soul experience, my brother. I'm rejoicing in being on the other side. But we both know these experiences transform us. I'll be honored to address the local church leaders as a humbled servant. The Spirit revealed to me now, that he is moving in a mighty way here. There will be a great downfall soon. Strongholds will fall."

He Is Risen Indeed!

HELP US, LORD

You are Holy
You are Just
You are Merciful
You are Faithful
You are Gracious
You are Love
You are Eternal
You are Everywhere

You know all
You see all
You gave us free will
You gave us the path

We fall short of the mark
We detour on the path
We ambush others
We are not good neighbors
We are fragile and broken
We refuse to accept this about ourselves
We do not extend ourselves to see others that way

Help us to hear you
Help us to know you
Help us to follow on the path
Help us to be unselfish
Help us to know ourselves
Help us see the truth
Help us be good neighbors

We can change if we choose
Please help us to change
To choose who we are
To choose what we do
We can pick this day whom we will follow
We must seek Him but He is not far
He can make us anew
His mercy is new each day

Listen or Don't

APRIL

CHAPTER 3

After Easter lunch with Pastor Rich, Justus returned home and resolved to return those missed calls, if anyone would talk to him.

Sitting on the one straight chair in his room, he called Ramone first. Much to his surprise Ramone jumped at the chance to have him back in the kitchen. "Trying to keep up with the patchwork of your students filling in was a mess. I backfilled the slot also, but your absence was noted and starting to hurt business.

"By the way, I'm planning on adding a catering business with the success of the restaurant and hoped you'd join me. The Esteban Rodriguez wedding planners asked me to cater the reception in a few weeks' time. It'll be a trial run all paid for in advance," said Ramone.

"I won't leave you like that again Ramone," José vowed. "I needed some time away to deal with the bombing, Da Wyz's death and some other personal matters, but I'm in a better place now. Things are back under control. Thank you for your understanding."

"I understand amigo. You were working too much as it was and needed a vacation. Just give me some notice next time please," Ramone said.

They agreed he'd start back Tuesday, after Monday's funeral for Jeremiah.

✥ ✥ ✥

His next call was to Father Menendez who he'd blasted a few days earlier.

"Father forgive me for treating you so badly on Thursday. You just wanted to help, and I hit you with both barrels. I feel horrible about it."

"I'm in the forgiveness business brother José," Father Menendez said. I'm glad to get this behind us but you did give me a fright when you rebuked me. I haven't felt that power before in any of my encounters with others. What was happening to you?"

José took him through the story and what the attack by the enemy looked like this time. They prayed for Miranda Michaels, Da Wyz's widow and her young girls as well as Hamsa and his situation. They rejoiced in the reinstatement of Pastor Rich.

✣ ✣ ✣

He then tried to reach Amena but got her voice mail in Arabic.

"Amena this is Yosef. I've been out of sorts for a time but am feeling much improved now. Please let me know how I can help with the situation in New Rojava. Know that I'm praying for you now. I'll reach out to Hamsa's attorney, Erica Miller to get an update also."

✣ ✣ ✣

Justus checked the phone list of recent and missed calls and saw Jacqueline Hyatt's name. The recollection of how he'd left things with her made his heart ache because of the fractured relationship between them now. *I regret how I treated her even more than Father Menendez. How do I mend this fence? The Lord does amazing things through me at times, but I'm baffled at how to fix this. She isn't in the forgiveness business, and I was more than rude when I left.* He ruminated through the conflict and asked the Lord how to proceed. Just then, Amena returned his call.

"Hello Amena."

"Yosef, I'm so glad to hear from a friend. I hope you're feeling better. We were afraid you abandoned us too. Please come to us when you can. Hamsa is still in jail under heavy guard, in solitary. We can only speak with him once each week on visiting days. Rima tried to go today but she couldn't get out due to a threatening crowd that has set up camp near the entrance to our apartments. They've blocked us in. We're all scared, and some are thinking of running."

"It's too late tonight but, I'll come by tomorrow later in the morning to see what can be done. I must attend a funeral for a friend before that. In the meantime, we can write to Hamsa and encourage him that way. He won't have to wait a week to hear from us. It won't happen in jail at this point, but this is a key area where young men get radicalized. We must be careful now. Any word from Susan or her group?"

"No, they're silent. But again, thank you, I look forward to seeing you tomorrow. I've missed having you around during this crisis. People are calm around you despite a storm. I appreciate your wisdom in these matters and your strength."

"Thank you for your kind words. Goodnight."

⚜ ⚜ ⚜

He decided to return Erica Miller's call next. *She's not likely to pick up on Easter Sunday night.* No surprise, he had to leave a voice mail message to call as soon as she could.

Weariness crept in now, he'd been up since before sunrise and needed rest. He laid down to sleep thinking and praying for the widow, Miranda Michaels and her fatherless daughters . . . Tony, who even now prepared for a funeral . . . Amena and the other refugees . . . Susan Hamilton and her marriage . . . Pastor Rich and the fund-raising campaign with over four hundred thousand dollars already pledged . . . Hamsa and how alone he must feel. *I remember those lonely nights in jail. At least I had the Master to comfort me. This must end soon.*

As he drifted to sleep his last thoughts were of Jackie. Was she the dark-haired lady in the vision given to him when he was sent here. Her compassion for her city, the strength of her convictions, the fact she would tell him what he needed to hear even if he didn't like it, and those delightful hazel, turquoise-green eyes.

The vision the Spirit gave him to call him on this mission came back to him now.

> *I saw a dark-haired lady, three partial men all of a different color, a well-dressed black man, strangers in the land,*

blood, a river, rain and hills. At the end a verse repeated like a welcome song, 'I know the plans I have for you . . . plans to give you a hope and a future.'

MAY

CHAPTER 4

After the funeral on Monday, Yosef made his way to the Syrian enclave of New Rojava.

The Syrian refugees made steady progress over their six months in Carlisle. They created a village out of an abandoned apartment complex and with federal assistance turned it into a very livable space. They centered their village around the former main office-clubhouse complex. While much more work needed to happen over time, the progress reflected the drive of a community trying to make the most of what they had.

On the bus ride, Erica Miller returned his call, and Yosef learned the FBI and the Department of Homeland Security joined the investigation into the bombing in Carlisle.

"It's a small story, since it appeared two of the perpetrators were killed. However, since Syrian refugees were involved, the Feds were now in control," she said.

"What does that mean for Hamsa?" Yosef asked.

"Hamsa got a new public defender, one with more experience in these matters. I don't have the time or capacity to represent him at this level. You wouldn't have been allowed to speak with Hamsa anyway, since DHS gave him a new translator that both the prosecutor and the public defender knew and trusted," Erica said.

"Thank you for that Erica. I wish you peace."

✣ ✣ ✣

The village leaders: Amena, Sami and Rima, along with more people than Yosef could count gathered daily in the main clubhouse. Some prayed in the makeshift qibla. Others busied themselves in the kitchen.

The main area, all one color now, was painted a very soft tone of beige. The mismatched chairs, tables and sofas made for a functional space for village meetings. The windows across the front allowed some natural light in but the room remained dim. The high ceilings kept the place from feeling stuffy but also kept it cold. The kitchen facilities improved markedly since Yosef was there last with a new set of stoves installed to make community meals more efficient. The wonderful aroma of baking bread filled the air.

Without the bombing and subsequent arrest of Hamsa, all would be progressing well for the group. However, under these circumstances, Yosef comforted the group as best he could and encouraged them to write letters to Hamsa even if they couldn't visit often.

The Syrian Kurds gave graciously to Yosef of the meager supplies they had. He knew this was a way to show their hospitality. *That's so important in their culture. I hate to take the small portions of manoushi bread and dips, but I won't insult them. Plus, it tastes wonderful. Reminds me of home long ago and far away.* He enjoyed their rich Mediterranean coffees and teas. This made him even more determined to bless them.

Ramone learned from Yosef's abrupt absence that he needed a better back up plan in the kitchen. He used some of his students to help with the cooking duties part time. The result, Yosef was allowed more time away.

Over the next several days, the refugees welcomed his interpretation of what was happening. He relied a lot on Father Menendez and others to help him understand the facets of the US criminal justice system.

Many in Carlisle didn't wait for the conclusion of the investigation. "The Syrians were guilty of terrorism and should be deported right now," many cried. None did so louder than a group that called themselves Pure Americans.

They protested near New Rojava every day with signs expressing the need to cleanse the city of the Syrians and other hate filled comments. They blockaded the main road, intimidating any who would enter or leave by various means including throwing bottles and rocks. Last night, the protestors set fire to the field where the Syrians planted their crops, using a flammable accelerant. It killed most of the young green sprouts. This just served to further dishearten the group.

Today, Amena told Yosef, "We saved those seeds and nurtured them for months. To see them go up in flames isn't only an insult, but also impacts our food supply. We've seen this before in Syria. You'd think we'd get used to it. We hoped it would be better here."

"Yosef, we can't leave this place," Sami said, "or we lose the money we're getting from the government. We can't stay much longer; the pressure is too great. Some of our people, even the women, want to go out and fight the protestors now."

"Please don't do that. This will pass over soon. Even if Hamsa is found guilty, it doesn't get worse. He's guilty in their eyes already. Unlike Syria, this country has a rule of law that most people respect. We must respect it too, if we're to stay here. We must wait for the system to work through the facts. I'm assured by those who know, that will be any day now."

Amena couldn't get over the crop burning. She stood in the kitchen of the clubhouse gazing blankly out the window at the charred field. Her black hajib covering most of her dark hair. Yosef always thought she had a lovely face that became distorted by the many trials in her life. "We lost our crop. This is dreadful. We've done nothing wrong except be foreigners in this land. They're doing to us what the Assad regime did in Syria. I'm not sure we're any better off. We should've just stayed there."

Yosef turned her around, put both hands on her shoulders and looked straight into her eyes. "At least there are no chemical attacks here.

This isn't from the governors appointed to watch over you. It's a faction of people who fear you. You must be patient with them. The police will find the right answer. When they do, Hamsa will be cleared, and the crowds will go away. I've seen these people repent. They'll acknowledge their wrong against you and accept you soon enough. I know it seems bleak now, but it won't stay this way."

Amena squirmed under his touch trying to get away. Yosef knew in their culture only married men and women touched in public, but he had to get his point across. She was the leader and as she went so went the village. He saw how uncomfortable she was, and he dropped his hands to his side.

Relieved, she looked down. "Yosef, thank you for what you're doing for us. You've been here and helped us through. You're right, of course. I'm not as hung up on the old norms anymore now that we're in America, but it's hard to forget so many years of tradition. I see this place is full of strong women and I plan to be one too. I'll take what I want when the time comes."

He wanted to comfort her more, but knew she'd be talked about if he did. "Amena, you are a strong woman. Few would get through what you have and still be sane. I admire you."

She smiled so wide he could see it around her eyes and then fell into his arms and held him tight.

Before things developed further, Sami interrupted them, stepping into the kitchen and clearing his throat. "What can we do about that scary crowd? They're getting bolder even coming into the village now."

Sami looked older than the last time Yosef saw him. This trouble aged him, hair around his cap looked grayer and the lines in his face deeper. His slight frame even more frail now.

Breaking away from Amena, Yosef said, "I'll speak with Susan Hamilton, to see if we can get more police help."

"Susan doesn't want anything to do with us now," Amena said.

"Perhaps she'll take my call," Yosef said. "After all she is the mayor's wife and your sponsor. Surely, she will make something happen."

"Susan, this is Yosef."

"Yosef, it's been a while." He could hear the warmth in her tone.

"I hate to ask but can you get Marcus to speak with Sheriff Ward. The protestors outside New Rojava are getting out of hand. They burned the crops last night. Who knows what happens next."

"Oh, you're not still involved with those people?" Her voice now turned cold. "This is awful, the political fallout from this bombing may sweep Marcus from office. We can't be seen supporting those people any longer."

"Please Susan, help these people one last time if not for them then for my sake."

"I'll speak with Marcus but don't count on much. Ward's got his hands full with gang wars as well as the Syrian investigation. I'm done with them. Yosef, this could've ended so much better."

Those people echoed in his ears several minutes after she hung up. *She showed no remorse. I dare not share this with the group. Help isn't coming from the authorities.*

Thinking it best to get the groups mind off the crowd out front he asked, "Sami, do we have any provisions left or do we need to go to the store and buy some food and supplies?"

"We're almost depleted. Our online orders get intercepted by the crowd. They won't let the drivers through. We need to go get loads of things. We have the money through direct government payment but can't get through to the stores. Yosef, what can be done?"

"Give me the money, I'll take it to a friend. Give me a list of what you need. We'll go today and bring it back later." They gave Yosef three debit cards, PIN's and some cash.

Yosef dialed Father Menendez, "Can you come pick me up at New Rojava? We need to get these people's necessities replenished. The mob near the entrance will harm the Syrians who try to leave, but they won't harm a priest and his friend."

"Are you certain, amigo? They look pretty agitated on TV," the Father said.

"The Master will protect us."

The church van of St. Francis pulled up to the mob and began to inch forward. The mob started hitting it with open palms, but they did let it through. Father Menendez collected Yosef and headed back out. He was sweating despite the air conditioner. Near the mob, Yosef got out and spoke to the crowd.

"Neighbors, I understand your fear and frustration. These people need food and supplies. We're going to bring those back. There are no Syrians in the van. Only myself and Father Menendez of St. Francis church. Please let us through in peace, we're doing this to show Christian love to hurting people."

The crowd quieted for a moment. Yosef got back in the van and drove past them.

"How do you do that?" the Father asked.

"I do nothing of my own power, it's the Master who speaks. It doesn't hurt that I know some angels who can help us in a pinch too." He smiled.

The crowd parted again when the van drove back into the complex a couple of hours later. All New Rojava turned out to unload the food, toilet paper and other necessities. They shopped in Villa Maya where the stores are less expensive but the selection more limited. Father M added some money from the meager church resources too.

Yosef's phone vibrated. Jackie's name flashed on the screen.

Jackie was all business. "José, there's going to be a press briefing at 4 on the Hamsa investigation. Someone needs to be with the Syrians to interpret the proceedings."

"I'm here now. I'll stay with them."

Yosef told everyone about the timing. He texted Tony and Rich to *pray for justice for Hamsa.*

Sheriff Wade sent a car for Rima and anyone else that desired to attend the briefing. Amena's English was better than Rima's, so she agreed to go along.

Sami and Yosef remained in New Rojava.

At 3:30 Yosef walked to the entrance where the mob besieged the village.

"There's going to be a press briefing on the investigation in a half hour. We'd like to invite you to watch it with us. We don't have much to offer but there are chairs, coffee and water. We have two TV's set up in the clubhouse."

The crowd didn't know what to make of this.

Yosef expected someone to throw something at him. It didn't come.

"We'll watch it out here on our phones," A spokesman said.

Most murmured and nodded in agreement.

"It's cooler and shaded inside. You're welcome to join us. You'll find we're all humans who suffer fear and pain. We are all created in God's image. He calls us to love one another. Please come."

"Not in a million years," said someone in the back of the crowd of about fifty people.

Yosef's countenance fell. Before he turned to leave, he looked at the crowd and said, "Listen or don't."

✢ ✢ ✢

Sheriff Ward was now at the podium in the briefing. "I want to thank the Federal Bureau of Investigation and the Department of Homeland Security for giving resources to move this case along faster than we could have on our own. Agent Reed has been of invaluable assistance to the Carlisle Police Department.

"Our joint investigation has discovered the following:

"Stuart Powell and James West were killed by the explosion of an improvised explosive device, or homemade bomb, last month. The bomb did extensive damage to an abandoned area near Eleventh Street and Riverside Drive. There were no other injuries reported or discovered.

"The construct of the bomb was an empty fire extinguisher filled with potassium nitrate and ball bearings. The detonator appeared to be a modified household timer. There was other material used but for the sake of brevity, I won't recount them here. They are in the full report, which you can find on our website.

"This type of bomb is consistent with bombs constructed in Syria. We did find correspondence between Mr. Powell and Hamsa Mohammed, a Syrian refugee, moved here by the federal government's refugee relocation program. The correspondence shows how to construct a fire extinguisher bomb of a very similar design to what we believe Mr. Powell and Mr. West created.

"Our team did obtain ball bearings and traces of other material used to construct this bomb in the backpack of Mr. Muhammed.

"We examined the computers of the Syrian refugee village known as New Rojava and did find a site from which the bomb making process could be obtained. We also found several communications between Mr. Mohammed and radical Islamists.

"In addition, we found video evidence of Mr. Powell ranting on his computer about how the Syrians must leave and he had a plan to get rid of them. We discovered some deleted texts with the cooperation of the families that indicate that the plan was to create a bomb and detonate it in Carlisle to implicate the Syrian refugee community.

"Finally, based on testimony of family corroborated by other witnesses, Mr. Muhammed did not associate with Mr. West or Mr. Powell over the weeks leading up to the explosion. While it is ill advised, it isn't a major crime to visit these sites or discuss bomb making. The crime occurs when you act on the information once obtained or fail to warn the authorities of impending terror attacks. Since Mr. Muhammed was unaware an attack was planned based on the evidence and further, he did not associate with them while the bomb was constructed. Mr. Muhammed did not commit a crime by these definitions.

"Based upon this evidence, it's the conclusion of the Carlisle Police Department, the FBI and DHS that Mr. Mohammed while supplying information had nothing to do with the actual bomb making, its intended target, or its detonation. He will be released into the custody of his family. This case is closed.

"I'll take questions now."

The cameras cut to Rima and Amena who were overjoyed and demonstrated it with hugs and smiles.

The camera also went to the West and Powell families. Yosef thought the mothers were crying. The men near them were angry.

After Yosef translated the news to the watchers in the club house, there was much dancing and jubilation.

He went to the door to look at the protestors. People were leaving, deflated. Some left their signs stuck in the ground.

※ ※ ※

Hamsa returned with Rima and Amena a few hours later to a welcoming party.

Yosef addressed the group before he left. "This country isn't like where you left. They follow the law, not a dictator. They don't always get it right. The people have firm beliefs sometimes before they get the facts. It's still better than a dictator, who lives only to feed his own lusts and ego. I'm proud of you as a people. You stood up to the worst in others without showing the worst in yourselves. Now is a time to heal."

Hamsa came over to thank Yosef for his kindness during this tragic time in his life. Yosef was standing next to the burned field garden and praying for abundance.

"Hamsa, you've been spared for a purpose. This could've been very bad for you, your family and your entire village. You must stay away from these radical places and look to contribute to the greater good in this land now. Not all get second chances. Stu and Jimmy received justice, but you've been granted mercy. Use it wisely." Yosef said as he hugged Hamsa with one arm.

"Please come back to cooking class once this settles down."

"I will Yosef. Thank you again. No words can express my deep thanks."

※ ※ ※

William West, Jimmy's dad went online to say he thought the whole thing was a conspiracy cooked up by the Feds to get the Syrians off the hook and we shouldn't believe any of it. He encouraged people to continue the protests until they were driven out. His comments got a small following and were reposted by the *Pure Americans*, but people had other things to do, and it fizzled until another incident might come along. A short time later, the West family moved away from Carlisle, not to return.

MAY

CHAPTER 5

A gang war moved into the void left with Da Wyz's death. The Biz worked hard to keep territory. The Mayans did everything they knew how, to take it. Sooner or later, it had to spill over.

Innocent people became collateral damage, the first were many of the family members of the gang heads on both sides, then it moved to the general populace in Villa Maya and Broken Wharf.

Sheriff Ward and Carlisle's finest countered with arrests of the gang heads. But it seemed that when one head was arrested or killed, another arose quickly to take their place. The allure of money and power was too much for the young, impoverished men to resist.

MX 60's leaders remained the only gang that didn't have lots of turnover at the top. Juan and Carlos were good partners in this. Especially now that Da Wyz was gone.

Carlos dropped out of José's cooking class a few weeks ago and now focused on staying free and staying alive. *I can't take much more of this. Too much bloodshed, but I see no way to stop it. Juan seems to enjoy this. He was like a field commander sending troops to battle. I'm weary, but I can't show that to the gang*, Carlos thought as he barricaded himself in another hide out for the night.

✢ ✢ ✢

Mario, now head of the Biz, determined to subdue the Mayan threat and started sending gangs into VM to shoot things up. If they hit bystanders, so be it. The shootings happened with too much regularity, and with plenty of Latinos in the emergency department of University Hospital.

Juan decided to strike back and sent a team into the heart of the Wharf in broad daylight.

"Diego, I want you to take three homies and go shoot up the residences on Commonwealth. That must be where the Wharf Rats are breeding. We got to send a message. You can't come to Villa Maya and shoot us up for free. It's time to take it back to them," Juan said. Carlos looked on and couldn't dispute the logic. He cheered the team as they left. His heart ached at the thought of the carnage about to be inflicted.

✣ ✣ ✣

As MX 60's cruised down Commonwealth, Officer Jim Lemoyne, on his beat, noticed them. The car, painted with such a luminous color looked out of place. He decided to slowly pursue to see what was going to happen.

What happened next horrified him. The Mayans got to the residential section and began to shoot out of each window in the vehicle.

"No!" Jim yelled to no one in particular. He was almost two blocks behind. *I never dreamed they'd just open fire.* "Base, this is Officer Lemoyne in Car Baker 15. We have active shooters on Commonwealth Avenue near Ninth Street. I'm in pursuit, send back up. Send Ambulances and EMT's this is going to be very bad. Dear Lord, help us." He hit the siren and flashing lights.

The sight of the police so close must've got their attention, the driver hit the gas. As they drove by Ms. Roberta's group of mothers meeting on the corner. They'd been meeting here for months now doing their part to stop gang violence. All the ladies ducked down to the ground as fast as they could, but not before two were hit by gunfire.

The hoopti sped down Commonwealth, side swiping a parked car. It careened back into the road into the path of on oncoming pickup truck. The impact set off airbags in all directions. The shooters weren't wearing seatbelts, so they were thrown all over the car.

Officer Jim caught up to them. One shooter hopped out and ran. The other three were injured. He pulled two from the car. He yelled at the driver, "Get out and show your hands."

"I can't officer, the door won't open."

"Wait there, help is on the way."

Backup arrived in two minutes. By then, Jim had one in cuffs and the other with hands behind his head face down.

The other officers extracted the driver, Diego Duran, who was missing teeth and still stunned from the impact.

Jim spoke into his chest mic, "We have a perpetrator on foot, last seen running north away from Commonwealth near Twelfth Street. He is a Latino male, with brown pants and a bright yellow t-shirt. Armed and dangerous. I need to go back down the street to search for victims."

As Jim backtracked a couple of blocks, he found Ms. Roberta's group of mothers. One of them already called 911. Shirley Smithson was hit in the back and was bleeding profusely. LaWanda Jackson died on the scene. Gunshot wound to the head. Officer Jim wept over her. *If I had only stopped them, when they drove by. These ladies were here trying to stop this. Dear Lord, something must change.*

Ms. Roberta was also crying over both of them. Before Jim arrived, she pulled off her jacket and tried to stop the bleeding from Shirley. The paramedics arrived fast and took over.

Jim got up and moved further down the street to see if there were any more casualties. He knocked on doors of homes, on each side of the street, with bullet holes in them. He grabbed his mic and reported, "No other injuries noted."

✠ ✠ ✠

Mateo was still running when the Wharf Rats caught up to him. There wasn't much left to identify the body when they finished their retribution.

WHERE ARE ALL THE FATHERS

I see the broken families tossed by the storm
There seem only to be mothers who hold them together
The fathers are gone to seek selfish gain
The fathers are gone because of their own pain
The fathers are in prison, on drugs or at war
They seem not to care for the children they bore

Their fathers left them
Why shouldn't they go
It makes the child tougher
When dads vanish

This is a lie
Convenient but not true
Do the fathers truly just not care
They are driven by lust that is instinct in most
They want to avoid the results that they host

Sons and daughters need fathers too
The holes left by absent dads are gaping and deep
Many try their whole lives to fill the cavity
They are not the people they could be
Because no father guided them

Fathers say they don't deserve such reprimand
They didn't ask to have so many children who demand
So much attention and resource
We want to be carefree
Ignoring the scars that our absence leaves
Even after completeness the wounds leave a trace
Both generations miss blessings abundant
When they reflect they are full of regret

Did he not see me worthy of love
Can she not stand on her own
We were made for relation
To each generation
It is easier to be gone than to wrestle the beast

Please fathers reflect on the path you have chosen
Your truancy is stinging to those left behind
Your children, their mothers, the rest of the land
Have hearts that are scarred by the absence of your hand
We must have our fathers in the homes
They can be safe places with you in the midst
Your frustration is clear
But you are needed here

We can try and be better at giving examples
Of fathers who love and give it abundant
We know that we all seek the love of our dad
If we reflect on what we missed they were not all bad

I lament the father who did not know best
I lament the father I have not been
Help me move on and let the pain rest

Abba Father forgive me for being a poor dad
Forgive me for being a sinful child
Help me to forgive my absent father
Empower me to break this pattern
Show me how to be a father like you

MAY

CHAPTER 6

The IRS audit of Paul Stanley's business, Stanley Builders, that began last fall, now moved from bad to awful. Mike Winter, the chief financial officer, made a frantic call to Paul.

"The IRS seized our bank account today. I suspect they're going to seize your personal accounts too. You should check with the bank. You may want to pull a bunch of cash, so you can live for a while."

"I am about to tee off with a very important potential investor. Can't this wait until this afternoon? What's going on with you anyway? I thought you had them buffaloed on the audit. You didn't tell me there was a problem. My name and the company name are going to show up as federal violators. You owe me better than this. I thought you were good at your job."

"Paul, I am good, we don't need to do this over the phone. Get some cash out. I've called our attorneys and out tax accountants. We can fight this, but you'll need money to live. After the initial seizure, they'll give us some cash to keep operating. We won't be able to hold them off any longer. We're going to have to show them all the books, for all the companies."

"Only a couple are under audit, we don't have to show them everything. They're not even looking at the investment company. Keep your head and earn the money I overpay you."

"You'd better focus on the cash and remember if you take out more than $10,000 at a time, you're going to get reported as a potential money launderer. Best to keep it below the ten K," Mike said.

"I'll get some cash, but you need to get the business unfrozen. Now!" Paul said.

Paul hung up and told his golf guest, "The business cannot run without me for a minute." He stepped to the other side of the golf path and called his attorney, Bill Shire. "I want a court injunction on them today!"

After his lackluster round of golf, Paul went to two banks where he had accounts and withdrew $9,000 from each. Then he went to his main bank, the Bank of the New South and withdrew $9,500 more. *That should be enough to live on for a month until we get this sorted. Mike better get this sorted or we won't make the next payroll.*

After locking the stash in the safe at his estate Up the Hill, Paul showered, drove to the office to meet with Mike and Special Agent Steven Moore. They met in the conference room adjoining Paul's office with it marble top conference table and fine black leather chairs. It was decorated with artist's renderings of all the projects done over the years by Stanley Builders.

"Agent Moore, I understand you've seized my assets today. What do you think you're doing? I'm the president of the Chamber of Commerce. An elder in my church. Everything I do is out there for all to see. What would make you do this to us?"

"Mr. Stanley, the IRS doesn't do such things unless we believe we're not being taken seriously. We have significant questions about your real estate dealings, your treatment of like kind exchange investments, and we aren't getting prompt and clear responses. All the data Mr. Winter provides is piecemeal and it's obvious to us you're trying to confuse our agents. After repeated attempts to clarify the data and multiple attempts to communicate with you, we couldn't find any other way to get your attention. Frankly, we're fed up, sir."

Paul looked at Mike, "Is this so? Have you been stonewalling this audit?"

"No sir, Paul. We've been giving them what we can, in the time we have. You know we're short staffed. We just can't go any faster. We have the business to run on top of these requests."

Paul shook his head in disgust and looked back to Agent Moore. "I'm sorry. I didn't realize how bad this has gotten. What do we need to give you to unfreeze our assets? We have payroll to make at the end of the month, less than a week away. You must want my employees to be paid."

"Now that we have your attention, we'll work with Mike to release funds for approved expenses. In the meantime, we need our data requests to be taken seriously and acted on promptly. I want the overdue requests filled before I'll release anything, for the payroll or other vendors."

Paul was pleased to see that the IRS didn't seize his personal assets also. He kept the cash he took out, just in case.

Once this is done, I'm going to get rid of Mike. He knows too much and he's not very bright. A proper payment will make him go away. What a pain this whole thing is. Why don't they leave business alone and let us create jobs? They just get in the way of folks who know what they're doing.

MAY

CHAPTER 7

The Saturday after the shootings in the Wharf was the day of the late afternoon wedding of Jesus Esteban to Maricela Rodriguez. The same couple whose Christmas time engagement party signaled José's arrival in Carlisle when he created a meal for the ages.

Saint Francis of Assisi Catholic Church, adorned in its finest, was the place for the nuptials with Father Menendez presiding. The church had a grand outdoor staircase leading into the sanctuary. Ideal for wedding photo shoots and staging the wedding party.

The May afternoon was a Chamber of Commerce day in Carlisle with a cloudless sky. The smell of fresh cut grass along with roses and peonies filled the air.

The bridesmaids all dressed in strapless, flowing lavender gowns gathered outside on the grand staircase awaiting the processional. The bride was in the lobby just inside the doorway in her off the shoulder dress with long train. She had eight attendants not including the flower girls. A gentle breeze blew.

Jesus was in his white tux and black tie waiting at the altar with Father Menendez. The whole community turned out in their finest dress for the occasion, everyone claimed to be a cousin of the bride or groom.

José sat with Ramone's family near the back. They needed to make a rapid get away after the wedding to be sure the reception, dinner and cotillion all came together.

José heard a popping sound outside then saw people begin to stir. Screams followed next. *Not today of all days.* He began to pray to the Master for help and deliverance.

José felt the power of the Holy Spirit come upon him in a way he'd not felt in a long time. It was like the first coming of old. He knew some of the local gangs were nearby for protection and enforcement. Dr. Esteban made sure of that. But that wasn't the solution for today. There would be no gunfight in front of St. Francis.

As he left, he told Ramone to take Jesus to another room. The bridal party rushed to enter the church for safety. They streamed in so fast that they jammed the doorway. The flower girls got lost in the shuffle. Flower petals and bouquets sprawled onto the floor and were crushed under foot. People were trampled. José squeezed past the incoming stampede of bridesmaids and groomsmen, stepping onto the porch at the top of the stairs. A car sped toward the church with guns blazing out of the two rear windows shooting at anything that moved, much like the attack in the Wharf yesterday. *Payback.* The local protection returned fire.

José closed his eyes and prayed. He felt like he was on fire. He opened his eyes and bolted down the stairs toward the car. Then, in a loud voice, he shouted, "Enough!"

The shooting stopped. The car stood still in the road. The Mayan gang approached it with trepidation. Guns trained on the occupants.

As he arrived at street level, everyone stopped to look at him. Guns turned toward him.

He continued to move toward the car. The occupants began to panic. They tried to restart the car, but the engine did not turn over. They fumbled with the door handles, but the doors wouldn't open. They aimed and tried to fire their weapons, but the triggers were frozen in place. They would've climbed out the windows, but the car was the only shield.

José arrived at the driver's door. "Who are you? Why are you here?"

"Man, I'm gonna pop a cap in your . . ."

José held up his hand index finger raised. "If you want to live, answer me." His other hand he held toward the approaching Mayan gang. Everyone stopped.

"Man, I'm Desean the destroyer. I'm here to kill some Mayans. We part of the Wharf Rats. Y'know the Biz, man."

"Who are the others? I need your names."

"Bilbo," said one in the back seat. José guessed he was the short one.

"Target," said the other one in the front seat.

"Equalizer," said the one behind Target.

"Tell me the names your mother gave you, not what the world has turned you into."

"I'm Barry," Bilbo said.

"I'm Dalvin," Target said.

"I'm Jaquan Cook," Equalizer said.

"My children, these you see behind me will take you out of this car and kill you if I walk away. I stopped your car and your weapons. I did all this in the name of Christ. I can stop your breathing, if I wish to. You would all go straight to see the Accuser with no way out of eternal torment. Do you understand me?"

"Yeah, man. What do you want?" Desean said.

"I want this to stop now. There's been too much killing. Too many injuries. Boys are dying. Mothers are dying. It must stop now! Go back to your boss and tell him that Joseph said 'This. Must. Stop. Now!'"

"Please, get out of the car. Climb out the windows." José lined the gang up along the back of the car. "Leave the guns and the car. They won't work anymore. Two blocks that way, there is a bus." He pointed north. "It will arrive in five minutes. Be on it. It's your only way out."

To the Mayan gang he said, "This is now a cease fire. These young men are allowed free passage to the bus. They are protected while they obey. They are defenseless. Do not harm them. This is a day of celebration, not a day for killing. We've had too many days of that already. If they are harmed, you will answer to the Master for your sins before the sun sets this afternoon. So says the Lord of Hosts!"

He looked at the Rats. "You may go. Don't tarry."

They ran like they'd seen the devil, in the direction of the bus. It arrived just like José said.

"Who do you think you are, man? I could have shot you along with them," Angel said.

"No, you could not, your gun won't fire, and I know it. So do you. They won't fire again. It would be best if your team would get this car out of the road. Sell it for scrap, that's all it's worth now. Give the money to the hungry. We have a wedding to celebrate. There's been enough distraction for one day." He walked back to the church.

Later, several poor-quality cell phone videos were posted of the incident. They showed someone approaching the car, but they were inconclusive as to who. The ones with the best angle were the gang members, but none shot video at that point. One video showed José coming down the stairs so rapidly they thought he was flying. A rumor started about El Diablo de Villa Maya.

✣ ✣ ✣

No one could see out of the stained glass and the wedding party and guests were ordered by Father Menendez to shelter in place so no one inside got a good look at what happened. All they heard was a loud, echoing, "Enough!"

Jackie and Karl were stuck inside with the rest of the attendees. Jackie felt like a caged animal, desiring both to get the story and stay alive.

✣ ✣ ✣

José returned to the group gathered at the top of the stairs. As he got closer, he saw concern on their faces, and he knew something terrible happened. He heard sirens from an ambulance and EMTs approaching in the distance.

Then he saw Dr. Esteban with a blood-soaked towel pressed against a young lady's head. She did not appear to be breathing. "What is it?"

"This is Renata, Maricela's teenage cousin. In all the commotion, she was trampled. She fell and hit her head when everyone panicked trying to get inside," said one of the groomsmen.

"May I help, Dr. Esteban?" José asked drawing closer for a better look.

The doctor shook his head slowly. "She hit the concrete too hard. Looks like a bad skull fracture. Not sure what happened, all those long dresses and high heels. She must've gone down hard and may have been trampled over by those fleeing the shooting." He whispered, "I can't get a pulse. I need my instruments to help me diagnose."

"No, you don't," José said. "Let me see her."

He kneeled over her and said a prayer in Aramaic. José reached out and held her hand, and then touched her forehead at the temples with his other hand. "Talitha cumi," he said. She gasped for breath and coughed, opened her eyes and blinked a few times.

"He said you'd come for me," she said in a whisper.

"He told me to come for you. You have purpose here first. It's not your time. Give him the glory, not me. Please don't speak of this until the Spirit tells you to."

José and Dr. Esteban helped her sit up. The EMTs were on the porch now. José slipped away unnoticed in all the commotion. He found the restroom in the basement and got cleaned up.

An hour later, Renata's hair now redone, joined the bridal party on the stairs. She was a little shaky, but ready to resume her place. The bridesmaids cleaned up her dress with the blood stain covered by a borrowed white shawl from one of the guests. The wedding went forward. The food and drink at the reception and dinner turned out even better than the engagement dinner.

Dr. Esteban sought out José after the father-daughter dance. "She was dead or at least had severe head trauma. How is it now that she dances with friends?"

"It is the power of the Master that healed her, not me. It was also the excellent care she received from you and the EMT's, that got her back in the wedding so fast."

"You are gracious José. What is your full name, again?"

"They call me José Sabio. Please don't tell anyone what you saw."

"José the wise. You are much more than that, amigo." The doctor smiled when he said it and raised his glass in a salute to José. "It's hard to tell people what I saw since I don't understand it. I'm a man of medicine and science. What you did falls in the realm of magic. I won't tell many folks about that. Might put me out of business."

❦ ❦ ❦

The Hamilton's were out of town, not wanting to make public appearances right now, so close on the heels of the Syrian embarrassment. Sherriff Wade had to work. Karl wanted to come because he heard the Latinos can sure throw a party. Jackie was a reluctant plus one.

Once Jackie realized Ramone's group catered the affair, she had hopes of running into José. She noticed Ramone but didn't see José anywhere at the party. On top of that, she didn't get to see what happened because of the shelter in place order. She was one frustrated news lady tonight.

She decided to shift into reporter mode thinking that would calm her spirit. She spoke with some who were outside on the stairs and heard that a man flew down the stairs of the church, stopped the car with his bare hands. He disarmed them and sent the homies home. No one was injured. The same man then came and healed a young lady named Renata. They said he appeared to be like an angel. As fast as he came, he disappeared.

❦ ❦ ❦

José caught a glimpse of Jackie at a distance. He wanted to go speak with her, but the duties of the Master and the catering overcame him. He tried to take a break and get out to find her, but when he did go, he couldn't pinpoint her in the large hall. *Had she left already?*

MAY

CHAPTER 8

The wedding celebration now moved to the reception hall, decked out with white tablecloths on multiple round tables all lining both sides of a huge dance floor. The stage at the far end housed the mariachi band as well as a DJ station. The multi-layered wedding cake was on the far end of the dance floor on display for all to admire. The scent of dinner coming from the kitchen was almost as intoxicating as the champagne flowing in the fountains near the cake table. There were several bars set up throughout to keep the patrons lubricated for the evening which could last until breakfast.

Much to Karl's irritation, Jackie was working the crowd at the reception to get the facts about the earlier incident. *I'm sure he had other plans for us tonight, but he knows once I get wind of a story, I'm not going to drop it*, Jackie thought. I can work it even in an evening gown and heels. She kept kicking herself for being so close to a giant story, and not able to witness it herself. *Angels, they say. These legends only distort what really happened.*

Jackie noticed a group of the wedding party gathered around a phone and had to intrude. "May I see too, por favor?"

"Si, señorita. Roberto shot this from the stairs," said one of the bridesmaids.

It was near impossible to make out much, except an average sized, clean shaved man approached a car and stopped the shooting. He moved quick but didn't fly.

"Where is Renata? Sorry, I don't know the Spanish?" Jackie asked embarrassed but steadfast.

The bridesmaid with the video pointed her out across the room. She was still wearing the white shawl.

After pulling her away from her friends, Jackie said, "tell me what happened to you, por favor."

"I speak English señorita." She gazed at Jackie with starry eyes. "It was amazing."

"Wait, it's too loud here. Let's step into the hallway for some quiet," Jackie said.

"Like I said, it was amazing. I still get goose bumps thinking of it. Wow, what a place heaven is!"

"I'm having trouble following your comments. Why are we talking about heaven? I want to know what happened to you."

"Oh señorita, that's where it starts. You see, I died on the steps outside today. I met Jesus. What a kind and loving face. He said, 'I had to go back for his glory.' I told him 'I will do anything for you.' I heard a voice call me back and I opened my eyes. I was back," Renata said. She had a glow about her Jackie didn't understand.

This story astounded even Jackie. *She did get quite a knock on the head*, Jackie thought. "Um, how did you get back?" That was all she could come up with to ask.

"God did it. When I opened my eyes, I saw Dr. Esteban and others gathered."

"Who called you back?" Jackie asked.

"He told me not to say. Please don't ask anymore, I can't lie after being in the Lord's presence, but I'm not supposed to say. I give God the glory."

"Wow, as you say that sounds amazing. Perhaps you should rest some. You've had quite a day," Jackie said. *First, Ms. Roberta won't talk, now her. Rumors of miracles but no ownership. Something big is going on here I've got to get this story. Maybe Dr. Esteban will talk.*

She found the doctor sharing a drink with others and asked to speak with him. He was quite happy at this moment. *Maybe the drink will get him talking.*

"Señorita Jackie, what may I do for you. Thank you for honoring us with your attendance today." He said as he reached out and gave her a side hug.

"You're welcome Dr. What a beautiful couple they make. What a wonderful ceremony and reception." She bit her lower lip. "I was wondering if I could ask you something. It's about what happened outside the church today?"

"Tonight, is a night for celebration," he said as he waved his hand in a sweeping motion around the room. "Not a time for interviews."

"Please doctor, this is driving me crazy. Answer one question for me then I'll go and enjoy the evening. Who healed Renata?"

"God did." He smiled at her.

"Not you too." She put her hand on his wrist. "Please Dr. I just want a name."

"He told me not to say and I agreed."

"Please."

"Do you speak Spanish Señorita Jackie?"

"Not much, how do you say 'no mucho.' Please anything you can give me will help me enjoy this celebration."

"I won't give you the name. I'll only say he is very wise. You should learn Spanish, cariño." He paused. "That means dear or sweetheart." They both laughed.

"He covers his tracks well too."

"Enjoy the fiesta señorita. I must get back."

That wasn't helpful. You should learn Spanish. He's had too much to drink, Jackie thought. *But he is very sweet.*

Karl caught up to her and asked her to dance. She agreed, but her heart wasn't in it.

"What is wrong with you tonight? This is a wedding, celebrate! You look wonderful tonight. That candy pink color brings out your eyes.

The V-neck directs me to other spots." His eyes and his hand moved down her side and rested on her hip. "You are an amazing, beautiful, lady."

"Well thank you Karl, I think you've had enough to drink though. I didn't look that good when you were sober." She placed her arms around his neck as they danced but wouldn't get too close. Too much on her mind for that. "I know I'm not a fun date tonight and you've clearly had more to drink than I thought. I shouldn't have left you alone so long, but I need to do something. I'm sorry but I've to get some air." She gave him a quick kiss.

She sought out Ramone or José, but again frustration set in. Ramone was too busy for a conversation and José was nowhere on the floor. She even barged into the kitchen, but her struggle with Spanish showed up again as she couldn't get the kitchen staff to give her José's location. The best she could discern was that he'd gone out a while ago. *He must be taking a break or maybe even gone for the night.* Her last effort was to dial his number but got no answer. She threw her phone back in her clutch. *Probably best, I didn't want to do this over the phone.*

She saw Ramone and asked him to tell José she asked about him as she headed for the door. "Where are you going Señorita Jackie, the fiesta is just getting started good," he said.

"I need some air Ramone, and I'm afraid I'm not much in the party mood right now."

"Let me get you something to drink, por favor."

"No thank you," she said as she left.

Others were there today. I bet the gang members doing security will talk. All that bravado, Jackie thought. *They're out there on the street somewhere close since they are protecting the party.*

As she stepped onto the sidewalk, the acrid aroma of the street hit her hard after all the wonderful smells inside the reception hall. A few cars rumbled by, some rusted out, others she wondered how they still ran, while others painted electric green or purple also passed by. No one was out at this hour except her.

She walked less than two blocks down the dimly lit street with short two- and three-story buildings on each side. Then from the shadows a gang enforcer named Iván greeted her.

"Que pasa señorita?"

"Do you speak English?"

"Si."

"Were you near when the gunfire began outside the church?"

"Si."

"Did you see who stopped the car?"

"I don't give information for free, I'm not the news."

"I am the news, I'm Jacqueline Hyatt, WWNS News investigating this incident. What if I give you fifty dollars?"

"In that dress cariño, you can give me more than that. Let me see the fifty."

"I'm not your cariño." She flipped open her clutch and produced a couple of twenties.

"What else you got in there?"

"For fifty dollars I need a name of the man who stopped the car."

"You must want it pretty bad. Fifty isn't enough. He's an amigo of mine. We do stuff like this all the time."

"OK great," she said with some disgust. "What is the price of the name?"

"I'll take the whole bag and while you are at it, my chica likes shiny things. Toss the earrings and necklace in as well."

"So now this is a robbery?"

"You're smart señorita. How much are you willing to pay for this name?"

Two more gang members appeared out of the shadows. Jackie realized just how bad an idea this was.

"The bag and the jewelry for a name and safe passage back to the fiesta."

"Si. He said his name was Joseph. He cost me my gun today. This will help me get a new one. You may go."

She handed him the bag then removed her earrings and necklace. He opened the bag, and she dropped them inside. One earring missed the bag, landing on the sidewalk with a tingle. He reached down to pick it up as she turned to leave.

"Oh, one more thing. I want the zipper off your nice party dress."

"Excuse me? I don't understand."

"I think you do. You came out here looking for some rough action and we'll give it to you now. I want that zipper."

"I can't do that and keep the dress in one piece. But you know that."

"Si. We'll help you remove it."

At that he reached out and grabbed her arm pulling her to himself. Jackie tried to raise a knee to deter him, but he blocked it and smiled. "Amigos, a feisty one." He laughed and kissed her hard.

She scratched his face deep breaking two of her nails at the quick. He backhanded her across the face calling her a name in Spanish she didn't recognize but didn't let go of her arm.

Just then another gang member stepped from the shadows. "What's happening here?" Carlos Rodriguez asked.

Iván waved him off as he struggled to contain Jackie. The bag hit the ground with a loud thud and spilled the contents.

"Now look what you did." He reared back to strike her again, but Carlos grabbed his hand and spun him around freeing Jackie who staggered away. Carlos moved in between them and drew his blade. The others fanned out around. Iván regained his balance and bull rushed Carlos. He stepped aside and spun Iván in the direction of the others. He turned to Jackie and yelled, "Run!"

She looked to grab her purse but gave it up and took off back toward the party as fast as she could go in those shoes.

One of the gang bolted after her and Carlos hurled his knife at him. It struck him in the back of the leg severing his hamstring and he fell face forward yelling obscenities. Jackie couldn't tell what happened next but got back to the party and went straight to the restroom. She had a bloody lip and likely a bruised check from the blow. Her hands shook as she tried to clean up the best she could. She found an open stall and cried, almost sick on her stomach. She took a large number of cleansing breathes to compose herself.

That was really stupid Jackie. What were you thinking? I must be an idiot! Wait, you're the victim here. You went to pay for information not get assaulted. Who do I tell about this? The cop's aren't around. The gangs are the ones here to keep the order and look how well that is working. I need to go.

She checked her face in the mirror to make sure her beating and tears weren't too obvious then went out to find Karl. He was now too well imbibed to be of much help, so she got him to order a ride share to take them home. *Time for a quick shot of whiskey before I go. Steady girl.*

After she got him in the car, Carlos stopped her and said, "You forgot your purse, Señorita Jackie."

Jackie hoped her mouth wasn't wide open for too long. This both scared and excited her. She stood amazed at this young man with a swollen eye and bloody shirt. "I don't know what to say. I'm glad you're alive. I didn't know what to do. I don't know how to thank you. You told me to run . . . ."

"It's OK. I'll be fine. Iván won't bother you anymore. Dr. Esteban paid for protection for his guests, I'm doing what was agreed. Ramone was worried about you too. He sent me after you. I'm glad you're alright. What were you doing out there?"

Her hand shook as she took the bag from Carlos. "Looking for the name of the man who stopped the shooting today at the church."

"Did you get it?"

She exhaled sharply, "Yes, it was Joseph. Whoever that is."

"Not many Joseph's in the barrio señorita. Lots of José's but not many Joseph's."

As she got in the car, she smiled. Karl was passed out. *Lots of José's,* she thought. Then her lip started bleeding again and she got a tissue out of her purse that still had her jewelry and money in it.

As she massaged her cheek, she rolled the name José around in her mind. *What did the Dr. say? 'Do you speak Spanish?' No, wait after that. 'He is very wise.'* She pulled out her phone and to the translator app and typed wise then translate to Spanish. The screen flashed up: Feminine 'sabia'. Masculine 'sabio'. "Oh my heavens," she said. "José Sabio is José the Wise. I've heard this before." She recalled her interview with Pastor Rich back in April. They spoke about Justus or José and his other names. "I'm a word nerd and looked up Sabio, it means 'wise' in Spanish. So, he is Wise Justus or José the Wise," he said back then. She pulled out her phone to check her interview notes. There it was. *It must be José.*

I can't believe I said such harsh things to him. I'm almost scared to speak to him again. But now I must. No way I can report this yet. People'll think I'm the one with the head injury.

Sure, perform miracles and just leave. Just like a man. She glanced at Karl sleeping. *No, wait . . . it doesn't sound like a man at all. A man would want to be the center of attention after this. Not stay in the kitchen or sneak out the back door. Who is this guy? I need to talk to José, but not yet, got to get my facts straight.* She rubbed her cheek again, *I hope I can cover the bruise with makeup.*

Karl was snoring quietly. She poked him and he turned toward the window.

Her mind flashed back again as she remembered Ms. Roberta's doctor and his words from several months ago. 'Unless some unknown miracle worker has come to town . . .'

I'm beginning to believe one has.

MAY

CHAPTER 9

A month passed after his near termination, before Pastor Rich got the local pastors back together. He wanted to catch everyone before they scattered, when summer started, and school let out. Some went on long sabbaticals. Others attended denominational conferences and lingered afterwards for a while.

They met in the back room of a large Italian restaurant near downtown. It smelled of garlic, onions and fresh bread. There were red and white checkered tablecloths on each of the tables all arranged close enough together to be able to eat family style. Overhead fluorescent lights buzzed highlighting the old, discolored paintings of Venice hanging around the private room.

Justus attended, a guest of Pastor Rich, Reverend Tony, and Father Menendez. There was over a dozen clergy in attendance.

After lunch, Pastor Rich stood and said, "The rumors of my demise were greatly exaggerated. I'm glad to report." The room laughed and applauded. "The Lord's not done with me and Carlisle yet. Let's not dwell on me and the past. I want to introduce you to a friend of mine who helped me through this ordeal. He's a wise counselor and a trusted ally in our mission to unite the Church for our city, to combat the poverty that threatens to unravel us. He's known by several names around town, but I call him Justus. I've asked him to share what the Lord put on his heart."

"Ladies and Gentlemen, it excites me to join with a group of the Master's fellow workers in this city. I've worked with Reverend Tony and his ministry in the Wharf. You're making a difference there, brother. I've worked with Father Menendez both in Villa Maya and with the refugees in New Rojava. It's been a blessing to see the Master work there. I've counseled Pastor Rich up the hill on his sermon series on helping the impoverished of our city. I'm jubilant at what the Church of Carlisle is doing to raise money for affordable housing in our city.

"I know many of the churches here aren't comprised of wealthy members. I know some of you are working to help the hurting in Carlisle on your own. You don't have to do that anymore. Whether your membership is up the hill or by the river, there is one body and one church. Just as the body has many parts so the church has many elements. I ask that you look at the bride of Christ as one body. Just as each congregation is made up of many gifted members, so the bride of Christ is too." He paused to take a drink of water.

"I've seen the work done by the Episcopal membership, for the hungry. I've seen the work done by the Presbyterian membership, for the sick. I can go on, but my point is made. The mission of the local congregations can be aligned with the whole bride to be truly what the Master prayed for in the Gospel of John, chapter seventeen. As he prayed, so to do I. For those congregations with means, follow the lead of Pastor Rich and create a fund for the poor. Combine it with the work of Commonwealth AME Zion and Carafe Homes, headed up by Reggie Saunders. We don't have to wait for government to address this. We can't wait for business to. We, as the church, must do this for his glory. We must swallow our pride, embrace our common ground. Deemphasize our differences, instead of using them to create barriers to unity. Let's use our diversity in debatable doctrines to be all things to all men. Let's exploit where God has placed each in this. View your placement like his spiritual gift to you. Use it just like you implore your members to do acts of service. Just as our Lord told us at the Last Supper, we must love one another. Carlisle will know we follow him by the love we show first among the brethren, the bride and then to the greater community. Our biggest witness is that we love one another." He was speaking from the Master. He could feel His power in the words.

"He brought the needy to us. He brought the mission field to us by the international students at Carlisle State, the Latinos and the Syrians in our midst. If we don't rise to these challenges, he won't embrace us as good and faithful servants. He'll instead look at us as those whose works were too focused on themselves and get burned up by the refiner's fire. Listen or don't."

Justus sat down. There was some polite applause, but most were staring at him. Some had their mouths open.

Rich waited for the comments to come.

Harry Morrison of First Presbyterian spoke up. "Thank you for your challenge, sir. Tell me again, are you an ordained minister of the Gospel?"

"I'm what you'd call a lay minister. I once was a Jesuit priest, but I identify with the Bride of Christ, not one denomination. They're all parts of the same body, if we believe that the Master was crucified, was buried and was resurrected on the third day."

"I don't argue that sir. I just want to know who you think you are coming in here and challenging us like this. You haven't been to our churches. You've not seen our challenges. I see a pastor new to our city who's looking to grab power and glory for himself. I see others who would follow him to be a part of this human ambition. I mean that with respect but Rich, you've not been here long enough to understand how things are in Carlisle. Justus, I appreciate what you may have done for my colleagues, but we're doing many excellent things at First Pres and don't need to submit ourselves to a lunch group for church governance. I've got a busy day ahead. Rich, thanks for the lunch and the fellowship. See you later."

With that tossed his napkin onto the table and left. Several others got up to leave also.

✥ ✥ ✥

Justus almost pleaded with them to stay, but he knew they weren't ready for the message. He looked down and rubbed the back of his neck with one hand. He knew what this outcome would bring. *There must be more trouble before these hearts would listen to the Kol Yahweh.*

"Well, we now know who wants to be a part of this. I learned the hard way last month how to get to a holy consensus, when there are warring factions. Now we can be of one mind on this topic," Rich said.

Justus surveyed the room and could see Brother Bruce Cochrane of Bible Baptist; Lucy Saunders of St. Marks Methodist; Joan Clark of St. Luke's Episcopal; and Brother Leroy Alexander of Riverside ARP church. This was in addition to Rich, Tony and Father Menendez.

"I guess we're the seven churches of Carlisle," Rich said.

"No, we are the Church in Carlisle. Others may help, many will detract. We need to decide what each church's gifts are and see how to use them for his kingdom. We must be very honest about our assessments. Some gifts are more sought after than others, we all know. Don't let pride interfere here. If you can say one thing about your church, what gift shows most? Please take a napkin and write the top three gifts that show most in your church," Justus said.

"Now write your church name at the top and pass the napkin to your right. Please check the one or two you see in that church or feel free to add to the list."

They worked on this exercise until all seven napkins passed before each of the clergy.

Justus collected the napkins and read them with care. "Based on my read we have a whole body of spiritual gifts. We do have room for other congregations to join, but you're here by divine appointment. He wants you to lead the efforts using these gifts. Some congregations will lead two projects since you're so large."

He shuffled the napkins. "Our gifts and churches are:

Bible Baptist is Evangelism and Teaching

St Mark's is Intercession

St Luke's is Mercy and Creativity

St Francis is Hospitality and Service
Commonwealth is Discernment and Administration
Riverside is Encouragement and Faith
Church at Carlisle is Giving, Leadership
My gift is prophecy."

He paused to let it sink in. "Did everyone get that?"

"I wrote it down and will email it around later today," Tony said.

"I'll put it in an anagram so everyone can remember it," Joan said.

"That would be soo cool," said Leroy.

"I'll see if I can spread the word around to some other sister churches," Brother Bruce said.

"We'll welcome them with open arms. We should help the staff clean up these tables," Father Menendez said.

"I knew you all would say that" Justus said, and everyone burst into laughter.

"Seriously, brothers and sisters, the Lord is moving in this place. I know it. We must move with him. Listen or don't."

"It took us a while, but now we're listening, my friend. Help us to hear the Master," Rich said.

"I'll close us in prayer," Lucy said.

When all were gathering their things, Justus sought out Rich once more. "Rich, what happened to ones who tried to oust you?"

"That's a sore subject my friend. I don't want to talk about it."

"You must reach out to them and try to restore them. We can't leave them out of the body without any loving contact."

"I know, but I'm not sure I can do it. I'm not sure I've forgiven that far."

"That's where evil festers. Please pray through this. Please remind me of the names so I can pray for them."

"The big three were Paul Stanley, the builder; Thomas Spratt and my former assistant pastor, Randall Pendergraph."

"Thank you for those names. I'll pray for them and you. Let me know what you've done to reach out to them when next we meet.

You're allowed time to heal and forgive, but you'll be surprised how much healing comes from reaching out to confront the enemies here, to make them brothers again."

"Don't say it brother. I can't take another 'listen or don't' from you today."

"I don't have to. The Spirit has said it for me. I'll pray for you. You're strong and courageous."

JUNE

CHAPTER 10

Mario, the new head of the Biz, stewed on the incident in Villa Maya for days. He didn't like having his Rats rebuked by Joseph and sent home on a bus. He didn't know what to do about it since word got around that the devil lives in Villa Maya. Now most of the homies didn't want to go there at all.

He reflected on the earlier account from Desean. "It was scary man and I ain't afraid of nothin'. You know it's true. We was just ridin' along shootin' the place up. Ya' know, like you said, had to get revenge on them coming into the Wharf and killing that lady. Suddenly, the car just cut off, stopped dead in the street and the guns wouldn't fire. Everything just kinda froze. He yelled 'enough', and I almost messed myself. Said I was going before the Accuser without any way out forever. When we got back, I went to see Preacher Leroy to get right. I ain't facing that man or whatever he is again."

"You homies'll do what you're told, or I'll send you to the devil today myself. You need to quit talking like the Mayans got some angel or demon on their side. It ain't helping us. Guess I'm gonna have to take this Joseph character out myself. Show the Mayans who's in charge. That might do the trick. I like the idea. Just got to set it up right. Get outta my office!" Mario said.

Today, Mario and Deion were seated in Da Wyz's mahogany paneled, high-ceilinged office which still smelled of smoke and musk. Same over the top fine wood with gold inlays. Becoming the boss hadn't changed Mario much. Except now, he was on the other side of the desk in the big chair. It was the right size for him, a man who could easily throw a Sumo wrestler. He was the man mountain Da Wyz always sent to intimidate but he did enjoy both the fear and inflicting pain. *Must give him some morbid jollies*, Deion thought.

Deion, the sleek enforcer, was back at work now after a few weeks' recuperation from his injuries during the hit on Da Wyz. "What we gonna do 'bout them takin' out Da Wyz? Got to be blood for blood at the top."

"I think we go after this Joseph guy. Looks to me like he's the one trying to take over anyway. Kinda like Da Wyz of VM. Although who'd want that? He took out our Wyz by trickery. He's a con man, not an angel. He's gonna unite VM against us. They got less to lose than we do. We got to take him out, 'fore they get any stronger. You know what he looks like and where he works. You do it."

"I'm not one hundred percent yet. Still can't move like I did. It'll be at least a few more weeks at the gym to get me all the way back. Do you want to wait that long?"

"You not scared, are you?"

Deion looked at Mario with a dead eye stare. "Do I look scared?"

"No."

"So, you don't want to wait, I'll need some backup then. It's a man's job, not for the Rats."

"I can recruit a few contractors I know from outside. Get it done clean and right. Won't be the first time we used pros," Mario said.

✣ ✣ ✣

Restaurant Tapas was closed when Carlos came by night to see José. He knew what happened at the wedding and wanted to talk alone. Carlos Rodriguez was a muscular young man, who had to mature fast to lead one of the toughest gangs in VM. José cultivated a relationship with him since he came to Carlisle last fall. They had some run-ins but mutual respect. Carlos was athletic but not a body builder. Lethal with gun and blade. Some tats on his arms and neck. A scar over his left eye from a fight no doubt. Some cigarette burns on his arms he told José an uncle did when he was little because of spilling his milk. The uncle, now dead, José did not ask about.

"José how'd you do that with the car and the guns?"

"The Master gave me certain gifts which he allows me to use when it is in his will. I pray and meditate on his word, and he does the rest through me. It's his timing and his direction."

"Can you stop this war with the Wharf? I'm tired. Too many people dying. Too much evil. Too many goin' to jail. We seem to be fightin' each other, with the cops just watching most of it. They didn't respond to the wedding incident for hours. Seems like our lives don't mean much. What can we do to stop this?"

"It takes a desire for peace first. It sounds like you have that. Then it takes courage to face them without weapons. Do you have that?" José said.

"Some days I do, not sure if I can get others to go along."

"Then those are the ones you must face first."

"What if they kill me as a traitor or a coward?"

"Are you ready to meet the Master?" José asked.

"No, I got lots more livin' to do."

"But if your time came tonight, would you be ready to face him?"

"No, I've done too many bad things. Need time to make up for it. Maybe he'd send me back for a second chance to get it right. One where I wasn't in the barrio."

"That's not how it works, Carlos. You've heard that from the priests all your life. You've got to make it personal. You must let him do it. If you can earn it, you can lose it. What kind of Master would he be if that happened? He would seem like a human one, not a God-like one."

"Yeah, I know, I'm just hopin' it don't come to that."

"It will one day, if not today. What will you do?"

"I guess I better get right, because we may not make it through today. I know that about the life of a VM gang member. My tomorrow ain't certain. What do I have to do?"

"You need to accept the sacrifice he made for you. You have to believe in something bigger than what you can see, taste, feel, hear. Are you ready to do that?"

Carlos looked at José and said, "I guess so."

"If you are, you need to pray this prayer with me. It has no magic unless you mean it."

José went over and stood over Carlos with his hands on his shoulders and began to pray in Spanish. Carlos repeated each phrase.

"Dear Father . . . I know I am a sinner and have missed your mark so many times in my life . . . I cannot save myself . . . I need you to do it for me . . . Thanks be to you that Jesus died for me and rose again . . . I believe that and accept your forgiveness, your free gift of salvation . . . In his precious name I pray. Amen."

José felt the Spirit indwell Carlos. He was reborn.

Carlos wept for his sins but mostly just enjoyed the joy of forgiveness. He had peace for the first time in his life. He looked up and said, "Thank you Father."

"I'm not a priest."

"Yes, you are."

JUNE

CHAPTER 11

Two days later Carlos brought Juan to Restaurant Tapas along with Aguila, the new leader of the Salvadorans and Angel, the new leader of the Puerto Ricans. Aguila was young and tough-looking, with tats on his face and neck. Muscular under his tight t-shirt and jeans. Long hair in a ponytail tight behind his head. Angel had tats on his arms and hands but none visible on his face. His hair was short and neat and his face that of a child. He had a thin mustache, trying to make himself look older. Juan, the most authoritative looking and sounding, wore a tight red t-shirt and jeans. His hair cropped close and eyes that seemed to dart all around the room. *Was he on something?*

After cleaning up the kitchen, José awaited the start of the meeting. He prayed they'd listen this time. He already closed the blinds to the main room so no one could see in. The diner style tables already arranged for the morning breakfast rush, served as a makeshift conference room. The well-lit space gave everyone a clear view of each other. Suspicion hung over them like a rain cloud. They were all seated in a circle at different tables. Far enough apart to defend themselves if the meeting went bad for them. José sat with his back to the kitchen door.

"It's about time we got back together. We tried this before, but when Da Wyz got killed, everything went crazy, fast. It's time for us to organize and unite. If we can beat what's left of the Biz, there'll be lots of money to go around," Juan said.

"That's not why we're here," Carlos said.

"Oh," said Aguila, "then why are we here, man?"

"I asked Carlos to bring you here to talk about peace with the Biz," said José.

"You a brave man, señor. I saw what you did at the wedding with the Rats. That was so cool man. How did you do that?" Angel asked.

"Not here to talk about that tonight. We're here to talk about peace," José said. "Who killed Da Wyz?"

Everyone shook their head while shrugging their shoulders and turning their hands up in unison.

"It was a pro hit. We don't have that kind of money. I wish I'd done it, but no, it wasn't MX 60. He was fortified. The limo was supposed to be one like el presidente rides in," Juan said.

"Wasn't us either," Aguila and Angel both said at the same time.

"Cops don't even know, nobody arrested," said Carlos.

"Thank you for telling me that. If the Mayans didn't do it, why are we at war with the Wharf?" José said.

"We don't answer to you. We want what they got, saw our chance to get it. You'd do the same if you was us, man," Juan said.

"It's time for this to end señors. Angel, you were at the wedding. What did I say?" José asked.

"Enough!" He shouted and laughed.

"Did you hear it? Did you believe it?"

"Man, I'm not going to lie, that scared me to the soul. Glad you ain't talking like that tonight. Someone thought the devil was there."

"Not the devil, Angel. Quite the opposite. You know I serve the Master. He is more powerful than the devil. We just don't give him that kind of credit. He's the one who said 'enough.' I was just the one he used. So, if he said 'enough' are you ready to quit and make peace?"

Carlos and Angel nodded yes. Juan and Aguila did not.

"Why would we want to do that, man? I think we're winning and shouldn't quit until they surrender, we go marching in and take over everything. You guys are acting like home girls, not home boys.

What're we waiting for, if José will stop their guns, no one else has to die. This'll be quick and easy," Juan said.

"Is that what you think the Master wants? Help you take over the drugs, protection and sex traffic in the Wharf? That's not why I'm here, and you need to be careful thinking like you do. I've seen very bad things happen to those who seek to use God's gift for selfish, sinful gain," José cautioned.

"Juan has a point. Why give up our advantage now? We must be close to breaking the Biz. We got their money flow already, and the new boss ain't got control. We should keep pressing. I'm not ready for peace yet. Not sure I'm ready to unite with this bunch either. Looks to me like MX 60 ain't united on this," said Aguila.

"Man, I'm done here. Carlos, let's go, MX 60 is not a part of the peace treaty."

"No man, I'm staying, I want to be a part of the peace. We can make this work. Stop all the killing. You heard that mama scream when you popped that boy months ago. I can't get that out of my mind. Not until a couple days ago when I accepted Jesus," Carlos said.

"Oh no, man. Not you too. You're out of the 60s man. Be glad I don't pop you right now."

With that, Juan grabbed his stuff and headed out the door slamming it behind him.

Aguila lingered but was also fidgeting. He looked at Carlos. "Man, I don't think you speak for the 60's anymore."

✠ ✠ ✠

Outside, Juan didn't see Deion and two others waiting in the shadows around the corner just toward the parking lot. They'd already taken care of the streetlight, so the darkness hid them well. Juan went down with two shots from a silenced pistol.

"Do we wait for them to leave one at a time or take out all the leaders at once?" One voice whispered while he checked his gun and reloaded. The other dragged Juan's body over and tossed it into the nearby dumpster.

"Let's go in. I want to see them all go down," Deion said.

Deion opened the front door and the other two went around back.

"I need a night cap," he said. "Looks like buy one get four free. Happy hour comes late in VM."

The three homies jumped for cover, José stayed in his chair and closed his eyes.

"This was a set up!" Aguila said, pulling his pistol out of the small of his back.

They scrambled for cover with tables turning over and condiments crashing to the floor, but no shots.

José stood and said, "Why are you here, Deion?"

"I'm here to end this. I figure to take you out and all the gang lords at once. I just came for you, but what a bonus I've found. Mario's right, you are trying to unite the barrio against us."

"Before you kill me, don't you want to know who killed Jeremiah?"

"I'd like to know that, especially if it's one of these homies."

José heard the back door open and close.

"It was not one of them. Look around, these young men didn't do it. There is enough bravado in the room to be sure, but they had no means to go after him themselves. You're believing what you want to, not what's right. Think for a moment, they don't hire pros. The Biz does that. Mario had Jeremiah killed and didn't care if you died too. I suspect one of the men in the kitchen still has a bullet in there with your name on it. If this goes down like Mario hopes, you and I both will be gone. The one in the kitchen with the kill order takes your place by his side. I'm just a tapa's cook but think about that."

One assassin stepped out of the kitchen and said, "A shame you not a police detective, you could've figured this out sooner. Might've saved your life." He fired at José hitting him in the back. He went down hard. Pierced through the lung. Blood and tissue sprayed out when the bullet exited.

"No!" Carlos yelled.

Deion took careful aim and shot the shooter in the head. Blood and brains went everywhere. Deion spun around, with a loud groan, down by the cash register.

Carlos had a good bead on the other shooter who knew he was exposed with his compatriot taken out. He bolted from the kitchen to a table to flip it down for cover.

Angel shot him in the leg before he could set. The best Angel could do from his vantage point on the floor. The second shooter went down, and Deion jumped up firing twice into his torso and then as he walked closer, once more to his head.

Angel and Aguila scrambled around the table to get a good shot at Deion, but Carlos stood up and said, "Deion, no more killing. We need this to stop. Enough!"

Deion lowered his still smoking weapon. The body beneath him still twitching. "No, there is one more killing to be done. Once I do that. Stay out of the Wharf and we'll stay out of Villa Maya. Cease fire and peace."

"We agree. Right?" Carlos said.

"Si," Angel said.

Aguila exhaled slowly and lowered his weapon then said. "I don't like it but okay. What about Juan?"

"Do you mean the dead guy outside in the dumpster?" Deion said.

"You shot him in cold blood," Carlos said.

"Not me, one of them did him. But I would've before I knew what I know now."

Carlos ran across the room to José now. "I'll call 911. We got to keep you around. Just breathe easy."

José didn't speak. His breathing erratic. His eyes were closed, and he just held unto Carlos' arm. Mustering some strength, he said, "Take me to St Francis . . . Father Menendez."

"Man, you'll bleed out."

"No, he'll get me to the hospital. Leave me at the church."

Angel and Aguila did the sign of the cross before touching anything.

"Help me get the bodies into my car, I have a way to make them disappear. I'll be in touch soon about the territorial lines," Deion said.

"Not Juan. He needs a decent burial. The cops'll just mark it up to one more gang murder. We need to clean this place up," Carlos said.

"Anybody call the cops?" asked Deion.

"I don't hear anything," said Aguila. "Even if they did get a call, it'll be hours before they get here."

After they loaded José into Carlos' truck, Angel and Aguilla got the bodies of the hitmen in Deion's trunk and he drove off toward the docks.

Carlos took José to the church and dropped him off near the back. He called Father Menendez, refusing to identify himself, and told him to go out back. After he saw the Father call an ambulance, and saw José getting treatment, he went back to the restaurant. He had to supervise the clean-up, he knew where all the cleaning material was. In the restaurant, they cleaned up blood in the back all the time, where all the meat was cut, so he knew how to sanitize and make it look spotless. He got some of the MX 60s to come over and help. Angel and Aguila helped as well.

While they were all together, Carlos announced the truce and warned of severe reprisals, including losing precious body parts, if it wasn't kept. They were all tired of war and ready for truce, so it stuck.

After they finished cleaning, Carlos didn't know what to do with Juan's remains. He took them to St Francis left the body around back where he left José. He made the sign of the cross and prayed for Juan and his family.

Later that night Mario received a call that woke him from a sound sleep.

"Man, we got Deion like you said, what do we do with the body?"

"Take it to warehouse fifteen at the Wharf dispose of him there like always. I told you that already." The line went dead.

Deion stepped through the bedroom door of Mario's room. "You didn't tell me. I guess I missed a meeting. I don't miss often." He emptied his clip into Mario. *Guess I'm the Da Wyz now.*

JUNE

CHAPTER 12

Jackie was watching the 5:30 am edition of the news on a competing station while she ate her bowl of granola and almond milk sitting at the kitchen bar in her patio home. *Got to keep up with the competition.* She heard a report about a shooting in Villa Maya. The body was found at St. Francis church. The victim's name wasn't disclosed.

She crunched on her cereal until her cell phone hummed, Mitch's charming face appeared on the screen. "Yeah boss, what's up?

"The guy they found shot in Villa Maya was the cook you know from that tapas place."

"What? Is he dead?"

Her mind raced. She was the one who convinced him to stay and now he was gone. Despite her efforts at wedding, they hadn't really spoken again after that. She was calloused over with all the shootings in Villa Maya and the Wharf. While on the phone she realized how cold she'd become. Now it was personal. This was a friend and a good man. *He's not just another shooting victim. He has a name. I guess, they all do.*

"I'm sorry to say, there was a body there, sounds like it."

"God no. Please." Jackie closed her eyes and prayed. It was the first time she'd done that for many years. She felt her stomach tighten up. "I'll call Sheriff Ward and see what I can find out. Then, I'll head over to the morgue. This is terrible Mitch. I just can't believe it. He was a force for good, I'm convinced."

She called Ward on his cell. No answer. "Arrgh!"

She clicked off the phone, half-cleaned up her breakfast, and was out the door with a cup of coffee to go. She had to pause and check herself in the mirror, sleeveless black and white striped blouse, a knee length pencil skirt with some jewelry to highlight. "Looking good Jackie." *Not feelin' good but lookin' good.* She double checked her cheek where she was assaulted last month. *Lookin' good lady.*

On the drive to the morgue, her anger erupted. She started in a low voice but the further she got into the trip the louder her voice got.

"God, how can you do this? He was your man here. Doing all you asked of him. I made him stay and now he's gone. Why do you treat us like this? No wonder so many struggle to believe in you, when the good die for no reason. How can you do this to us and still say you love us?"

She composed herself as she arrived at the morgue, then found the junior medical examiner in charge on this shift. "I'm Jacqueline Hyatt, WWNS news. I can identify the body found last night in VM. I'm a friend. He has no family."

They walked back to the drawers with the bodies. Her senses were in overdrive. She noticed the dim lights in the hall; the burning stench of death and the chemicals used to cover it. The granola wasn't sitting well. *What am I doing here? How will I know it's him? Bodies get distorted in death. I don't know where the shots hit. This was such a bad idea. Oh, what am I doing here?* The click of her high heels on the floor started to deafen her. *I wish I'd worn sneakers. Wow, it's cold in here. I'm starting to shiver. God, please no. I'm sorry for my outburst. You must have better plans than this. Please, please no. I can't bear them treating him like a John Doe. He's so much more than that. Please no.*

"How far have we walked? I had no idea this place was so big," Jackie asked.

"Almost there now," the ME said.

"Here we are Ms. Hyatt. Juan Doe."

He pulled out the drawer with a dull roar. The cold jumped out of it like a freezer being opened. "Are you ready? Do you need to steady yourself?"

After a deep breath, she nodded and said, "I'm okay."

He pulled the covering back and revealed the face of a young man with a bullet hole on both sides of his head. One the entry wound on the left. The other the exit wound further back on the right. She gasped at the violence of the death. She also found herself rejoicing that she didn't know who he was. It wasn't José. "Are you sure this is the body from last night?"

"Yes Ms. Hyatt, you can see on the label the time of arrival. There were no others last night from VM. Can you identify him?"

"No, I'm not sad to say I don't know who this is. I thought it was someone else." She swallowed hard to keep her breakfast down and took a deep breath.

The ME closed the drawer with a thump and a click.

"Who did you think it was? If you don't mind me asking," he said.

"Wow! I thought it was a good friend. I know it's sad because someone has been killed. But doc, I'm tickled my friend is still alive. You just don't know. Thank God. Wow!"

The doctor handed her a tissue from a table nearby. She dabbed her eyes, whipped her nose and breathed deeply.

"He must mean a lot to you."

She swallowed hard. "More than I realized."

The long walk to the body now seemed very short as she went back to her car. Her anger now redirected at Mitch as she phoned him. "How could you do that to me? Get your facts straight, bud! I don't enjoy trips to the morgue in the early morning . . . "

"Whoa Jackie, that's what I read on the police wire. A shooting victim found at Saint Francis. Latino male. Wearing a Restaurant Tapas t-shirt and chef's pants. José on the name tag."

"I don't get it."

At last, Ward called her back, so she clicked off Mitch in disgust to pick up.

"This is Ward. What can I do for the media today, Jackie?" *I wonder if he talks to everyone with such condescension.*

"What happened in VM last night?"

"José the chef was found shot, outside of Saint Francis last night. He's critical at University Hospital now. Another gangbanger wasn't so lucky. He was found outside the church a couple of hours later. Other than that, we don't know what happened. My officers say no one is talking. We'll get a statement from the chef, if he survives."

"Thank you, Sheriff, that clears up many of my questions. You've been most helpful."

"Always glad to help the media, they're so good to us." The tone was filled with sarcasm.

Other days she would've had a comeback, but not now. She called Mitch to apologize and let him know she was heading to the hospital.

As she drove, Ward's last comment rang in her ears. 'If he survives.' *He must be bad. He's not like other men I've known. As she drove on, she began to pray out loud in a much different tone than when she drove to the morgue.*

"God, thank you for answering my last prayer. I know it's been a while. I'm sorry for what I said earlier. You and I have some history of disappointment and frustration. I don't feel right asking twice in one morning but please let José survive. We need him here. I like having him around. He is special to me. I see that now. I didn't know how special."

Earlier that morning, Father Menendez went with José via ambulance to the emergency department of University Hospital. A gunshot wound to the back. The kind of injury that gets reported to the police. Father Menendez couldn't help them. He knew nothing of how it happened or where it happened.

Amena, now a tech in the emergency department, was getting her credentials from the University, but she had already seen more emergencies from violence than almost any of the health care professionals there. She saved many lives in Syria, but still needed to learn the procedures and the language in Carlisle. She refused to leave José's side, who was in surgery for much of the night. He got to his ICU room about seven o'clock that morning.

The Father called Pastor Rich, Reverend Tony and Ramone too. They were all in the waiting room when the ER doctor came in, with Amena right behind. "The bullet passed through. It broke one of his ribs on entry and nicked another on exit. We re-inflated the lung without major issue after the surgery. He has a head injury from a fall. Vital signs are good but could be better. He's in critical, but stable condition. The next twenty-four hours will tell. He's going to be very sore."

✣ ✣ ✣

Jackie arrived just after the ER doctor's report and found the three clergymen already there, looking somber and had a horrible thought. Then she saw Ramone, and was comforted by that, for some strange reason.

"How's the patient?" she asked the group in the waiting room.

She assessed the room as she always did and saw multiple single chairs and recliners. TVs in two corners opposite each other one on the news and one on a sports channel. The lights were inviting, not clinical. There was a desk to the left as she entered with a solitary phone on it. To the right was the entrance to the ICU with a coded keypad to regulate entry.

Pastor Rich and Ramone both knew who she was. "Didn't know this would make the news," Rich said.

"José's a friend. I didn't realize how much of one until now. How is he?"

"Stable and resting, but critical. He's heading to ICU as a precaution. Lung injury. He must be breathing on his own for twenty-four hours or so, before they move him to another room," Ramone said.

"Obvious question, what happened?"

"Father Menendez found him outside the back of the church late last night, after an anonymous call. The Father got him here as quick as he could. José has a gunshot wound, looks like he was shot in the back. It pierced the left lung and exited the front. He lost so much blood. We don't know where he was attacked or who did it," Rich said.

While Rich finished his comment, Amena came by to see Father Menendez. "You met me at New Rojava. I work here in the trauma department. I've been with Yosef all night. It made my boss mad, that I didn't attend other patients. I only cared for Yosef."

"I'm sure Yosef is very grateful for your loving care. Can you tell us anymore we can do for him? Any further updates?" Father Menendez said.

"He's very strong and seems to be improving quite fast. I'm happy to tell you. I've seen lots of shootings in Syria that didn't end so well. I was very concerned for him when he came in."

"Again, we thank you for caring for him."

"I have to go home now, but I'll be back later today. I'll make sure he's taken care of. But you must know, the police want to talk to him. The file is marked to call them as soon as he awakens. Someone should be with him when the police come. Yosef told me a while back that he's nervous around police."

"Thank you, Amena. I know he'll want to see you when all the drugs wear off."

The rest of the group overheard her and thanked her for attending to him.

"We should set a schedule to stay with him in case he wakes up and the police want to interview him. Father, go home and get some rest, you've been here all night. Rich you want the first watch? I can be here around noon. Who can take from four to seven?" Tony said.

"I'll take it," Father Menendez said.

"I can be here after nine tonight. I'll stay overnight," Ramone said.

"I'll take seven to eleven. You can relieve me then," Jackie said.

"Ms. Hyatt, that's too much to ask. I didn't know you two were that close," Rich said.

"We're not, but this guy grows on you. Besides, there's got to be a story here and I'll get a great shot at it. Plus, that'll be after my news shift."

"OK. Everyone have each other's cell phone numbers? Any change, text us all immediately."

✢ ✢ ✢

There was no change until Jackie's shift. "His vital signs were improving all day long." the Father told her when he left. José was breathing on his own by the seven o'clock shift. Jackie arrived after she ate dinner and was allowed to stay in his room for longer stints than most in ICU, due to her celebrity and his improvement. She had her tablet for the night alone, listening to the various devices whir and beep. The smell of sanitizer filled her nostrils. Still better than the morgue. She sat nearby and began to read the New York Times on her tablet.

She remembered the conversation with Father M as he left. "When I got to St. Francis around noon, they told me the other body found around back was Juan Ricardo. He was a leader of MX 60. Two shots, one to the torso, one to the head. The police have been all over the area today. They said, 'he didn't die there but was brought there.'"

"First José, almost dead and now Juan. Is someone trying to send a message to you Padre?"

"I don't know, but I hope it stops. They must be related somehow."

✢ ✢ ✢

Around 9:30 José awakened with a jerk. His eyes searched the room.

Jackie reached out and held his hand gently. "How you doing, Señor Chef?"

"Not sure. Where am I? So thirsty, may I have some water?"

"Only ice chips for now. Take it slow. You must've had quite a night."

She spooned some ice chips out of the plastic cup past his parched lips. His eyes tried to focus. He licked his lips and closed his eyes. "Some more, please."

She obliged.

"You're in the ICU at University Hospital. You were shot last night. We almost lost you. I made a pact with your clergy friends to notify them if you came to."

"How . . . how did I get here?"

"Father M found you outside the church. You remember anything?"

He closed his eyes and appeared to strain as he swallowed hard. He took in a deep breath. "I cleaned up. After dinner. Maybe around nine or ten. I don't . . . " His voice trailed off.

Maybe I don't need to tell the group just yet. Jackie thought. *Not sure he's really awake.*

"Mayan gang members came in . . . talked about peace with the Biz," José strained as he spoke.

"Who were they? What were their names?"

"More ice please."

Again, she obliged.

"After we talked, someone was mad. Threatened everybody. People from the Biz came in. Everything else a blur." He shook his head.

"Who was it?"

"Don't want to say. Too fuzzy. I may not be remembering right. Don't want others in trouble for no reason." He kept trying to focus his eyes.

"I understand that. Look, once you're awake the police are going to ask harder questions. Amena told us you don't like the police. So, we're staying with you. I got this shift until Ramone comes on at eleven."

"Thank you. I owe you a story. This one's about peace in the city. I don't want to say names, but there's a cease fire now. No more shootings. We have peace. There was justice too. The leaders agreed, but peace doesn't come without suffering and sacrifice. I guess that's why I'm here."

"So, you're saying you brokered a peace deal between the Mayans and the Biz. That's a big story. How does this end with you getting shot? Or is this just a very good dream?"

"I guess someone didn't like the deal." He laughed and then grimaced in pain.

She stroked his hand as she held it.

He turned his head toward her, looking in her eyes. "A very good dream would have you in it, Jackie . . . Sorry I'm still groggy. But I confess, I'm glad I woke up to see your face instead of Ramone's."

"Now you're a sweet talker. I think your pain meds are talking. I was beginning to think you were a traveling miracle worker. But I figure a miracle worker would heal himself or at least know to how to dodge a bullet."

"The things I must do to throw you off track." He smiled and winced again.

Just then, Amena stopped by to see if there was anything she could do.

"Our friend's awake." Jackie looked back at José, "Amena's here. She's been making sure you get all the care you need."

"Thank you for being here and all you've done," Yosef said.

"They couldn't keep me away, Yosef," she said while coming over and adjusting his pillow. "They knew better than to try." She checked his monitors and his IV and then took his other hand to check his pulse.

There's more here than just good nurse patient relations, Jackie thought.

"You're my two angels of mercy." He smiled, coughed and grimaced again. "I got to stop doing that."

Jackie didn't realize there was competition for José's affections until now but dismissed it after looking at the black hajib on her head. *Although, she is quite a pretty lady, in a rugged sort of way.*

Jackie let Amena attend him as she sat down to text the friends. 'He's awake'. She sent a second one saying, 'It doesn't look like there will be any police inquiry tonight. He's too weak and it's almost 10:00.'

"Who are you texting?" José asked.

"Pastor Rich, Father M, Tony, Ramone. They wanted to know when you came to. We made a pact that we'd be here in case the police want to speak with you. Amena said you may want a friend nearby for that."

"Might be best to tell them I'll only speak with Officer Jim Lemoyne, if they want a statement from me. No one else."

"Now you're dictating terms to the police from a bed in the ICU. I like your style señor. That's something I should handle since I know the Sheriff better than they do I suspect."

"May I bring you anything?" Amena said.

"When can I have real water, instead of ice?"

"Soon Yosef, you've been through much. Take your time. I'm praying for you," she said the last part in Arabic.

Jackie didn't like being left out of the conversation. Before she could reinsert herself, Ramone arrived ahead of time with a purple overnight bag.

"Welcome Ramone. Our patient is awake and wants to go from ice to water. I think we have progress."

"That's wonderful, Señorita Jackie. Good to see you awake, amigo."

After the exchange of pleasantries, Jackie pulled Ramone aside.

"Did you see anything unusual at the restaurant when you went in today?"

"The dining room wasn't quite right but nothing else. It was clean, but the tables were out of place."

"I think he got shot there and someone cleaned it up."

"In my place! Ay-ya-yi! It'll be a bad crime scene now. We cleaned it again today." Ramone thought for a moment. "I told him not to have the meeting with the VM gangs at my place. Things could go bad. Looks like they did. Good thing Carlos was there to fill in today."

"What meeting with the VM gangs?"

"It was to happen a couple of months ago. I don't think it ever did."

"Sounds like it happened last night. If José isn't dreaming, a peace treaty was agreed on last night. I guess, the shooting was part of it. Not a good part."

Ramone rubbed his forehead and temples with both hands. Then he developed a case of nervous twitches and fidgets. "Peace is good señorita, but not in my place. The police will be everywhere tomorrow. I should just close for the day, maybe the week."

"Don't panic, let's take one step at a time. I'll let Ward know José will speak with Lemoyne and then we can see what happens."

"You might want to let the other members of our team know what's happening," he said.

"I'll do that when I get home. Since you're here, I'll head home now after I say goodnight to our peacemaking patient."

Jackie got home and showered to get the hospital smell off her. She enjoyed a glass of wine and sent the text outlining what she suspected but couldn't confirm. Her phone rang almost immediately. It was Father Menendez.

Jackie recounted the conversation with Ramone, and finished with, "Let's see what comes back to him in the morning. I want to be there when Officer Lemoyne does the interview. Based on what you know, we should both be there. Meet you there tomorrow at eight o'clock?"

"See you then, Ms. Hyatt."

MIRACLES OR MUNDANE

The first breath of life
The love of a friend
The touch of a hand
Warm sunshine
Gentle breeze

Feel the heartbeat of your lover
Savor the saltiness
Relish the sweetness

See the beauty of the mountain
Let the majesty of the sea breeze touch you
Taste the salt
Embrace the order of nature

The seasons teach us to change
The change comes back again
Life is change
Death is change
Rebirth comes after

JUNE

CHAPTER 13

José moved early in the next morning to a private room since he improved so fast. The room was a typical hospital light gray with a fluorescent light overhead. The standard issue recliner sat on the far side of the bed. A small desk chair nested under the table near the bathroom. It smelled of cherry scented air freshener attempting to cover up antiseptic.

Jackie and Father Menendez arrived at José's room at the same time. Jackie overheard Officer Jim Lemoyne joking with José about being tough, but not very quick as she entered.

"Is this official police business or can anybody join?" Jackie asked.

"I'm doing an interview here, or rather will be in a moment. May I ask you two to wait outside?"

"I'm the one who found José outside the church, you may want me here," the Father said.

"I agree, yes that'll save me from hunting for you later. No press though."

"Officer, I'm hurt," Jackie pretended while her lower lip turned down. "I'm a friend, anything he tells you; he'll tell me later. He promised. He told me some things already that may prove useful. I won't jump ahead of the police report. On my honor as an old girl scout." She held up her hand in a mock pledge.

"José, you okay with these people hearing what you have to say?"

"Yes, Officer Jim. I'll tell them anyway. It saves me some oxygen which is in short supply for me right now." He took a deep breath.

Jim got out his note pad and his cell phone. "Mind if I record this?"

José shook his head no.

"OK, for the record state your name."

"They call me José Sabio, I'm known by others but that is what's relevant here."

"What happened to you two nights ago? What do you remember?"

"It's still fuzzy. I cleaned up at Restaurant Tapas and was getting ready to leave. It was a busy day, so the clean-up took longer than usual. While I began to lock up, some leaders of the Mayan gangs came in. They wanted to talk peace with the Biz."

"Why come to you?"

"The restaurant is in the center of where several gang territories meet. It's as close to neutral ground as there is. I convened such a meeting once before, before Jeremiah was killed. It ended in frustration. After his death and all the fighting, it took a long time to bring people back to the table. Recently, one of my cooking class members came to me asking for spiritual advice. He accepted Christ as his Lord and Savior. He didn't want to fight anymore. I told him to bring the other leaders, if he could. When, they showed up, I guided the conversation. They fought with each other and Juan Ricardo, one leader of the Mexican gang stormed out. He didn't want to be a part of the peace process. The other MX 60 leader was going to be removed from the gang. Next thing I knew, Deion from the Biz entered the front door. There were two shadowy figures that came in the through the kitchen. I didn't see them. One shot me, not sure what happened after that. Everything went black. I keep remembering the words cease fire and peace. I hope it's so."

"José, we found Juan Ricardo's body outside St Francis where you were left. It was after the ambulance picked you up. Two gunshot wounds at close range. Could've been this Carlos kid. I know you didn't mention his name, but I know who he is. He had a motive—didn't want to be out of the 60s. I'll check it out. Anything else?"

"Yes, this just came to me. Mario set up Jeremiah. The shadowy figures were hit men. They were there to kill me and Deion. If you can find them, they may testify against Mario."

"I'll go talk to this Carlos kid and his amigos, Aguila, the eagle, and I think the new leader of the PR's is Angel. I can't keep up; the churn is so high. It seems they never run out of gang bangers."

"They were running out. Depleted by the fighting and the arrests. It needed to stop. Hallelujah, if the cease fire happened that night. You need to be careful Officer Jim. If there is a cease fire, too much investigation may pull the scab off," Father Menendez said.

"Okay Father, I promise not to tell you how to do mass, if you don't start doing police work. To keep it equal, sounds like I better pick up Deion too. That'll be a barrel of fun. Anything else, José?"

"You must do what you think is right Jim, for justice to be served. If peace is achieved, arresting the leaders that brokered it, may well be very disruptive. Please don't do that yet." José coughed for the first time in a while and grimaced. "Might be best to visit Deion first, then see if the other interviews are necessary."

"OK, I'm getting all kinds of advice here. I'm gonna tell you how to make paella next. Sorry man, I'm a little edgy. Don't mean to be irreverent to either of you."

"Do three Hail Mary's . . . " Father Menendez said, while he grinned. "These are tense times for us all. Would you like me to speak with the gang leaders? Carlos and I are close."

"Maybe we go together. I'll call after I catch Deion. I know where he eats lunch most days. What I'm hearing is that there's no one else in imminent danger and the crime scene is so corrupted, I doubt it's worth the effort. My CSI guys got to go through it though. I'll tell Ramone we'll have to shut him down for a while. We won't come in with sirens blaring. We'll go in this morning.

"José, you get better, man." He clicked off his phone and put his pad away.

Jackie clicked off her phone too.

Looking at her he said, "I didn't get any advice from you. Rare for the media to be so quiet."

"They seemed to have it covered, I'm just a fly on the wall, officer." She smiled the smile that melts hearts of her fans. Jim nodded to her and walked out.

"See you around."

Officer Jim caught up to Deion at the Excelsior club at lunch. It was dingy lots of low lights and dark furnishings. Appeared to be black leather booths with dark brown tables. A bar with lavender neon lights buzzed in the back along with a few provocative paintings hung in various places around the room. There was a stage for performing and he could only image the performances that happened here. *Poor girls*. The smell of old booze and cologne assaulted him as he entered. He couldn't help but notice all the beautiful young ladies, that were tending bar and tables. The bouncer didn't want to let him in. "We can do it here, or I can come back with a warrant and a few dozen officers to arrest him and you. Plus, we'll investigate this place, like you won't believe."

The bouncer sent one of the bar maids to ask Deion's group for permission. She returned fast signaling to bring the officer over to Deion's table.

Deion was enjoying a bowl of low country okra soup and miniature loaf shaped corn bread. Jim was getting hungry, but work comes first.

"Greetings officer, didn't know you were a fan of the finest soul food in Carlisle. What'll you have? On me."

"Not now. What I need is information. I got a witness says you were at Restaurant Tapas two night ago with some of your heavy hitters. Care to tell me what happened, in your own words?"

"Not really. Don't recall where I was. There was a lady or two involved, I'm sure. Perhaps you could ask around here. See if anything strikes your fancy."

"Let's not play this game Deion. You know me. I do my research before I confront. What'd you go there for?"

"Why do you think I'd go to Villa Maya? It ain't for the food, Officer."

"I think you went there to kill the VM gang leaders on a tip. You brought your hitters 'cause you knew they were going to be armed and dangerous. My guess is you're still recovering from that run-in where Da Wyz went down and needed back up."

"Don't need back up now."

"Oh, I'm scared. You think that's gonna work on me?"

"You're taking up precious time, Officer Jim."

"I think it got complicated when José was there. He can be a very persuasive guy. So, everyone backed down. Then one of your hitters goes rogue and shoots the man talking, José. Am I close?"

"Close but not right. Joseph revealed the truth to me while we were there. The man speaks truth. The hitters were hired by Mario to take out Da Wyz. They were there to make sure I didn't come back. Even hurt, Mario knew he needed two to take me down. Turned out he needed more. Thing one shot Joseph. I took them out before they got me."

"You boys take out Juan Ricardo too."

"Maybe he was someplace he shouldn't have been and got popped. Thing two took him out, before we got in the restaurant."

"So, the Mayans didn't take him out."

"You have a bear trap for a mind, Officer."

"Are we going to find bodies all over town?"

"I doubt it. Mario knows how to clean up just like Da Wyz did. He can make people disappear."

"So where is Mario this fine June day?"

"I hear he's out of town on business."

"He hasn't gone missing has he?"

"I don't miss him. Do you? Doubt anyone else will. He may like it so much he may stay away."

"So, you're Da Wyz while he's away?"

"No, I'm just Deion."

"The peacemaker," said Jim.

"The fight with the Mayans is over. They didn't kill Da Wyz, we all agreed to respect each other."

"They helped save your life, didn't they?"

"Don't matter. I'm the peacemaker." He smiled a wide grin.

"You know Carlisle's finest will come for you, if you get out of line. I'll be there in the front of the charge. But not today, Deion. Today, we'll celebrate peace."

"With liberty and justice for all," Deion added.

JUNE

CHAPTER 14

Yosef continued to improve as the day went on but struggled to get comfortable in the bed. He couldn't lay flat or on his left side. The nurses propped him on the right side with a pillow behind that he couldn't reach to move. While trying to doze, he got interrupted by the constant cadence of staff taking vitals, giving meds, cleaning the room and then came the welcome visitors.

Amena brought Hamsa with her for the afternoon shift, so he could visit Yosef.

They knocked on the door of his room. "Yosef, you awake?"

"Yes, my friends, thanks for coming to see me. There's been quite a parade though here today."

"Can I do anything for you before I start my rounds?" Amena asked.

"Oh yes, could I please move out of this position not sure any others will be more comfortable, but I need a break from the right side."

"How long have you been like this?"

"Since lunchtime."

"I'll let the nurse in charge know that is unacceptable care. She's gonna get an earful."

"No, please don't, I'm sure they're doing their best. I just want to try something else."

"OK, but they shouldn't leave a lung patient in the same position for that long. Someone's got to learn from this. I'll be nice," Amena said as she left.

Yosef now on his back with the bed tilted up to take the pressure off the wound, breathed deep as he could. He adjusted the supplemental oxygen tube to fit his nose better.

"I just wanted to come by and wish you well. I'm very happy you're not dead," Hamsa said.

"Thank you for that, Hamsa."

Hamsa moved toward the window to look out. He changed his speaking from English to Arabic. "Yosef, Carlos told me something about you I find hard to believe."

"What's that?"

"You stopped a car with gangbangers in it. Dead in the road. Their guns too. At a wedding last month. You stopped the gang war. Is this true? How'd you do it? Man, I'd love to have that kind of power. I'd fix loads of stuff." Hamsa now turned to look at Yosef.

"I don't remember everything yet, but I'll say it wasn't me who did these things, but the power of the Master within me. He did them through me. I know that's hard to understand."

"He's such a wise teacher and now I see he's very powerful too. Why'd he let you get shot?"

"I'm not sure yet. I don't know everything he does all at once. He shows me his plan over time."

Hamsa's mood turned somber. He looked down at his shoes. "I don't know what'd happen to me, if you were dead. I've lost so many people. I thought I was going to die in jail, but you made sure I got out. You helped my mother and the others through all that. You stood with us. You mean so much to us and to hear you were dying, I just couldn't take it." He looked up with tears in his eyes. "I said I'd never cry again but I can't lose you too."

"Come to me, Hamsa," Yosef said with his arms as open as he could get them.

"I don't want to lose any more people ever," Hamsa said sniffing back tears.

Yosef patted his back with his IV'ed hand. "You know better than many that death is a part of life. You also know there's life to come after. It hurts to lose those we love, and you've lost more than your share. But I know we'll live forever. We can choose, if we want to be in God's presence, or not. I made that choice to follow my Master a long time ago. While it has struggles, some dark nights, there's no better place to live than in his presence daily. You can make that choice too."

"How do I do that?" Hamsa said as he grabbed a tissue from the bedside table to wipe his nose and eyes.

"You must pray this prayer with me. It's counter to what you've been taught in Islam. It's similar to the Shahada, in that it must be sincere, but it reconciles you to the God of the Jews, through the sacrifice of his son Jesus, Isa as you call him. This will create many strained relationships in your family and your village. Are you sure you want to do this?"

"Yosef, I've been looking for answers since I got to America. Why was I spared? Why am I here? What happens next? I just don't know. I do all I'm supposed to do for Islam, but I don't get answers."

"Perhaps the answer isn't doing your duty but in being in relationship. Knowing the one true God. The god of Islam requires you follow rules and perform good deeds to see him. My Master, Jesus, the Holy One, has done all the work. He was the only one who could restore relationship between us and the Father. That's why he came. We must accept his gift and live for him. He speaks to those who seek him."

"I want that. How does it happen?"

"What do you know of Isa's teachings?"

"Over the past many months, I've spent time reading his words in the Bible. He was loving, wise, kind, powerful. Very much like you. I spent time when I was in jail searching for answers in the Bible. Much of what I read, didn't help me. Many of his sayings agreed with the teachings I grew up with, but the difference seemed to always come back to a God who wants us to know him. What you say, a deep relationship with a Holy God. That's very hard for me. How do you go to God when we aren't good enough?" He looked down at the floor again.

"I do all the daily prayers to Allah and other good works, but I don't feel this presence you say. I don't have the peace you show. The followers of Islam killed my father and family. I see your living faith in your Master. I want that. What can I do?"

"Hamsa repeat after me as I pray for you."

Still speaking in Arabic Yosef prayed, "Dear Father God, creator of the universe . . . I come before you now a sinner in need of saving . . . I've done bad things and can't save myself no matter how good I try to be . . . Please save me from my sin . . . Through the sacrifice of your Son Jesus . . . He died, was buried and rose again . . . I accept his life saving sacrifice . . . and will live my life for you from now on . . . It's in Jesus' name I pray, Amen."

Yosef could feel Hamsa indwelt with the Spirit.

Hamsa, looked up smiling from ear to ear and grabbed Yosef in a big hug. "Thank you, thank you, thank you. I don't know what to do next, but I feel peace I've not felt . . . Oh, thank you."

"Don't thank me, praise the one who saved you. You're a child of the Master now." Yosef pointed to the Gideon's Bible on the bed table. "This Bible can be yours now. It's the Father's love letter to us. With his Spirit within you, you can better understand the teachings now. Please take it." He showed him how to find the books in the index.

"Have you read the book of John, in your studies?"

"I skimmed through it, but it was very confusing."

"Read it again with new eyes now. Focus on how much Jesus shared a loving relationship with others. His compassion shines throughout the Gospels, but so much brighter in that book. Once you've read John, I can show you some remarkable things in the word. You know so much about the Quran. Compare the Bible's teachings to the ones you know. It will be good to see the differences and the similarities. Your mother won't understand this. The others may see you as an outsider now. But the Master will guide your way now and forever if you'll let him."

"Thank you, Yosef. I feel so different now. Does this feeling last?"

"It is joy you feel, one of the fruits of the Spirit. It's wonderful feeling that can last but we often let go of it. Hamsa, I'll answer more questions later. Once I get out of here, we'll get you baptized. I need to rest now. You may stay and read if you like." Yosef closed his eyes to rest.

Hamsa decided to let him rest but took the Bible and re-read almost all the book of John on the bus ride home stumbling through the English translation.

Later, Amena came in to help bathe Yosef. "I told them, I'll do this part for you since they were doing such a bad job of caring for you earlier."

"Please tell me you were kind. I don't like to complain and wasn't trying to get anyone in trouble. Amena, I know you're not supposed to be with a man in such a setting as this, unless he's your husband. The others in the village would shame you for it."

"I've been in this country for many months now. The old ways don't always work here. I've seen women like Susan, and your friend Jackie, who lead and pursue what they want. I've decided, I'll do that too. I'm as strong or stronger than they. Yet I play the docile role. My husband and children were murdered, but the docile woman could do nothing but flee. I'm done with that kind of life. I found something new and encouraging here. I still embrace the teachings, but not all the rules of the old country. You've done wonderful things for us and I want to express my gratitude in your time of need. I'd like us to be more than friends. Besides, since I've been in this hospital, I've suspended many of the old rules of men and women I learned in Syria. They don't allow me to just treat women here. I'm used to it now. Let me do this for one I care for and owe a great debt to."

He took a slow deep breath unsure of what to do. He conceded the inevitable.

"I can show you how to care for this wound, to keep it from going septic. You need this for hygiene reasons also. Besides, there's no one here from the village to know. Our secret."

"I agree. Please proceed but only from the waist up. That's where the wound is."

She tilted the back of the bed up higher and untied the back of his gown and draped it across the front of the bed.

The cold air hit his chest, he shuddered and then remembered the scars on his back.

"Tell me about these." She started the bathing with welcome warm soapy water and listened.

"I've been many places where they don't follow my Master. Sometimes, people violently resisted anyone who brought his message. I've been scourged several times."

"And yet you stayed true to him? Kept preaching his words?"

"Yes, I've tried to be true to him all my life. I stumble. All men do. The key is to repent and rest on his free gift of mercy through his sacrifice and resurrection."

"I'm here to minister to you Yosef, not the other way around." She rubbed with a gentle but firm touch around the wounds, front and back. "When you go home, you won't be able to shower until these heal. You'll need to do this yourself. Please notice what I'm doing and how. Unless you want me to come and do it for you."

The last comment made him uneasy. "That won't be necessary, Amena. You're a good teacher. I think I can follow your guidance."

Yosef enjoyed the ministry of another and rested in her care.

Susan Hamilton knocked on the door and walked in without waiting. She found Amena helping José get a fresh robe on.

"Oh, am I interrupting something?"

"No. Mrs. Hamilton," Amena was embarrassed and felt accused by Susan's stare, "We were just finishing up his sponge bath."

"Sorry I missed that. Let me know if I can help."

Amena looked puzzled and José covered as fast as he could with his sheet and blanket.

"I'll check back in on you soon." Amena gathered her supplies and started out of the room.

"Don't leave on my account," Susan said. "I'm surprised but also quite glad to see you. I owe you an apology for running away like I did. It was a bad time for us all. I feel bad that I didn't stand up for you."

"Yosef stayed by my side the whole time. Even with the haters blockading the street. We could've used more help, but we're survivors. We did okay without you." Amena wasn't one to mince words any more.

"I deserve that. But please accept my deep apology. I've resolved to do better, and we can renew our mission with you, if you're willing."

"I accept your apology, but we don't need the charity you once offered any longer. There may be a different kind of help you can give, now that we know you're willing again. I'll get with the other leaders and let you know. Will other refugees be joining us anytime soon? We could use an Imam."

"A what?" Susan said.

"An Imam, a Muslim leader. He could lead us in our prayers and speak to us about Allah. Once our group gets large enough, we should have someone to lead us in spiritual matters."

"I guess she isn't ready to embrace my Master," Yosef thought.

"Oh, I understand now. I'll look into that. Yes, there are others who want to come, but we put a hold on it for a time. Sounds like you could accommodate more refugees now."

"Let me get with the others and I'll reach out to you. Now that you'll take my phone calls again."

"Yes, I'll answer. Again, I can't express how bad I feel about what I did," Susan said looking intently into Amena's eyes.

With that Amena took her gear and left. Susan and José were alone.

Susan looked at him with those dark brown eyes and beautiful Greek features. She was well-dressed and didn't appear to be there for seduction. The over tight clothes were gone replaced by more modest attire. José was already impressed with her contrite spirit toward Amena. He knew she treated the strangers in her land with contempt that she held for others who did the same thing. *Has she recognized her hypocrisy at last?*

"José, while I'm apologizing, I should say why I'm really here. I didn't expect to see Amena. You two seem to be quite happy together. I'm sorry for what I did to you a couple of months ago. I put you in a horrible place." She looked down at her shoes. "When you turned me down, it got me thinking. It made me very angry. No one did that to me before. Then you scolded me for the life I was living. It shocked me more than just a little. It made me reflective. Between that and the bombing implicating the refugees, I fell into a tailspin so to speak." She looked back into his eyes. "I didn't like the person I'd become. Your comments reminded me of the man I loved and married and of the vows we each took. Thank you." She paused to collect her thoughts.

She appeared to be giving a speech she'd rehearsed and now lost her place. *Perhaps she's surprised she got this far through it.*

"Marcus and I went away for a while and refreshed ourselves. Sorry I missed the fireworks at the wedding. We got counseling, which I won't tell anyone but you. When I heard you were near death, I was afraid I'd lose the chance to say these things. I decided I needed to put on my big girl pants and stand before you and apologize, if you got well enough to hear me. That's what I'm doing now. José, I'm sorrier to you than to the Syrians."

Her eyes welled up, but she didn't cry. She looked to one side, clenched her jaw and swallowed hard.

José adjusted himself in the bed. "Thank you, Susan. I've been praying for you and your marriage since that day. I rejoice that you and Marcus are reconciled and working things out. I know marriage is a journey that needs constant care. I'm in the forgiveness business, you know. You are forgiven, my sister. I'm reminded of my Master who would say 'go and sin no more.'"

With that, the tears did flow. He invited her in for the comforting embrace of a friend.

"Thank you for that. A weight is off my shoulders. Wow, you are quite a man. I should go. Is there anything I can get for you, before I do?"

She sniffed back tears and grabbed the last tissue from the box at the bed side.

"Some tissues perhaps and another cup of water. Thank you for coming. This is wonderful news. You've encouraged my heart more than you know. Please help Amena and the refugees while I'm recovering."

After she left, José thanked the Father for saving that marriage, and drifted off to sleep.

JUNE

CHAPTER 15

Evening brought another knock on the door. It was Ms. Roberta, who did not barge in. She brought some homemade chicken soup. It was the best thing José had eaten in days. She talked about many things as he ate, and he savored the soup while she went on. The warmth and salty flavor so distracted him he found it hard to follow her conversation.

"After he got out of the Biz, D landed a job at Wallace's garage. He loved it. In his spare time, he fixed up an old junker with parts from Wallace's and the junk yard. Old man Wallace took a liking to him. He helped him fix up the car after a while. Now he's got his own car. It won't go for long. He says he needs to add oil too often, but it's his own. He's proud of it."

Joseph continued to enjoy the soup with its soft noodles, diced chicken, carrots and celery scented with garlic and lemon pepper. The subject must've changed while his mind was immersed in the delectable experience. He tuned back in.

"Reggie is enjoying moving those folks up the hill. They got some trouble. The boys like chasing the rich girls. The rich boys don't seem to like the competition. I told Reverend Tony, 'I know boys from the Wharf could compete with those rich kids, if we give them a level start.' They doing well in school too, but I guess we'll have to wait 'til next year to see how well . . . "

One last bite of soup. He turned the bowl up to get it all.

"Ms. Roberta, that was an absolute blessing. I think they'll have your chicken soup in heaven as part of the wedding feast."

"You're goin' to make an old lady blush, Joseph."

"I heard about the shooting at your lady's gathering. It's a terrible thing."

"Yes, Shirley and LaWanda both got shot. LaWanda died. Left her husband and two teenage boys. Shirley had a hard time, but we think she's over it now. We still have the meeting out there every day. It seems like more mothers are coming all the time and there's more of these groups popping up all over. Who'd of thought that a group of mama's sitting outside would cut down on gang violencey. But it works! I even told Reverend Tony, 'if you get shot at, it's 'cause you're in enemy territory.' That's what my Lucas used to tell me from Afghanistan. Lord rest his soul."

"Has the church reached out to Lawanda's and Shirley's families?"

"Oh yes, they've been good as gold. Reggie even has the Jackson's, LaWanda's bunch, in the next group of folks to go up the hill. It'll be good for them to start over. Reggie's been targeting families with kids that might get into the gangs. He gets them out of there before they get hooked. I think he said he moved twelve families and is waiting on the churches now to deliver on their promised help. He offered to move me, but I told him I'm where God wants me. I know that thanks to you, Joseph."

She gathered her purse and the soup dishes, "I better get back home. You need some rest. I'll keep praying for you."

"With that soup and your prayers Roberta, I'll be home in no time."

"Do you want your TV on before I go?"

"No, I don't watch much."

"Man can get depressed all alone in a hospital room by hisself. Let me put on some music."

I've not been alone today very much. Knowing he had little choice in the matter he allowed it.

She found an easy listening station with singers and standards of the Great American Songbook. "There that'll do nicely. Relaxing but also nice words."

She gave him a big hug and a kiss on the head when she left.

José laid his head back to rest, drifting along on the melodies and clever lyrics.

✢ ✢ ✢

As she was waiting on the elevator, the door opened, and Jackie Hyatt stepped off. She remembered Ms. Roberta from her earlier interviews on the mother's neighborhood meeting and on the shooting last month.

"How are you, Ms. Roberta?"

"I'm doing very well my child. I hope you are too."

"Yes. It's always good to see you. What brings you to the hospital?"

"I'm here visiting a friend who got shot the other night. I brought him some chicken soup that he seemed to enjoy."

"Well, I hope he's doing better. I'm here to see a friend who was shot also the other night in Villa Maya. Did you come to see José? Wait, but I'm coming empty handed. I have to get him something. I'll ride down with you to the cafeteria. We can catch up along the way."

"I came to see Joseph, but I think he goes by José with the Mayans."

With that they got on the elevator and headed to the lobby.

✢ ✢ ✢

José heard another knock on the door. Looking at the clock he must've slept for almost thirty minutes. Jackie came in with two cups of ice cream.

"I've got to get shot more often."

She looked confused but undaunted, "Not sure if you're a chocolate or *banilla* person."

"I like *banilla*," he said with a grin.

"Good 'cause I can't stand it and was afraid you were going to eat the good stuff. I was willing to sacrifice for you though."

"Thank you, Jackie, I appreciate you coming here to see me. I enjoy seeing you very much."

She was dressed in her news outfit from earlier that evening. Tight sleeveless red dress with a wide black belt and high-heeled shoes to match.

"You are welcome, Señor Chef. You're one of the unique ones. I've not met anyone quite like you. You're a mystery to me and I'm not often mystified." She sat on the bedside chair and crossed her legs and let her shoe dangle as she bounced her foot and ate her chocolate ice cream.

"I shall try to stay mysterious, if that keeps you coming back." José couldn't help but notice her legs.

He opened his ice cream cup and enjoyed it almost as much as the soup.

"My dad was in and out of the hospital when I was young. Back then they didn't tell kids much, so I didn't know what was wrong at the time, but we always brought ice cream to him. He loved it so much. I still remember his face when he ate it. It looked very much like yours right now. Whenever I visit a friend in the hospital, I try to bring it. Easier than flowers." She looked around. "How'd you score a private room anyway?"

She grabbed a napkin and wiped a drip off José chin. As she did, her hand brushed his face. José smiled at her. "Thanks for that, I'm not very good at eating in bed. Dr. Esteban pulled a few strings for me. Said I should be under police protection, since I was shot. The perpetrator may come and try again. Least they could do is not endanger other patients."

"Nice to have friends in high places. How're you feeling?"

"Getting better with each visit. I hope to be out of here soon."

"Does that mean I can't come and see you anymore?"

"I hope not, but after a crisis, everyone wants to get back to normal. I know it's a challenge to come here each day. I know you have a wild schedule."

"So do you, Señor Chef. We can make time for what matters though. I'd like to spend time unraveling the mystery you present. Professionally speaking of course."

José at last realized she was more than just flirting with him. He paused and looked at her with a pleasant, yet sad stare, while he finished his last bite. "Jackie, my life is very unusual. I follow where the Master sends me. I'm not very attached to the things of the world. I do get attached to the people though. I have to tell you that dealing with me is hard for most women, because I must answer the Master's call first. My deepest relationships are with those who follow him too. Would you like to follow him?"

"Are you trying to convert me from your hospital bed? I love this. José, I know what you're doing is out of affection and a caring spirit. I've tried your way and it didn't hold up for me. I'm glad it works for you. I'd hate to think it would get in the way of bigger things we might feel."

"Jackie, it permeates all I am and all I do. I'm going to take you on as a special challenge though. I think we should continue to meet daily, and you should bring me ice cream."

She laughed and tossed a pillow at him. "I'll warn you I'm a project from way back. You've never had a challenge like me."

"I think you may be right. But I'll let you know. Further research must be done," José said with a playful smile. *If she can flirt so can I.*

"There's something that's been on my mind since our Sushi lunch. I spoke quite harsh to you and felt we left things splintered. I don't like messes like that to linger. I stand by what I said, but think I could've said it with less of an edge . . . "

José held up his hand, "you told me what I needed to hear. I was under attack on the spiritual level and needed a friend to snap me back to what matters most. I don't think the Discourager thought it would come from you or he would've labored more to keep us apart."

"So, what matters most to you?"

"Love of God and love of people. God called me here to care for the people and I could do both by staying the course. Leaving abandoned both and would've caused me even more grief, not to mention those around me. Someone needed to speak that truth to me. I didn't like it at the time, but I'm not sure what would've happened if you didn't tell me to be strong and courageous. It had to sting, or I wouldn't have listened. Rather like smelling salts needed to awaken us after a fall."

"Not sure I like being called ammonia. Is my perfume that strong?"

José tried to respond.

"I'm just kidding Señor Chef, I understand what you mean. You're being very gracious to an impatient news lady. So, are you going to come to me with your next problem?"

"How can I resist counsel from such a wise and beautiful news lady."

"I hope I didn't spoil your dinner with the ice cream."

"No, not at all, a friend brought me some chicken soup earlier that tasted heavenly."

"So how do you know Roberta Saunders?"

"How did you know it was Ms. Roberta?"

"I met her getting on the elevator."

"Oh. We met in the Wharf months ago, she's a very active member of Reverend Tony's congregation. What a wonderful spirit she has."

"She's very protective of you. I asked her about you, and she was both admiring and evasive in equal parts. She used to be blind, you know."

"Yes, I heard that. Strange thing the human body. Always keeps science guessing."

"She says she was healed by God. Sounds like something you'd know about."

"Maybe I do. It just adds to the mystery."

Her phone vibrated. She glanced down to cut it off and found it was Mitch. "I better take this. What's up boss . . . Wow, that is news . . . I'll be there." She clicked it off.

"I need to go. I enjoy our talks so very much. If you tell anyone else that, I'll deny it." She leaned over and kissed him on the forehead. "I enjoy being near you. When I thought you were dead, it hit me very hard. There were so many things I wanted to say to you. Now that you're here, I find I'm tentative in sharing them. That's very strange for me. You've gotten past my wall. I don't let many in that far. Not sure how you snuck in. I'm not sure where it goes from here, but I want to keep exploring, if you're game. My mysterious Señor Chef." He couldn't help but notice those hazel eyes, now with a green tint, so close to his.

He reached down and held her hand. *Such velvety skin. Such fabulous eyes. The exhilarating jasmine scent of her hair.* "Jackie, I'd like that very much, but you must remember who I follow."

Jackie leaned over and kissed his forehead once more. "I do need to go, big story brewing." She wiped the spot on his head in case her lipstick left a mark. "That's all you get from me right now. You can't take anymore. Get better soon. There's more I wish to give."

She smiled and left. José watched her until the door closed all the way then drifted off with good dreams as the American songbook continued to play.

PRECIOUS ONE

My Lover is Precious in diverse ways
Lures me into her wonderful maze
Where we will stay for many many days

I long to have her near me

Her Passion for what is right and true
Often frustrates and makes her blue
After a time, she does come through

She beguiles me

She is savory and sweet
She comforts and brings heat
Whenever we meet

Thoughts of you cling to me

How alluring her curves
She is one who deserves
All the love I reserve

You're a part of me

Her hair smells of jasmine
Her eyes tender and green
Her misty rose lips a dream

I yearn to see her in moonlight

My lover is precious in ways even more
How could I help but adore
My longing for her is hard to endure

I dream of her day and night

JUNE

CHAPTER 16

After several days as an uninsured charity patient, José was sent home to Maria's boarding house. He paid through the end of the month so despite the interruption in income, he'd be alright until July.

Maria was almost as kind to him as Amena and Roberta were. She brought food to his room for several days. He was able to manage the pain as his healing progressed more with prayer and meditation. So, he didn't use all the pain meds they gave him. He was certain, he couldn't afford any more. He improved fast but needed time to get his stamina back.

Carlos was a constant visitor each afternoon. He was seeking counsel and cooking advice. The police came to see him. While they didn't believe all his story, they also didn't have any evidence for charges. They appreciated the cease fire with the Biz and decided not to prosecute, if the peace held.

José didn't see Jackie in person for a few days. She called to check on him but told him about the big news happening in town. In the common room, he watched her on the news, to hear all about the big bank takeover. He found himself just watching at times, not listening, just admiring her on this small screen. The curve of her face, the movement of her mouth, the flash of those eyes. *I should keep my distance, but not sure I want to.*

✣ ✣ ✣

The Bank of the New South was going to merge with a bank in the Midwest. The corporate offices were all moving to Ohio. Jackie interviewed several bank board members and executives. She spoke about the many negative impacts this would have on Carlisle's economy, if it goes through. Many high paying jobs would move out of state. In addition, the impact on the psyche of the city was going to be huge. The bank was its pride and joy. The new owners were going to keep the name for a time but wanted to rebrand everything in their image. *They were the conquerors.*

Eric Reynolds made a frantic visit to Stanley Builders. Paul's assistant offered him a drink. He declined. He sat in the small waiting area in Paul's offices near the top of the Hart Building. He almost jogged over here from the Bank of the New South headquarters and was glad for a moment to catch his breath before his meeting with Paul.

"Mr. Stanley will see you now, Mr. Reynolds."

In Paul's office, he saw the usual photos of Paul shaking hands with the Governor and Senators. There were golf photos with famous pro golfers. A signed baseball from Pete Rose, Paul's idol growing up. Paul stood behind his desk trying hard to get off the phone with someone.

Eric didn't know if he should sit or stand. He opted to sit. Paul finished the call with, "Pastor Rich, I've got to go. No time for this right now." He hung up the phone and remained standing.

"What's so pressing that my banker pays an unscheduled visit?"

"We've got a problem. The acquiring bank has pulled several of your loans for review as part of due diligence. You know all the documents aren't there. I made the loans with promises of documents. I know you guys are busy, but I can't cover for lack of docs. They'll have me fired, if I don't produce them pronto."

"What's missing?"

"On a quick review, we don't have financials for the last two years on three of your neighborhood developments. We're missing personal guaranty docs on three others. I brought the PG's with me now. I need those financials too."

"You know I can't sign those without my attorney looking them over first. My financials are under IRS audit, and I've been told not to give them to anyone until that's done. I can't make up for your lack of follow through, Eric."

"Maybe not, but I've got emails where we requested these multiple times and were told they were forthcoming. That's the only reason I approved the loan advances. I relied on your word. If we don't get these quick, the buyer may exclude them from the purchase. If that happens, the loans get called by the bank for document deficiency. You'll have to pay, or they'll take the collateral. I'm sure your investors won't appreciate that any more than I do your attitude right now."

"Okay, okay. Let's figure this out. Susie," he said over the phone, "find Mike Winter and get him to join us now in my conference room."

They headed into a plush conference room with a marble tabletop and eight black leather chairs. In the center was a tabletop conference call phone and on the far wall, a large monitor for displaying presentations. The opulent structure of the conference room contrasted with a disheveled Mike Winter as he came in with files and a note pad. He dropped one of the files and the contents went all over the floor.

"Sorry, what's happening boss? Oh, hello Eric."

"Eric needs our financials for the last two years for the due diligence team. What's the hold up?"

"You know we were advised to withhold issuing those until the audit is complete. That way we don't have to restate anything."

"We could give him some unaudited ones and mark them preliminary, if that'll help."

"That's a start but I need real ones soon. When will the audit end?"

"You know how the IRS is. This is going to take a while and our accountants won't sign off on the financials until the IRS is done," Mike said.

"That may work on some people but not on me Mike. I'm your banker. I know you're delaying this. Give me the prelims. I want the others by mid-July, or we are going to call the loans. Paul, I need those PG's by the end of the week or we will do likewise. I can keep the buyer's diligence team busy until then but after that, your fate is up to you."

"Eric, we've been friends a long time. I'll have my attorney look these over and get back to you by Friday."

"Guys we're all up the creek together, if I don't get those documents quick."

I'll send you some preliminaries by ten o'clock tomorrow morning," Mike said.

"I'll get these PG's to my attorney today. Not sure what else he's working on, but he'll get on them quick," Paul said.

Eric thanked them and left.

※ ※ ※

"What are we gonna do Paul? I can make up some statements and get them to him, but the auditors won't issue because they don't like the transfers of funds between projects. They know we're robbing Peter to pay Paul. No pun intended. They're not gonna issue statements."

"You're getting way too worked up man. Relax. You're a mess. You just let me work on funding, I have some new sources for cash that may make BNS unnecessary anyway. Some investors aren't very sophisticated, and we can get creative with them without their knowledge. We've been doing this for a while. Momma Stanley's little boy isn't out of tricks yet."

※ ※ ※

Mike sent over the preliminary statements that he and Paul both knew were very erroneous, even deceitful. He was afraid time was running out on all their schemes, but he was already in too deep. His best hope was to keep this going until the big payoff when the Hilltop Neighborhood started selling.

A great downfall is coming to this place. I can feel it, he thought.

JULY

CHAPTER 17

José didn't start the month so well. He still struggled with stamina and could only work partial shifts at the restaurant and stopped his training classes altogether. He was stiff and sore in the mornings and often needed a nap in the afternoons. His rapid improvement early in the recovery, now turned into a longer convalescence. The short work weeks put him in a cash crunch.

"Maria, I can't pay the full rent for July. I can pay for the few days I've been here already, but then I'll have to go."

"I don't know what you mean. José, you're my longest boarder now. Ramone came by on the first and paid your rent for July. I thought you knew," she laughed.

José felt a burden lifted and thanked the Master for his provision. When he arrived at work that day, he thanked Ramone for his kindness and promised to repay him.

Shaking his head, Ramone responded, "It was a gift for you, amigo. Nothing to repay. You've blessed me so much since you arrived. It was the least I could do. I look forward to when you're fully recovered. I put the catering business on hold for now just to keep things together while you were out. It'd be good to bring that back when you're better."

As he went to put on his apron for the morning shift, his phone vibrated in his pocket. It was Jackie.

"How is Señor Chef this morning?" She liked to elongate the señor part with a faux Spanish accent. He found it endearing.

"I'm still stiff and sore, but each day seems to bring some improvement. Ramone's is closed for the holiday tomorrow, so I plan to rest and continue to recover."

"That's why I called, the production team is having a Fourth of July cookout tomorrow up at Bass Lake. It'll be the crew along with their families. The juniors will be running the station so all the senior staff can enjoy the holiday. I did my time back in the day. Just part of the gig. Anyway, wanted to see if you'd be my plus one. It'll be a relaxing time. Mitch has a boat. There are trails to hike, if you're up to it. Lots of kids swimming. What do you say? Will you join me?"

"That's a very kind offer." *I just wanted to rest and recuperate.* "What time does it start?"

"It'll be going on from noon 'til dark. I thought we'd arrive mid-afternoon and stay through dinner. We could head back to the city in time for the fireworks at Hart Park. I promise to get you home before Maria's curfew," she snickered.

"That sounds like a wonderful day. I'll rest up in the morning, so I can make it through the afternoon. What should I bring?"

After he got all the specifics, they bid each other adieu and he went on to work quite excited about the prospect of spending some time off with Jackie.

❊ ❊ ❊

She picked him up at Maria's near two o'clock and they headed to the lake. José brought a towel and some swim trunks he bought yesterday at a second-hand clothing store, along with a couple of bottles of his own brand of homemade spicy pepper sauce. A small contribution to the event, but one many would come to appreciate, he hoped. It was all he could afford at this point.

Jackie was dressed in cutoff blue jeans with a loose-fitting white mesh blouse that revealed a black one-piece bathing suit underneath. She wore sandals with straps around her ankles. Her eyes were covered by big sunglasses and her hair pulled back into a tight ponytail. There was a cooler in the back seat with a big sun hat on top of it. Next to that was a beach bag. She looked ready to do the beach. José felt underprepared with his towel, trunks and hot sauce.

"Thank you again for the invitation. I've not spent any time on the lake this summer. It's good to go and enjoy God's natural creation. You look enchanting today, by the way."

"Gracious, señor. Both for the compliment and for your company. I hate going to these things alone and couldn't think of a better person to join me."

He smelled her sweet cologne something he grew to like more each time the scent teased his nose.

"It takes about thirty-minutes to get to the lake. Tell me how you're feeling now that it's been several weeks since the shooting."

"I like to say I'm getting better every day. Some days that's only just a little better. I should be my old self in another couple of weeks, I hope. Still have a hard time sleeping on my left side. It's such a beautiful day out today."

"Yes, this is a scorcher, but it'll be great to be on the water. Find some shade and a cool adult beverage."

"Not a cloud in the sky. I came into Carlisle on this road," José said. "Got a ride with a trucker who told me all about the town. I've not been out this way since I got here. I forgot how peaceful and quiet it gets when you get out of the city. Nothing but telephone poles and trees to watch as you ride along."

Jackie cleared her throat.

"Oh, and of course my lovely driver."

"You've such a unique almost naïve view of the world. It's very refreshing being near you José."

"Thank you, tell me about the big story with the bank."

"No, not doing the news today. I did hear Sherriff Ward say he reaally appreciated the drop in violence with the gangs. He's calling it the

Pax Carlisle for the peace of Carlisle. Tell me again, how did you pull that off?"

They continued chatting on all sorts of topics, but José found himself admiring her tanned and toned legs often and tried to avoid staring. She was a very beautiful woman, but he vowed a long time ago not to think of women in a lustful way. Still, she seemed to know how to distract him from that vow.

When they arrived, they found the picnic shelter. He helped haul the cooler and the rest of the gear to the site. She pulled a couple of folding chairs out of the hatch. Once they got all the kit settled, she went to go find Mitch. José took the moment to sit down in the shade, to catch his breath and wipe his brow. Between the load and the lung injury, breath was hard to find in this heat. But he didn't want to look weak in front of her. *I haven't been out in this heat since coming home from the hospital.* Jackie came back with an older man, he surmised must be Mitch. Big mustache, well-groomed reddish-brown hair. A little portly. He wore flip flops, a faded Bar Harbor blue t-shirt, and yellow and blue striped swim trunks. José stiffened himself to look better than he felt.

"José, this my boss and our host today, Mitch. He's also the one who interrupts my life all the time."

"The news never sleeps," he said looking at Jackie.

José stood up fast and extended a hand.

"I could always give those stories, or interruptions as you call them, to others you know. But I think you wouldn't have it any other way." Turning to José and shaking his hand, Mitch said, "Mitch O'Conner, pleasure to meet you at long last. I was beginning to think you were a figment of her imagination. She speaks of you often, but we never got to see you. I have a wife and two teenage boys around here somewhere."

"I'm very much flesh and blood sir. Pleasure to meet you too. Thank you for the kind invitation today. I haven't been out much since the incident. I brought you some of my homemade hot sauces. The green one will go well with chicken and pork. The red one with beef dishes. Either will work with fish depending on how it's prepared."

"Perhaps you should do the cooking. I hear you're quite the chef."

"That is very kind and I'm glad to help . . ."

"No sir, he's still recovering. I know once he starts cooking, I won't see him for the rest of the day. No cooking for him today and no news for me," Jackie said.

Mitch put his hands up, "Got it, ma'am."

"I thought she said you were the boss?"

"We all know how that works, José. That's what they tell us and then they proceed to do what they like." He laughed and turned to leave. He turned again walking backward and said, "Good to meet you. We have the ski boat here, if you want to try. Come down to the dock in about thirty minutes. It'll be all gassed up and ready to go."

José looked at Jackie and smiled. "I just got put back together, I don't think rattling my innards on water skis is a good idea. You can if you wish."

"I might but let's mingle and meet some of the crew." She grabbed his hand and they headed into the newsroom crowd sprinkled around the hillside leading down to the beach.

After the meet and greets, José changed into his trunks in the nearby men's room. Jackie set up the chairs near the water and was now out of her cover up, showing off her curves in that black one piece. José left his shirt on to keep the scars covered. She persuaded him to apply sunscreen to her back which made him very uncomfortable at first. However, since he was behind her, he could mask his awkwardness. Her skin was tanned and soft. There were a few freckles and moles, but they just served as beauty marks from his perspective. Her shoulders were very taunt, so he gave her a neck and shoulder rub while he massaged in the lotion.

"Oh yeah. Wow, didn't realize how tense I was. Must be all that's going on now." She leaned into the strong hands.

"There is so much happening in Carlisle now with the bank deal. Does your work always make you tense?"

"Umm," she continued to enjoy his hands on her neck. She tilted her head to the right inviting special attention to the left side of her neck. José obliged. Her skin was warm under his hands.

"No, the work doesn't often get to me."

He realized it was this date that had her so keyed up. She was a tough lady to read but he knew he was making her as nervous as she was him. The rub was taking longer than was comfortable now so José patted her on the shoulders and couldn't resist blowing on her neck. She shuddered when the goose bumps hit her.

"Oh my heavens, you're going to make me light-headed señor," in her best southern belle accent.

"Just trying to relax you. No need to be nervous around me."

He took his seat next to her and held her hand while they watched the children playing in the waves made from the wakes of the boats and jet skis on the lake. The screams and shouts of children at play always gave José much joy. He sipped a beer while Jackie drank a diet soda.

"You seem to like watching the children."

"There is such innocence there. So few worries. Not that they're saints, but oh to be that carefree again in life. All their life ahead of them."

"Don't get all somber on me now."

"Not melancholy, just observing. They're sources of great joy, but also such challenges the parents can't imagine at this age. Near death experiences can make one philosophical."

"I think that's your natural state. Sometimes you seem so much older than you appear. Your views are almost that of my father or grandfather. How did you gain such insight in your thirties?"

"These days I feel like a grandfather. I avoid many vices of the world and spend much time with the Creator. He shows me things I don't see myself in his Word and in his world. My wisdom comes from him."

"OK now it's getting too heavy. Let's head to the dock and enjoy some time on the lake he created. Mitch is back and this may be the last run before dinner. No, you don't have to ski. But it'll be loads of fun just to be aboard."

Mitch shuttled various groups out on the lake to water ski while Jackie and José watched from the beach. Now it was their turn.

José was rested after their time on the beach, so he was game for the boat ride. They lurched forward and hit the wake of another passing boat as Mitch hit the gas. José came out of his seat and almost landed in Jackie's lap. He laughed with delight as they jumped one wake after another. He'd never been in a boat this fast before. It seated six people including the captain.

José became the full-time water ski spotter after the first one showed him what to do so she could ski next. He watched and mastered the hand signals and made sure Mitch could understand by yelling them to him as well. "I feel like a talking mime," he said to Jackie standing nearby. "I have no idea what it takes to be good at this sport. They all seem to be having a great time on the water."

"You should try it, the key is to get standing," Jackie said over the roar of the engine. "Not today, with all that bouncing, it would be just too much for me right now."

Jackie's turn came after the other three aboard finished theirs. It took her a couple of failed attempts, but she was soon up and hoping across the water like a pro.

She gave José, the spotter, a run for his money using all the hand signals he learned from the previous runs. "Go Left! Go faster! Go right! Just right!"

After about ten minutes in the water, she gave the slashing signal to stop and circle around to pick her up. José took her hand as she stepped back into the boat from the ladder.

"Wow, what a rush! That was great!" she said out of breath.

Now faced with a dripping and glistening Jackie, José again tried to remember his vow. He handed her a towel and hoped he wasn't staring too long.

She squeezed the water out of her ponytail. It splattered the deck.

José offered her a drink. She opted for a light beer this time. José decided he should just stick with water. It wasn't alcohol which intoxicated him now. He enjoyed the feeling but feared it.

They zipped across the lake and jumped a few more wakes as they headed back in for dinner.

Hamburgers, hot dogs, bratwurst, pork ribs, and all the fixin's. José hot sauces were gone in short order. They finished up with watermelon, homemade ice cream and various other deserts. José took a piece of Key Lime pie and brought Jackie some chocolate-chocolate chip cookies.

She was in a sheer, black cover up with v-shaped stripes. It was more modest but still distracting. She had on her sun hat now. "Let's walk down to the beach. I want to see it once more before we head back," she said.

"Don't get lost, we're going to have a bonfire down there later." Mitch hollered after them.

They walked away in silence. He held out his hand and she accepted.

"Jackie, I'm very tired. This has been a wonderful day and I couldn't think of a better person to spend it with. I don't want it to end, but I think I need to go."

"I understand, I'll make our apologies for the bonfire portion. That's new this year. I wanted to head back to town to see the fireworks at Hart Park, if you think you can last that long."

They stopped as the sun was setting on the water. He turned and faced her.

"Perhaps, if I rest in the car on the trip home. Sorry to be a party pooper."

"Nonsense sweetheart, you've made my day."

The gentle breeze by the lake caught a wisp of Jackie's hair that broke loose from her ponytail. It danced around her face pointing first to her eyes, her nose and then her lips before returning up to her forehead.

"Jackie, I must say something that is on my heart. I made a vow years ago to not look at women as objects of desire. Yet, I find myself desiring you. More than any other women I've known for a very long time."

"Nice to know the outfits worked. I was beginning to think you weren't interested, just trying to be polite."

"While they are stunning, it isn't the outfits alone. It's the woman and all her gifts that were wrapped in them."

"You say some of the sweetest things. They'd seem like just come on lines from other men but from you, it's so sincere." She swallowed hard. "Why are you alone?"

"Oh Jackie, I won't go there now. I don't feel alone when I'm in the presence of my Master but somehow, I'm wondering how I'd get along without you too. I have a mission . . . I just can't get involved like this . . ."

He turned toward the lake, and she moved back in front of him guiding his gaze back to her. "José, this isn't easy for me either. I know why I'm alone but you're so caring, so sweet, so loving. I'm not that except near you. Please don't turn away."

He cupped her face in his hands. *These hands perform miracles but not sure they ever held anything so lovely.* He brought her face to his and kissed her tenderly then with more passion.

He lowered his hands to her waist, and she kissed him. He closed his eyes but didn't want to miss any of it. She leaned into him, and he held her so tight a hurricane couldn't separate them. He just held onto her and enjoyed the marvelous feeling that swept through him. He took a deep breath and held her.

She pulled away looking into his eyes. She said nothing. Just a long look. Then she smiled and held him again. "I've got one more outfit to show you. I need to get out of this wet bathing suit. I'll tell Mitch we have to go."

After a quick change they headed to the parking lot. She'd changed into jeans with the knees out, a charcoal gray tank top with a red, white, and blue eagle in flight across her chest. A Carlisle State Red Eagles baseball cap sat on her head, with her ponytail sticking out the back.

She carried a white shawl. "Got to cover up in case of mosquitos," she said while she climbed into her SUV.

On the way back to Carlisle, José took a power nap to be able to enjoy the fireworks. They were set for 9:30. They didn't get back in time to clean up, so they parked and walked a few blocks to the park. The crowd was large and the fireworks impressive. They were set to patriotic music not all of which José recognized. Jackie and José were back at the car after 10 pm. Jackie had to let him lean on her to steady himself the last block of the walk. He did too much and needed to work the next day.

She walked him to the door of the boarding house. Before they parted, José looked into her delightful eyes again, glad the sunglasses were gone. He held her tight once more and felt himself melt into her and she into him. He kissed her again and then moved down and kissed the left side of her neck before moving back to her lips.

"Thank you for today, mi corazón. I've not enjoyed a day like this for a very long time. I enjoy being with you like no other. Everything seems to be moving so fast. We need to take this slow please. There's so much you don't know about me. If you can be patient, there's much we can share. I follow the Master and am on a mission here. You're a part of that, I know that now and am glad. Please bear with me while I try to understand all of this and get over my injury. Mi corazón, I'm sorry we have to part, but I must rest, and you need that shower." He held her once more.

"The pleasure was all mine señor. I can move slowly. A refreshing difference yet again. You are a mystery indeed. We should do this more often."

"I'd like that very much."

"Me too. Buenos Notches." She gave him one last kiss.

"Hasta luego, Señorita Jackie."

He couldn't help but watch her walk back to the car. She turned and smiled as she went adding some extra sway to her steps.

JULY

CHAPTER 18

Like José, Deion's summer started rough too. The Carlisle police probed Mario's disappearance which cramped the Biz early on. Deion was a shooter and loyal, but never led a business before. He didn't like it and wasn't good at it. With the reduced ability of the Biz to control all the territory Da Wyz once did, he worked out the territory split with the Mayans in late June. Running the Biz gave more trouble than Deion liked but such was the price of peace. The war depleted the ranks and Carafe Homes was taking the potential new recruits.

Deion had few trusted advisors. With his intimidating management style, there was no one who would tell him honestly what was happening. His management style worked with the gangs, but not the shipping business. Several of the experienced barge captains decided they could work elsewhere and be left alone. That left the Biz with inexperienced men running the river barges. On several occasions, they damaged cargo and barges, hurting the little legitimate business they had. Administrative work and bureaucracy were not the life he wanted. Deion wanted to spend his days at the Excelsior club with beautiful ladies by his side. He did like the cash flow through and decided a smaller Biz may serve his needs and allow him time for fun with the ladies too.

As barges were damaged, he diverted the insurance money to repair them to fund his lifestyle. He began to like the barge accidents. The Biz continued to shrink.

No one from the inside or outside challenged him knowing his reputation. But that couldn't last forever.

※ ※ ※

Hamsa was having a better summer than most. His conversion to Christianity wasn't received well in New Rojava. However, Rima seemed resigned to accept it.

"I understand that Islam let us all down in our homeland. It's hard to believe that Allah would allow all the suffering among good Muslims. I also know that teenagers rebel and this is part of that, no doubt. I've seen a change in you. There's joy in your life, my son. For that I'm grateful to Yosef for helping you. I don't follow this new Master of yours, but after so much strife over religion where we came from, I don't have the will to create a battle here in America. As a Christian, your life may well be easier here," Rima told him.

Sami and Dijlin didn't see it that way. Sami said, "You're just a troublemaker and have been since I met you back in the refugee camp in Jordan. If you want to follow Yosef's God that's up to you. You must know for me there is no God but Allah and Mohammed is his prophet."

Dijlin echoed that sentiment. Most of the adults in New Rojava felt the same and told Rima, "If he starts converting others, we may have to turn him out of the village."

※ ※ ※

The garden they planted on the vacant lot next door began to produce many vegetables and leafy greens. The burning of the field seemed to help the soil. They plowed under the burned section and replanted. While that crop was delayed, it had an even more impressive yield. The field must've been fallow for years and was ready to give up its nutrients to the community garden. New Rojava celebrated the harvest. Only Hamsa knew that Yosef prayed a blessing over the fields a few months ago. He told Rima who tried to dismiss it. Hamsa knew Yosef had power from God. He believed.

Many now spoke fluent English thanks to Yosef and the children spending so much time in school. Hamsa was teaching them some

Spanish he picked up in the cooking classes at Ramone's. Valentina Rafael, one of the waitresses, told him she was going to Carlisle State to study teaching. She offered free Spanish classes to the adults over the summer after she graduated high school. The refugees were thrilled to have her, but none more than Hamsa.

Hamsa went to the classes to learn, but also because he liked to see Tina. He loved to watch her annunciate the words to a group with Arabic accents. His attendance was limited, because he was now working almost full time in the kitchen at Restaurant Tapas helping Carlos. They were both young Christians and enjoyed sharing stories of how the Lord was working in their lives. He learned conversational Spanish working at the restaurant too. He used the money to help his mom, but still had spending money.

Tina was a typical high school senior in many ways, she had a round face with long black hair, thick dark eyebrows and mocha colored skin. Hamsa would say she had deep, dark brown eyes and was almost equal height which made them easy to see. She dressed with modesty, for a teen, and seemed more interested in academics than boys. Her plans were to study teaching and language arts at Carlisle State and return to VM to give back to her community. Hamsa wasn't sure what she saw in him, but she did seem to like it when he taught her Arabic.

After Tina finished up the latest class, she headed to the bus stop. Hamsa called to her, "Hey Tina."

"Que?" she asked.

"I'd like to take you out to dinner on Saturday," he said. His heart raced. His mind jumped from one thought to another. He shifted his weight from one leg to the other, while he waited, for what seemed like forever, for her response.

She didn't know how he left class early to make himself look just right for this moment. Every hair in place. Shirt neat and tucked. Chest out.

"Si," she said.

He thought he'd soar to the clouds. Then he realized she was still standing there and smiling at him.

"Was that *si* for "I understand" or for "yes, I want to go"?"

"Si, I want to go. Where will we go?"

"I'll meet you at Restaurant Tapas at seven o'clock. I'd like to dine there instead of work there for a change. Let them take care of us."

"That'll be fine. I'll see you on Saturday at seven. After, maybe we could go to hear some salsa music at the club down the street?"

"I'll look forward to it the rest of the week," said Hamsa.

The bus arrived and she had to go. Hamsa watched her hurry away and enjoyed the view. Then, he floated back home. When he told his mom about his date, he beamed, and she was thrilled to see him so happy.

JULY

CHAPTER 19

Pastor Rich listened to the chatter in the room coming from all those at the monthly pastors' lunch meeting. Today's lunch was Asian fare at the Shangri La Palace, up the hill. Scents of stir fry and chow mien wafted from the kitchen nearby. As usual they had a private room with several tables, this time, set in a U shape. The room was dark paneled with large colorful paintings from the Orient. There were plenty of statues of old dynasty emperors and lots of Chinese symbols on the walls that Pastor Rich did not understand.

The meeting consisted of attendees from the seven congregations that agreed to work together in May. It also included a few new pastors from other congregations who wanted to see what the group was all about. The seven main congregations needed to be more organized now since they had a mission to go along with the vision—of moving many families out of poverty and up the hill. They also invited Reggie Saunders, Managing Director of Carafe Homes, and Justus.

Pastor Rich called the meeting to order and opened in prayer. "I'm pleased to report that we've received pledges and cash offerings of almost two million dollars which came from three churches predominantly, to add to the endowment that Jeremiah left. In addition, with his estate settled Miranda Michaels added another million dollars to the corpus of the Carafe endowment.

"Thus, overall, we have almost eight million. As you know, we won't spend the corpus but will use it as an endowment to make this program self-sustaining. We'll only use the earnings off the endowment to supplement the housing rents to make them more affordable to our neighbors. The fund is in good shape right now but after the summer break, we'll restart the fundraising. Reggie, give us an update on the work of Carafe."

As Rich sat down, spontaneous applause broke out across the room.

"I need to say a couple of things. As you know, I've been an executive on loan from BNS since we started. With the sale of the bank, I don't think, I'll be able to stay on their payroll and benefits so, if you're willing, I'll need to move fulltime to the payroll of the trust. Unless any of you have a better idea," Reggie said.

"I think we can hire you through the Carlisle Baptist Cooperative. The benefits are good for a young family, and they already have several folks on payroll. They won't fund it though. So, we'll have to use money from investment earning to pay you. We could have an admin fundraiser, but most don't like to give to that kind of thing," Brother Bruce said.

"Thanks Bruce, but this seems like a problem for the Wharf," Tony said. "I'll squeeze my deacons and see if we can hire you full time at Commonwealth. We got good health care and if anyone wants to help fund it, I'm all ears. What's the second part of your report?"

"Now for the positive news, with the rent subsidy program using only earnings off the endowment, after allowing for expenses, we can move up to seventy families into our units and keep them there indefinitely. We've moved twenty families up the hill out of the Wharf already. Most had teens at risk for gang membership. So, over all we can move maybe fifty more. By the fall, we'll have placed forty families into new schools locating them away from poverty, giving new opportunity to a new generation in our city with the goal of moving the remaining thirty families by the end of the year. This will help break the cycle of poverty. We can do more, but this is a great start. I have several cities across the country who are watching this and want to know how we do. Pardon the pun, but we're movin'. If we can double the fund, we can make it almost one hundred fifty families sustainably in affordable housing we didn't have to build. That's my target over the next twelve months. I've also approached several large foundations to see if they will help us," Reggie said.

There was another round of applause with a few whoops and fist pumps.

"All the news isn't good. Some of the families are struggling to integrate into the new neighborhoods. This is raising tensions over adding more. Some HOA's are trying to prevent subsidized rents from being allowed in their neighborhoods. It appears these are more growing pains than serious issues. We're going out of our way to keep from having too many Carafe Homes in one area. I'm also looking into the apartment complexes up the hill. The supply of rentable houses is starting to run dry. We're watching the integration tension issue, but I could use some help from the local churches in those areas to welcome and keep everyone cordial. I do speak with each family each month. That's beginning to become more difficult, now that there are so many. I'll need some help by the time we get the forty families moved," Reggie continued.

"The next group of families should be from Villa Maya. We should target five families with the next wave. In addition, we should also look to the poor white families in the Wharf, to see if any of them should move up the hill," Justus said.

"My team can help you qualify families at risk in Villa Maya. Are we going to ask for immigration status?" Father Menendez said.

"What does the rest of the team think?" asked Rich.

"No," was the unanimous vote.

"If they're here and in poverty, we should do our best to help them out of it. The police will have to check immigration status." They all agreed knowing this may create negative publicity, if an illegal got deported from one of the homes.

"Who can help with qualifying the poor whites in the Wharf?" asked Tony.

"St. Marks is near a white area in the Wharf. We're helping many families now. We'll make some recommendations," Reverend Lucy said.

The meeting continued and excitement built despite the nervousness about Reggie's new role once the bank deal closed.

The meeting ended with Lucy's prayer for success and pledges from the churches up the hill to keep monitoring the temperament of the neighborhoods with the relocated families.

As the servers began to clear the tables, Rich noticed that Justus was distracted. Rich and Reverend Tony asked him after the meeting. "How are you feeling now?"

"I'm doing well. I'm back at Ramone's full time and enjoying cooking. The cease fire is holding. We're successful with the family relocation program, and it will be available to all regardless of race. However, something's still missing. The wealthy still aren't embracing this. Seventy five percent of our fund has come from Jeremiah. If people knew what life was like in poverty, the fund should be double or triple this size. The city still can't get new affordable sites designated. I fear the Master is losing patience with us and I don't know what to do about it. I keep getting the vision of a great downfall. I don't know what it means. I'm afraid something monstrous is coming. Pray with me this week and next. Pray every day for wisdom and mercy."

"We'll do that. Shouldn't we get everyone doing that?"

"Yes, make it a general request to the rest of the group. I'll tell Father Menendez about this too on the ride back to Ramone's."

Before he left, he pulled Rich aside, "tell me about the three United for Jesus leaders that tried to have you removed. Have you contacted them?"

"Randall moved to a new associate pastor role out of state. He and I reconciled before he left town. I gave him a good recommendation. He learned a tough lesson, but he did the right thing in the end."

Justus smiled at that report. "What of the others?"

"Thomas Spratt spoke to me over the phone. We had a cordial conversation. He joined another congregation down the street. He told me, I pushed him too far with my challenges and he hadn't grown to that point in his walk. He split with Paul Stanley and hasn't spoken to him in weeks. We should continue to pray for Thomas."

"Mr. Stanley?"

"He was the hard nut to crack, so to speak. He was the most vocal one and I think the instigator. Not sure what I did to offend him exactly, but he won't speak to me. I reached out to him via phone and email. Even wrote an old-fashioned letter telling him I forgave him and inviting him back to the church. The letter was returned unopened. I did speak to him a couple of weeks ago, once he found out it was me, he lost interest and hung up quickly. Not sure what else I can do."

"Sounds like you've done what you need for your walk with the Master. Mr. Stanley will need to address his own. Perhaps he'll reach out to you one day. I'm very pleased you listened. You're healed now. Look at all the good our Lord has done through you. I look forward to seeing what he does in your ministry going forward."

With that Justus grabbed the Pastor's hand and drew him close. "Well done my brother!" He said so only Rich could hear. After that, Justus stepped outside of Shangri La heading for Father Menendez's car as it started to rain.

JULY

CHAPTER 20

These days, Jackie stopped by Restaurant Tapa's around 9:30 as both hers and José's work was winding down. They began to meet many evenings for a late supper. She checked on his progress after the shooting and he caught up on the news of the day.

With all the rain of late, it appeared the news slowed down with the weather, so she started to have some extra free time. She always primped herself at the studio before heading out to see him and then checked her make up once again in the car mirror before going in to be sure she looked just right. Had to be certain her outfit was attracting but not too over the top.

"How are you holding up today Señor Chef?"

"Still have some pain when I turn a certain way. I'm a little slow to stand after sitting for a while, but overall, back to normal," he said and took a sip of his beer.

Jackie enjoyed a glass of New Zealand sauvignon blanc from a bottle opened earlier that evening, but not finished. Only one, in case a call to go to work came through and she had to anchor the 11:00 slot. Still, it was good to relax with José. They were seated in one of the booths near the window. The traffic on Belleview Boulevard went splashing by. It had a quieting rhythm to it.

He wore his chef's pants and jacket. She noticed he used to wear a t-shirt for their meetings, but now, was dressing up. *I guess I am a special case for him.* Jackie sported her workout clothes, black yoga pants and a fitted royal blue t-shirt with her WWNS News rain jacket drying on the back of a chair nearby.

"What's happening in the news world today?"

"Didn't you watch my excellent report on the ever-changing bank deal? Seems once others found out BNS could be bought, several suitors showed up. It looks like the front runner from Atlanta is edging out the bunch from Ohio. Everything's getting complicated now. It'll sell, just don't know to who or how long it'll take."

"Sorry I missed it. Sounds interesting. We had a busy dinner rush, so I didn't have time to watch."

"Most of the city finds it riveting, but not you. Why is that?"

"Big business deals like that tend to make the wealthy wealthier. At best, it's neutral to the poor. Usually, it harms the locals. People get laid off in the interest of efficiency most of the time. In their ego, the buyers overpay for the business and take it out on the workers after they close."

"For a tapas chef, you seem to know all about business. Where'd you learn all this? Did you go to college?"

"I did in a place far away, a long time ago. Now I just listen to the businessmen and women who come to the restaurants and pubs I work in. They're complaining often to each other about such things. Or at times they're worried about going out of business because of recessions and such."

"You sound like you don't approve. You know these businesses employ many people in Carlisle. They give families a good living. Nothing wrong with that."

"I agree. It just seems that in the chase for efficiencies they lose the human touch. Because it's about numbers and not people, it changes the way they see the world. The owners and managers get used to looking at numbers and not people. Then when the tables turn and their world is rocked by change, the owners and managers complain they're being treated like a number. Ironic justice." He took another pull on the beer.

"So, what's the solution the chef is cooking up to that?"

"Cute . . . it's a very tried and true solution. Treat others as you want to be treated. Competition is a good thing in some ways, but when overdone, it becomes destructive. When it does, it causes us to stop loving our neighbor as ourselves. The bigger the business, the more competition drives it away from people, toward things. When the business gets too big to focus on people, it's too big."

"Where did you say you learned this?"

"The schools I attended are long gone. I just read Scripture now and try to apply it to my life. It allows for simplicity. It requires solitude and time to study."

She leaned forward. "You don't get off the hook that easy, señor. Where did you get your degree?"

"I spent time several places. Never graduated in the sense of how you mean it. Studied theology at the Sorbonne . . . "

"In Paris? Sorry to interrupt."

"Oui Mademoiselle Jacqueline," he smiled and continued, "others were in Rome and Florence. I traveled around to some of the Spanish monasteries also. Researched in the libraries of North Africa. Most of those places are long gone."

"So how did you, a man of letters from Europe, get here, Señor Chef?"

"The last few years, I've been in Latin America. I came to America last year about this time. The Master sent me to Carlisle."

She leaned back and crossed her arms. "Europe, Africa, South America; what are you running from, José?"

"You forgot the middle east. I'm not running from anything. I'm running toward something. I go where I'm sent. I try to help in that place. Most of the time, it's a place that's in dire need of help. Often people don't even realize how dire a situation they're in. They prefer to deny any real issue exists until it erupts."

"So, do you help?"

"I help those who'll listen to the counsel of the Master. Over the years, I've grown impatient with the wealthy and the comfortable. I close my comments to them with 'listen or don't'. Rich tells me that comes off harsh. I tell him the Master used a similar saying in his teaching. 'Let him who has ears . . .' I want them to listen. I pray they will. We're all creatures of free will and most don't listen. It's sad because, I can see what will happen if they do, or if they don't. I want to help save them from the pain of bad choices, but they're too self-deceived to listen most of the time."

Jackie took a sip of wine. She liked hearing him share his heart. *With that subtle Latin accent, I think I could listen to him for a long time. I'd like to hear his French accent more.*

"What about me? Am I going to listen to you?"

"I don't know yet. We shall see. I hope you will. The way of the Master is work but the burdens are lighter than those of men. His way brings shalom to those who embrace it. I pray that you will. Listen or don't," he said in a soft, longing tone.

Jackie took in a deep breath and let it out slow. "You don't give up, I'll give you that. I told you I tried that before. I appreciate the concern. I can see it's sincere. I'll keep you guessing for now."

She took another sip of wine, reached out to grasp his hand and bit her lip. "I've tried to find a way to ask you this, but get nervous about how it'll come across. I know it's hard to believe I can get tongue tied. I'm not sure I want to know the answer anymore, but I have to. So, hear it is. You brokered peace between the Biz and the Mayan gangs. It's holding. That's impressive, almost miraculous. I've spent time researching some happenings in town. Some of this research came at great risk to me. I put a few things together while you've been out of action and need to ask you. Did you heal Renata at the wedding? Did you stop the gun battle in the street that day? Did you heal Ms. Roberta of her blindness?"

"Is a reporter asking me this, or a close friend?"

"José, I'm both. I can't separate the two. But I'm also a seeker of truth. I can be trusted with it. I don't broadcast everything I learn."

José put his other hand on hers. She was trembling.

"Why do you fear the answer?"

She swallowed. "I don't want what we have to change. You're one of the most remarkable people I've met. I like what we have now. I fear the answer will change that. It'll require me to go somewhere I don't want to go. If you answer *no*, I need to understand how these amazing coincidences happen around you. I may also doubt your answer and thus your sincerity. If you answer yes that requires the scientific method I've trained myself in for years to doubt itself and what it knows for sure, but now is challenged. It requires me to renew a faith journey, I'm not ready to embark on. I have to wonder, if you're of this world or if you're delusional. Either way the answer makes me look at you in a new way."

She steeled herself for the answer and sat up straight. "It's taken me days to work up to this moment and now I've asked. Please tell me."

"Yes. The Holy Spirit did these things through me and more you don't know. I've been given gifts of the Spirit. He shows me what to do. I can't do these on my own. Most of the time I'm just José. A man listening for the Kol Yahweh and striving each day to follow it."

Jackie moved her gaze from his eyes to the tabletop. "I see. I've never been around that kind of power. I have a hard time believing it's even possible. You could be the biggest story I've ever covered. Yet I know I can't say anything. That's what you tell the ones you touch. That's why no one will speak about it."

José leaned forward in the seat, "Jackie, the time will come when you will tell others about me. I feel that is part of His plan for us. But I also ask for discretion now. Look at what happened in the Scripture to the Master and the apostles when it became known the power of the Spirit was in them. The crowds flocked to them. That's not why I'm here. I wish it was. I'd love to heal all those around us. There's so much pain and suffering the Spirit could relieve with a touch. But it isn't the way now. He has the church in place for this. I won't usurp the Bride of Christ. That would be against his will. I know that's very hard to understand from one who no longer believes, but you shared your heart and now I've shared mine." He lifted her hand to his lips and kissed it.

She gazed out the window into the dark wet streets while another car swished by. She had to process this. *More than a kiss on the hand please, señor.* "José, I . . . I don't know what this means. But I . . ." Her phone buzzed and Mitch's face appeared on the screen. "No!" She looked at the phone. "Arrgh! Duty calls."

By accident, she clicked the phone on speaker. She didn't realize her hand was shaking until José let it go.

"Jackie, a barge broke from its mooring upriver and then rammed one of the supports on the Lumber River Bridge a few minutes ago. Police and river keeper are on the way. I'll send Bradley for an "on the scene" spot, if you're up for it."

"Mitch, I'm close but I'm in workout gear. Need to get back to the station and change." She was trying to make excuses. A first in a long time for her with a story.

"Do you have your station raincoat?"

She snapped back to news professional mode. "Yes, great idea. I'll head there now. Get Bradley out there ASAP. I'll call in a report for the 11:00 if he doesn't make it in time." She clicked the phone off.

"Oh, what's wrong with me? We just enjoyed a wonderful moment and I let work lure me back. I'm so sorry José. I think I need some time to process what you just told me. I think you just loosed me from my mooring as well. I hope I don't crash into a bridge. We must continue this conversation soon. I no longer fear your answer for some reason, but I'm also not sure what to do with it. I wanted you to tell me a believable 'no.' Truth be told. Let's meet next time at my place. I feel like I'm going to my parent's house here. I need to show you a change of scenery. I live up the hill in a small patio home. You still get to cook though." She smiled, grabbed her purse and raincoat and started for the door.

"No. Wait," she said and turned back to help José out of his chair. As he stood, she leaned into him and kissed him with great intensity and warmth. *That's the kiss I wanted. His embrace is much stronger now,* she thought as she rested her head on his shoulder both scared and comforted. "I need some time to think about what you just said. I promise I will. Please be patient with me. You don't know where I've been, where I've come from. Be patient. You told me you wanted to go slow after our Bass Lake date, and I agreed. Can you be patient with me too now?"

"I'm here for you Jackie. I'll be patient. I'm human with shortcomings, but I don't lie. I love truth too much for that. What I told you is true."

"I know. But wow, does it upend things for me. I must go. Come to my place on Sunday night. I'll text you the time and the menu. Ingredients on me, cooking's on you. We can complete the picture then."

He tilted her face up to his and kissed her again. They parted breathless.

"Gotta go, señor. Please come Sunday."

"Let me know the time and I'll be there."

She headed to the door and smiled when she looked back and saw him watching her go.

JULY

CHAPTER 21

Susan Hamilton and Yosef arrived in New Rojava in late July on a day prearranged with Amena, Sami and Rima. They brought a small group of friends and met in the revived club house gathered around a few mismatched tables and chairs. The roof still leaked in places due to the rain. They collected the leaks with various bowls and buckets.

"My friends, I failed you at a time when you needed friends most. I come asking for forgiveness and to see how we can work together now. I know Yosef stayed with you and that is why I asked him to come with me today," Susan said.

"We're used to the powerful letting us down. I told you in the hospital, you violated our trust and friendship. You decided we were guilty before we had a chance to defend ourselves. What happens when we have another setback. Will you be by our side or with the protestors out front?" Amena said.

"I was never with the protestors. My husband's the mayor. We couldn't publicly support you based on the way the evidence came to light. There were two dead young men with connections to New Rojava. We were advised to run for cover. We almost divorced over this. I was determined to bring you all here and he was against it. With the bombing, his worst fears were realized, and I bore the brunt of it. I retreated. And I'm sorry."

"So, what's different now?" Sami asked.

"You were vindicated. People'll think twice now before jumping to conclusions. And I realized how much you suffered from my neglect. A dear friend helped to put me back on the right path." She looked right at Yosef. "Thank you, my friend."

Yosef nodded and pointed toward heaven.

"I also want to let you know that after our conversation in the hospital. I reached out to the Feds, and they have another group of Kurdish Refugees now due to arrive in August. If you're willing to welcome them in."

Everyone was excited about that. The room filled with chatter and buzz.

"We'll need more apartments to be prepped. I'm afraid the ones that are left are in a very bad state," Sami said. "May we work on them along with some of the contractors? We've gotten good at the work, just repairing our own units. We need materials and we want to be paid a fair wage. We need to replace the roof here and a few other places also."

"I like that idea," Susan said. "I'll talk with the contractor. How many hands can you give?'

"We have at least twenty, off for the summer and needing work. They're girls but they work hard. They've learned to do it better than some of the boys did back home before the war. They'll be their own group. No outsiders please. I'll supervise. We must protect our girls from these men that ogle them."

"I like that even better," Susan continued.

"Our girls can speak English well after a year in the American schools. We're learning Spanish now too from Hamsa's girlfriend Tina," said Rima swelling with pride.

"When can we get started?"

"I'll call the contractor today and work it out with the Feds to get him funded so he has materials. We'll have money for tools as well."

"Make it new stuff this time. We got their cast offs last year, but I hear they got all new tools with the money from the Feds. Someone said that we stole the tools. That's not true." Sami finished and folded his arms across his chest.

"I take it you want us back and are willing to accept our help again?" Susan said.

"By all means. Thank you for what you've done and what you will do," Rima said.

Amena signaled to Yosef to come into the kitchen.

"We need to talk. You converted Hamsa to Christianity. It's causing problems for us. He has converted three of our younger teens and two of the mothers. He talks about Jesus and reads his Bible to them. It's causing strain in our village. I hold you responsible. I don't like it at all."

"Amena, I only presented the story of my Master to him. I didn't convert him. I spoke loving truth to a hurting young man. It's made him a better man. For that, I refuse to apologize. This is real to him. So, he shared it with others. It's only natural when you receive good news. That's what I do also. I can see where this will cause issue in the group, but you can't stop the good news from spreading."

"We'll deal with this in our own way. We accept we're in a new land. I can't argue that Islam didn't stop our war or make it better. But it's still our way, and it must be respected. I had great admiration for you Yosef. I even hoped we could be more than friends. After this, I see you won't come around to Allah and I won't move toward Christianity. There's no hope for us in this world."

"Amena, I do respect you and your group. I appreciate the leadership you've shown in these difficult times. I didn't mean to mislead you into thinking, I wanted more from you. My intention was and remains to treat you with love and respect, welcome strangers in this land. If I can help, I will. I do this out of love for my Master first, but out of love for you too."

"Yosef, I must ask that you stop coming here. We no longer need English lessons and we've reconciled with Susan. We have what we need.

You coming here will just encourage this group of Christians to continue to make inroads. I won't stop them from what they believe, but don't want it to divide our community. I ask that you stay away." She said with a firm clinical tone.

"Is this the wish of the whole council of leaders?"

She nodded.

"I respect your wishes and will honor them. I'll also continue to teach Hamsa the Bible if he asks. I only ask that you maintain an open mind to his message. It's a message of love and hope. Something we all need. Something the new refugees will need to. Let me know if I can help you again. My heart is grieved by this parting, but I understand."

With that she handed him a bag of manoushi bread. "This is a gift from us to you for all the good you've done for us. We don't wish to part as enemies."

"Salam my friend," Yosef said.

He made his apologies to Susan and the rest of the group and headed to the bus stop. Sami stopped him outside and extended a hand and then a hug.

"Take care of Dijlin," Yosef said. "It didn't have to end like this. There's still good that could be done."

"Salam."

On the bus he wept for their hardened hearts and prayed for the small group of Christ followers in their midst. *The seeds were planted, may they take deep root.*

JULY

CHAPTER 22

Paul Stanley and Mike Winter met on a Saturday in late July in Paul's art deco office. The Atlanta bank's offer delayed the ultimatum from their banker, Eric Reynolds, a couple of weeks but the day of reckoning still fast approached.

"Mike, where are we with the IRS and the financials? I signed the personal guaranties for the loans a couple of weeks ago. Our boy Eric is freaking out. Swears his job is on the line and he'll take us down too."

"Any luck on finding other funding?"

"Not yet. I did get Alexandra's dad to give me some cash to keep us liquid until Summit Spires is ready to presell. So glad he doesn't ask too many questions. Anything for *daddy's little girl*."

"This rain isn't helping our project. We're well underway but now we're stopped dead for a week by the blasted weather. In July yet. Unbelievable," said Mike. He looked at his notes. "The IRS isn't happy they're days away from shutting us down again by seizing things. I have to give them the detail on all the like kind exchanges. We're outta time."

"How long do you think it'll take, for them to find the issues?"

"A week at most, could be just a couple of days."

"Mike, we got the bank on one side squeezing and the government on the other. The weather's been against us for days. Is someone trying to tell us something? I'm just a businessman trying to create jobs in our corner of the world. Why do they have to make it so difficult?"

"Boss, if we don't get a break soon, we're done. Maybe Hill Top was a *bridge too far*."

"Stop calling it Hill Top! It's Summit Spires!" Paul said.

"Yeah, yeah, whatever we call it, they're going to call us bankrupt if we don't get a break soon."

"You see Mike, that's why I'm the boss. I have a clearer view from the top. I can see we need a break. I know it's coming. Not sure what it is yet, but it's coming. Go ahead and give the IRS their requested information. We've kept it going for over a year now. It's time to face them, let them pronounce their view and we can appeal it up the chain. The way the Feds work we can keep this spinning until after Labor Day. By then Summit Spires preselling starts and we're off to the races again."

"I'll work on it this weekend and give it to them lunchtime on Monday. What shall we do about Eric?"

"Bank of the New South is gone and Eric'll go with them. Good riddance. Let's just not respond next week. Tell him the IRS is keeping us from issuing anything."

"That's not gonna work."

"Mike, I pay you well enough to make it work. Do I need to remind you that you're deep into this too? If I go down, you go with me. But I'm not going down. Stall him. Make it happen."

Mike left with his hands shaking and the blood pressure ringing in his ears. *This is going to kill me. I've got to get out of this. Maybe turn state's evidence?*

✢ ✢ ✢

José got a call from Father Menendez after Saturday mass. "Tony, Rich and I would like to speak with you on some matters that are concerning us. We've been praying per your instructions, but some things are coming to us that we find disturbing. Can you meet Sunday night for some dinner and a chat?"

"I have dinner plans on Sunday night, but they're not until later. Is there something we can do around six? How long do you think it'll take? Shall we meet at Ramone's?"

"No, best to be somewhere private. Rich suggested his house. I can pick you up around five?"

That should work fine since I'll be closer to Jackie's that way. "Let me see if Ramone will let me off that early. I'll text you for sure once I speak to him. Can you give me a set of topics I should prepare for?"

"Someone with your gift of prophecy should already know, mi amigo." Father Menendez chuckled.

"OK, who said I didn't already know just looking for confirmation perhaps." José continued the game of cat and mouse. "See you tomorrow, Father."

I'm surprised it has taken them so long to ask me who I am. Jackie already figured some of it out. I must seek the Master's wisdom on what to share. She isn't ready for the whole story. Perhaps these men are.

AUGUST

CHAPTER 23

José started an eventful Sunday with early morning prayer and worship at the Iglesia Pentecostal Camino a La Paz. He sat next to Carlos Rodriguez of the MX 60's. They enjoyed the animated music and the passionate message of the pastor. José didn't agree with all that was said, but the theological issues were minor.

The church remained much as he remembered it from the Easter service . . . chairs, not pews . . . small platform, no choir . . . big projection screen behind the pastor broadcasting the words to the hymns and other announcements. Like Easter, they still had ushers roaming the aisles with tissues as the more passionate parts of the sermon came.

He liked to visit different congregations around Carlisle and see the Lord worshipped in so many heartfelt and diverse ways. He remembered the Easter service with fondness when he came to be fully reconciled after his bout with depression following all that happened this spring. He felt this worship service would strengthen him as he prepped for the evening meeting with the pastors he mentored while on this mission. He prayed for them, for himself and for his dinner with Jackie afterwards. The Holy Spirit gave him no insight into how their evening would go considering the revelations he made to her a few days ago. He didn't like going in unprepared, but the counsel of the Master comforted him. . .

Do not be anxious beforehand what you are to say, but say whatever is given you in that hour, for it is not you who speak, but the Holy Spirit.

May it be so.

He went to the restaurant to work the lunch shift. Ramone granted him an early evening to attend the meeting at Rich's house provided he opened the breakfast shift on Monday. Father Menendez collected him around 5:30 in an old, domestic light brown sedan. It smelled of old clothes and animals.

"I tried to clean it up as best I could. My dogs roam free in here when I travel. I hope you don't pick up much dog hair."

"Not a problem for me. I enjoy dogs very much, and I appreciate free rides when they're provided. I'm not picky."

"I missed you in mass this morning José. Is everything alright?"

"Yes Father, I visit a number of the local gatherings in His name to enjoy the different styles of worship. Today I went to the Hispanic Pentecostal church in VM."

"Under Roman Catholic teaching, that doesn't count." He smiled when he said it.

"Father, you know I don't follow strict Roman Catholic teaching any longer. I'm called to a more ecumenical ministry. It is the Church, not the churches, as far as the Master is concerned. That is plain to see. After all, we're going to the home of a protestant minister to discuss deep matters of theology this night."

"I understand José. It is a remarkable thing the Spirt has done through your ministry here. I'm glad to be a part of it. However, I won't disavow my own convictions. On the other hand, the Lord is moving here. There is no denying that."

"So, what's the purpose of this mysterious meeting, Father?"

"All will be made clear soon. I hear you and the news lady are quite an item these days."

"She is a special case for me. We enjoy each other's company very much. I'm attracted to her like I've not been for a long time. I'm meeting her for dinner tonight after she gets off work. She's invited me to her place."

The Father looked at him with a raised eyebrow. "You need to be careful there, mi amigo. Are you wandering into the spider's web?"

"Not sure I understand the analogy. She's no venomous creation. She's a wonderful lady, who seeks truth. I can take care of myself around women these days. I could tell you stories. But I won't."

"OK, amigo, but this sounds like a danger zone to me. Can she be trusted? She is quite an attractive lady."

"Noted, Father. I know you mean well, but not to worry."

They arrived at Rich's house just before six. It was a beautiful evening with a welcome break in the rain of the past many days. The house, a two-story home, looked much like the others in the neighborhood. They headed to the door just as Tony arrived in his black sedan. Rich greeted them at the door, before they rang the bell.

As they entered, Rich said, "this is my wife, Maryanne. She's a rock the Lord brought in my life to support me and the ministry. I would be in deep trouble in life were it not for her. She's a great cook, a teacher of ladies, a fantastic mother . . ."

"Stop it," she said, extending her hand. "Justus, it's good to finally meet you. I've heard amazing things about you. Welcome to our home."

Justus shook her hand and looked into her eyes. "It's always a pleasure to meet a strong woman of God. It sounds like Rich knows how blessed he is, but let me just say, there are too few of you. You're a blend of Mary and Martha. You serve well, but also know the value of the greater things."

She blushed at his remark as her eyes welled with tears and looked at Rich unable to speak.

"I told you he had great insight." He took her hand as Justus let it go. Looking back at Justus, he said, "her mother used to tell her that when she was growing up. She passed a short time ago."

"My sincere condolences for your loss, but I know it's heaven's gain. She is singing his praises even now."

She regained her composure. "Thank you. May I get you all anything?"

"I'll have what others are having," Justus said.

"We have both kinds of tea. Sweet and Un," Rich responded.

They moved to the study after choosing their iced tea.

As Rich closed the door, Justus said, "what a splendid lady she is. I should like to see your children again, if they're home."

They were all seated around an oblong maple colored coffee table in three green and brown side chairs with Tony on the dark green sofa.

"They're out at church youth meetings. They'll be home around 9:00."

"Shame, I remember from Easter that they're all so precious."

"Thanks for that my friend. We need to get to why we asked you here today. I know you have another engagement tonight," Rich said.

"I'm also most curious about this called meeting. Have I done something wrong?"

Tony took the lead. "Joseph, we're convinced you're a man of God. We know he does amazing things through you. Healing Roberta Saunders, conversion of Jeremiah Michaels."

Father Menendez continued the thought, "The way you stopped the gun battle the day of the Rodriguez wedding. The healing of Renata Vega. The peace between the gangs."

Pastor Rich chimed in, "The moving of the poor and downtrodden out of the ghettos that held them for generations. Awakening the comfortable to the needs of the others. These are just some of what has happened, I'm sure. We could list more but that isn't our purpose here."

"I think you give me more credit than I'm due. You were involved with much of this. I was a participant in the Master's plan along with you. You still haven't gotten to the point," Justus said.

Tony picked up where he left off. "I'm preparing to preach a sermon series on the book of Acts this fall and came across a passage that intrigued me. I shared it with these men because it concerns you. They encouraged me to have this conversation to allow you to answer my question."

"What is the passage, my brother?"

He opened a well-used Bible to a bookmarked page and read the story of the selection of the apostle to replace the traitor Judas in Acts 1.

"Before you go on, I always like to know what version you're reading from."

Tony held up the Bible for all to see the ESV on the spine. "The English Standard Version is my preferred version these days."

"Thank you," Joseph said. "That is a good choice. Please proceed."

Tony paraphrased as he spoke. "The Holy Spirit led them to select Matthias. The passed over potential apostle was named Joseph called Barsabbas, who was also called Justus. It didn't escape my notice, that you go by both these names. As well as Yosef to the Syrians, the Arabic version of Joseph."

Father Menendez continued, "It took me a while to recall that you also say, 'they call me José Sabio.' You never say your name is José Sabio. The resemblance to Sabbas is what caught my eye, when Tony mentioned this."

"I'm not sure how to respond, gentlemen. Are you saying you think I'm a two-thousand-year-old almost apostle? Remember, I've made no such claim. Perhaps my mother liked that name, or I was renamed by the church. What are you asking me?"

"Justus can you explain this or is it just a coincidence?" Rich said.

Justus took a deep breath. He looked down and prayed for a moment tracing his eyebrows with thumb and forefinger. Then he placed his hands on his knees. Looking up at the brethren he said, "Tony, look up John 21:22 and 23. Read it to us."

> "Jesus said to him, 'If it is my will that he remain until I come, what is that to you? You follow me! So the saying spread abroad among the brothers that this disciple was not to die; yet Jesus did not say to him that he was not to die, but, 'If it is my will that he remain until I come, what is that to you?'"

Tony looked up in amazement. "It is you. That's why you have such power. You were with the Master from the start . . . "

"The Spirit has revealed this to you. The Master told me after the encounter on the beach with Peter before he ascended to heaven. He said that he had a special mission for me. He also told me not to tell any of the others. I would not be spared suffering, but I would not die until he returned in the clouds. After two thousand years you have no idea, how I long for that day. At first, I thought I was to be an apostle, but his wisdom is greater than mine. You'll note I was mentioned first and, in more detail, indicating my prominence among the young church. I wasn't passed over because I was unworthy. An apostle's role would be documented in church history. However, no one remembers a loser. My story was never written. Matthias went on to be the head of the church in Alexandria, Egypt among other things. You'll find my brother's name a few chapters later. His name was Judas. He was martyred in the early days of the church. All you'll find of Joseph in traditional literature is that he headed a church, and drank poison, but did not die. But finding all this would require a fair amount of digging."

"I've done the digging. You're right. You were the Bishop of Eluetheropolis," said Father Menendez.

"You've been thorough, I see. Yes, the Orthodox Church speaks of that. Curious that it was a city that got that name in the third century." He reflected a moment. "The city of the free, I always liked that name. If it's true, how did a first century almost apostle end up as bishop of a third century church. Something doesn't fit, unless . . . "

"Wait a minute, now!" said Rich. "This is too much to take in. Not sure I'm buying this. Where've you been for two thousand years? What was the Master's mission for you?"

"I go where I'm needed. Where he sends me. I found after some tough lessons that it's best to work behind the scenes. Not draw attention. He has allowed me to be present at some of the greatest events in church history. He has worked through me to minister to those he chose to lead these movements."

Rich crossed his arms.

"You may find faint references to me in the lives of Martin Luther and Saint Ignatius of Loyola. I worked to reform the Roman Catholic church at the Master's prompting. I was a confessor of each of these men at different times. There was much strife with the emergence of Protestantism. I encouraged those who led the movement, because it was needed to bring the church back to its first love. After a few years, I tried to then reform the Catholic church from within by working behind the scenes as a confessor of Ignatius and Francis Xavier. Two prominent founders of the Jesuits in the Catholic Church. Despite our Lord's desires to see them as one bride, the split church continued to fight each other. There were sound doctrinal issues to be sure but all the forced conversions, and torture and wars in his name just grieved the heart of God." Tears filled his eyes while he recalled this. He bowed his head and put out his hand to pause the conversation. After taking a moment to compose himself, he resumed. "We tried to force men, who didn't believe, to follow him and motivate them with fear of God to do the will of men. This is so easily twisted and so evil. It is present even today. Perhaps even in this room. I pray it is not. It has taken lifetimes to work through this. In the meantime, I kept my vows of poverty and chastity. After a few lifetimes, I felt led to lose my vow of submission to the will of the order of the Society of Jesus. So, I left the Jesuits centuries ago. I journeyed all over to minister where the need was greatest, wherever I was called. I was in Nicaea at the adoption of the Creed. I was there at the great Schism between east and west. I fought to stop the crusades before they started. I worked with the black plague victims. And down through the ages with victims of war, famine, pestilence. I tried to be Jesus with them each place. I was witness to the rise of Christianity in Africa. The last many years, I ministered in Venezuela, Ecuador, Peru and El Salvador."

He fixed his gaze back on the pastors.

"Now, he brought me here. I ask you, what do you think my mission is here?"

"This is a remarkable claim. So, I must conclude you are either suffering from the delusion you are this man, or you are who you say." Rich began to believe.

"The Master gave you the same choice, if you read his words with care." He paused again. "So, what do you think my mission is here?"

Rich recited what Justus told him months ago. "You're here to comfort those who suffer and make uncomfortable those in comfort."

"Correct. This we've done together, thanks to all your work. I don't want others to know about this. This is a private revelation. Not meant for the airwaves at this time. The Master has a plan for how this will be revealed. Brothers, I'm a man like you. I'm fallible like you. I bleed like you . . ."

"That's what threw me the last month or so. How was it that you got shot and almost died?" Tony said.

"I was lying in my hospital bed wondering the same thing too, Tony. What did I do wrong? He showed me, it was part of the plan. I don't know all of it even yet. He reveals it to me in pieces, when I need to know it. I didn't know what tonight was about, but knew it was serious enough to be in prayer much of the last many hours. I've been fasting all day. He did show me a vision to come to Carlisle. I saw many things in the vision but without context it made little sense to me. I saw the riots, the racial tension, the indifference of the wealthy, the unwelcome strangers, the gang wars, three partial men of different shades and one dark-haired woman whose face was unclear. Again, I didn't know who it was, since I didn't know the person."

"So, who was it?" Rich asked.

"I now know it's Jacqueline Hyatt. She has a major part to play, but I'm not sure how. I go to see her tonight after this meeting."

"You're older than Methuselah!" Tony said busting out with a boisterous laugh.

Justus joined him and tried to lighten the mood. "He was just a teenager. At one thousand, I was still waiting for my voice to change."

Tony got serious now. "This is going way to fast. There are so many questions. You were there at so many of these events. What was Peter like? What was Paul's thorn in the flesh? Who wrote the book of Hebrews? What was Solomon like . . ."

"Solomon was before my time. I'd love to share these other things with you my brothers, but you must have deeper questions you want to know."

And they launched into a series of questions that went on for hours. The hour of his date with Jackie was fast approaching and Justus stomach rumbled. "Gentlemen, you've no idea how wonderful it is to share such things with the brethren. You've blessed me so with this conversation. Can we meet again next Sunday night? I'd love to continue now but need to go see Jackie. Please pray for her. She needs to decide who she will follow. She needs to decide soon."

He stood up to go but continued. "One thing that has become apparent to me is that there will be a great downfall soon. I've seen cascading waters, news flashes, people weeping. These may not be literal since the Spirit sometimes conveys feelings more than actual events. Please continue to pray with me on this topic. Pray it can be prevented. Pray for wisdom to discern the meaning, before it's too late."

"We will do so," Tony said. Rich and the Father both nodded.

"There is one other thing. I won't be with you much longer. I'm not sure where but feel the Master will take me away from Carlisle soon. Please keep this conversation to yourselves until I'm gone. I don't seek publicity for me. Only to glorify the Master."

The Father interrupted him, "José, it seems like you're playing with fire here. A story of this magnitude you want to keep quiet and yet you're off to see a beautiful reporter. Alone. For one seeking to be in the shadows, it seems like a you're balancing on a razor's edge. Remember Samson fell over a lady."

"Again, I thank you for your concern Father. No need to worry here. I know what the Master seeks, and I won't let him down. I'd like a ride to her home. From what she told me it's not far from here."

The Father agreed to take him and asked if he could pick him up later. "No need, I'll take a ride share back to Maria's. I suspect you'll want to come back here to chat with Tony and Rich."

"No doubt."

AUGUST

CHAPTER 24

José rang the bell when he arrived at Jackie's. He hoped he had the right address. He'd look pretty silly standing out here at nine o'clock on a stranger's front stoop. But she greeted him at the door with a big smile, a hug and a kiss on the cheek. "Thank you for coming. I was afraid you'd cancel last minute."

He kissed her hand and said, "I wouldn't miss this. I do have one request though. Please turn off your phone. You're to be my assistant tonight and I don't want you distracted by another barge accident while you're using knives around me."

"Got it Señor Chef. Safety first. Or do you just want me to yourself?"

"Well, there is that too."

She led him into the living room. He couldn't help but notice the big mirror in the foyer when he stepped down into the open area. The home had a small kitchen to the right along with a dining area at the far end, all part of the open living plan. The light-colored wood floors were decorated with area rugs of various shades of burgundy, brown and beige along with a fine dark brown leather sofa in front of a glass coffee table and a very large screen TV, side chairs and floor lamps that hung over the seating. On the far end of the room, there was a sliding glass door that led to a privacy fenced patio with a small gas grill. Two bar stools stood in front of the island separating the kitchen from the living area. Granite counters and stainless-steel appliances adorned the cook space, with vibrant colors in the paintings and photos on the walls. He guessed it was a two-bedroom based on the closed doors and was sure there was a laundry room around also.

"You have a delightful home, Jackie. Thank you again for the invitation." He strolled around the living room looking at the paintings. "I know I'm here for a purpose. I'd like to do my job first. What did you get us to eat tonight?"

"Relax first, mi amour. I have your favorite beer chilling in the fridge. You can pour me a glass of the white wine. It's on the door. And you can check the fridge for ingredients. I'll get a wine glass. And oh . . ."

She picked up her phone with some fanfare and shut it off. She took a deep breath and said out loud but to herself, "You're going to be okay. You're going to be okay."

José smiled and headed to a fridge full of surprises. He retrieved his beer and her wine bottle. Pinot Grigio from Italy. *Good choice to start.* Inside he saw salmon, kale, lemons, fresh garlic, cucumbers and carrots among other things. *This has potential.*

"Show me to your spice cabinet please, señorita."

She sat at the bar with her empty wine glass. "It's to the left of the stove. I'll stay over here, where it's safe."

He opened the spice cabinet and found red pepper flakes, sesame seeds, sesame oil along with soy sauce, kosher salt and black pepper. *Excellent.*

He opened the wine and filled her glass, opened his beer and made a toast. "May there be peace in this home."

"Hear, hear." She took a sip. "Very nice. Thank you."

"Direct me to your pans and utensils and we can get this underway."

"No. Sit with me before you get to work. I want to chat for a while."

He leaned across the bar to look at her. "No, let's go outside on the patio, before it gets too dark."

She agreed and they walked outside. He noticed she was wearing light blue capri pants with ruffles around the knee going down to the calf. She wore a free-flowing white blouse with short sleeves and a thin white belt. It gathered in the front to show just a sliver of her tanned and toned stomach. She also had on white deck shoes, no socks. Her hair was off one ear with a gold hoop earring exposed. He could see a small gold chain with a cross around her neck. She was home and dressed to relax but impress too.

As they went outside, she pulled out a lighter from the wicker table nearby and lit two tiki torches along the patio rim. "Lots of skeeters out here this time of year." She sat on a love seat in between the torches. José took a seat in a chair right across from the grill. "You look captivating tonight."

"Gracious señor. I appreciate the dress up on your part also. No chef's coat or pants. Khakis and a dress shirt. I didn't know you owned one."

"Sunday go to meetin' clothes, señorita."

She smiled. They sipped their drinks and enjoyed the cooling evening air after a hot August day.

"So, what's in the news today."

"Other than the fact we got some sunshine at last, not much happening new. Just ongoing stories from the week. August is a dead news time. Congress is on recess; the President takes a few weeks off. It's too hot to do much and most of the world goes on holiday. Sundays in August are some of the slowest. How was your day?"

"Went to a Hispanic Pentecostal worship service this morning. Pulled the day shift at Restaurant Tapas and spent the last few hours with Reverend Tony, Father Menendez and Pastor Rich, just down the street."

"Sounds stimulating."

"They warned me about coming to see a lady in her home late at night. So, I must know, do I need to be afraid?"

"Well, my intentions aren't all honorable, but I promise I won't hurt you," she laughed. "So, what do four men of the cloth speak about for hours?"

"How the Lord is working in our lives and the life of His church. The lives of those we care for."

"You have a passion I don't understand. Why do you do this? Since our last conversation, I just can't get over it. You've been shot, beaten. You live way below your means. Are you trying to make up for the guilt of prior wrongs? What's in it for you?"

"It is the lack of guilt and fear that keeps me going. It's what we're created for. To glorify God. It brings me peace, fulfillment. The knowledge we make the world a better place by sharing God's love with those who are suffering. I know no other way. However, you know more about me than I do about you. Tell me your story. Why do you do the news?"

She launched into a well-rehearsed spiel. "I grew up in Virginia outside of DC. My dad was a military man who enjoyed too much alcohol. I told you before, he was in and out of the hospital for various ailments. I keep most of this to myself, so I didn't mention this part before over our ice cream. I found out his issues were liver related. He reformed and got better, but then started fooling around on mom. She divorced him and moved us to a suburb of Charlotte. A fresh start. Are you asleep yet?"

"Not at all. Please continue."

She leaned forward in the chair and took a sip of wine. "I got my start in journalism working for the high school newspaper. I interviewed teachers, the principal and brought injustices to light."

"Such as."

"Such as why do seniors get all those privileges, when juniors and sophomores work just as hard. Shouldn't we reward the high achievers with privileges and not those with seniority? It seemed reasonable to a sixteen and seventeen-year-old mind."

"What about friends?"

"I've been an introvert most of my life. Hard to believe that someone on screen doesn't want to have intimate talks with people. I talk to many people but not deeply with any, if that makes any sense. This is getting hard. I can't joke my way through this. I don't want to do this now. I need another glass of wine and I'm starting to get hungry. Plus, I don't think these torches are doing their job." She scratched her lower leg.

"Okay, let's head back to the kitchen."

He pulled the cucumbers out of the fridge. "Do you have a spiralizer by chance?"

"You're joking right? I don't even know what that is."

"May I use your knives?" There was an attractive knife set in a block holder on the counter near the stove.

"Of course."

He pulled one out and tried it on the cucumber to test sharpness. Then he pulled out the sharpener and sharpened it by rote. He didn't notice her staring at him until he was done.

"That was impressive, but you never did give me my second glass of wine."

He poured her another glass and then cut the cucumbers into smaller pieces, then into thin spiral slices with a vegetable peeler he found in a drawer. Adding some soy sauce, sesame seeds, garlic, chilies and sesame oil, and before long they had a spiral cucumber, garlic and chili salad. He plated it and put it in the fridge to stay cool while he prepared the main course.

"Wow."

"Now you get to help. Get the kale out and wash it. Pat it dry with a paper towel and bring it to me."

While she did her work, he found a large fry pan. Then he folded the kale, stripped out the stem and placed it on a cutting board. He grabbed a knife from the block, sharpened it with intentional flair this time and handed it to Jackie. "Your turn to cut up the kale while I get the pan ready."

She began chopping with great caution. He came behind her and put his arms around her, took her cutting hand tenderly and showed her how to hold the kale and cut without fear of losing a finger. She looked back at him over her shoulder and thanked him. "I feel like a klutz around you in here."

"I do this for a living. I'm sure I'd need lots of help to do an interview." When he let go, he couldn't resist kissing her neck beneath the hoop earring.

She raised her shoulders and leaned closer into him. "Oh! Are you sure I don't need more cutting lessons?"

"Best lesson is practice, I have to get on with the salmon. I'll roast the salmon on the grill outside. No need to smell up your place cooking fish indoors."

He went outside and lit the gas grill, cleaning it with the brush hanging on the side. While outside, he reflected on the kiss. *I liked the way she felt. Such soft skin and with hair that smelled of jasmine. Glad she didn't pull away. Keep your head man.* While the grill heated, he came back in and prepared the salmon. Jackie was almost done with the kale.

He mixed up garlic, soy sauce and lemon fast and was preparing the fish with the sauce and thin slices of lemon. He found a broiling pan to place the fish over the fire on the grill and came back in to sauté the kale with the remaining garlic, lemon, red pepper flakes along with some olive oil, kosher salt and black pepper. He moved almost like a dancer from stove to grill and back making sure everything would finish at once. "Please stir the kale while I retrieve the fish. We're almost ready."

While he was outside, she lit two candles on the table and put the music app on her TV to smooth jazz.

"I didn't know TVs could play music like that until Ms. Roberta showed me in the hospital. It's a neat feature," he said when he came back in with the salmon.

In what seemed like an instant, they were seated at the dining table with their gourmet meal for two.

"I think this needs a red wine," he said. "Do you have a pinot noir?"

"From Oregon of course," she mimicked a snooty accent.

She got the bottle from the wine rack near the bar and twisted off the cap with exaggerated flair mocking the knife sharpening. She poured them each some wine. They smiled and they raised their glasses. He reached out and took her hand and kissed it.

She smiled again and started to eat.

He bowed his head to bless it in silence.

"No, say it out loud please," she said.

He held her hand and blessed their food. They enjoyed a sumptuous meal together.

As they ate, he reminded her. "You promised me more of your story. I've shared some of mine, now it's your turn. You have home field advantage. I've got an idea. I'll interview you and you can tell me what I'm doing wrong." He picked up a spoon to be his pretend mic.

"I wouldn't interview me. Too boring. But okay, I'm game."

"So, who was your first love?"

"That's a softball rookie reporter, I fell in love in high school with Derrick McGee. A cute boy, who really liked me a lot. I was a chubby girl, who didn't get into fitness until college. Not many boys wanted the fat one. We dated until he went off to college and then we lost touch. I went to the University of Georgia for journalism. Got an internship with several news stations in Atlanta. I studied meteorology too, so I could be credible doing the weather and, on the scene, reporting too. Most of the time, I just got coffee for the personalities."

"Tell me where your name comes from. Jacqueline is an unusual name for the south."

"That's a good question Señor Reporter. My great grandparents lived on the border between Germany and France. Sometimes it was French and sometimes German. Frankfurt means French Fort. I think you know that already. Anyway, when the famines hit the area in the nineteenth century, they immigrated to the US. It was good for many reasons, but one was my great grandmothers was a Jewess. That wouldn't have gone well a few decades later. They wound up in the DC area. Which is where I was born."

"There's more, I know."

"Well Jacqueline means *to protect* or *protector*. I found that a good life's calling in journalism. Protecting the weak from the powerful. You and I are in a very similar business."

"Tell me of your spiritual journey."

"OK, like I mentioned before, after the divorce, my mom moved to the suburbs of Charlotte for a fresh start. She joined a Baptist church there.

I got saved when I was ten. Got dunked and, like the Baptists say, was set for life. Once saved always saved. I've got my fire insurance, as they say. Went on to school, fell in love, got married. Fell out of love, got divorced. Just like mom." She looked uncomfortable now.

He put down the spoon, reached out and touched her hand. "How about I get us some dessert? What are the choices?"

She seemed thrilled to be off the hook. "There's ice cream with chocolate sauce."

He cleared the plates, put them in the sink and found two bowls and the ice cream. She brought a few other dishes to the sink and retrieved the chocolate sauce. They moved back to the table with desert in hand. She poured them both more wine.

"You've told me several times you tried my way, and it didn't work for you. So why did you leave the faith behind?"

She pouted now. "I thought, we were done. I think we'll leave it there for now."

"Jackie, you skip from high school to the present far too fast, regardless of the path your story takes. What happened in college?"

She looked down at the table and began picking at her fingernails. She took an unsteady breath, bit her lip and looked up with watery eyes. And then looked past José to find a spot on the wall.

"Okay. I told you, I was the fat girl in high school. I got into fitness in college. I hit the residence life gym, learned about nutrition and started eating well. I had a vice, I liked to drink too. I was never the sought-after girl until then. I didn't realize what a prize I'd become. Frat boys started paying me much more attention than I was used to. I was desired and I was flattered by it. I wasn't even twenty years old. I went to a frat party with Randy Briscoe. While I went to the bathroom, he put something in my drink. He raped me." She took a deep breath to steady herself.

José wanted to hold her and comfort her. She held up a hand. "No, you pressed, now you get it all." She seemed to move into reporter mode now. Reciting facts from a distance.

"Date rape wasn't talked about or even warned about much back then. I had no idea what was happening to me. I later found out what he used, GHB. Clinical name is Gamma Hydroxybutyrate. Known on the street by many names but my favorite is Georgia Home Boy. It has different effects on people. It paralyzed me. I could see, hear, smell and feel everything. I couldn't say or do anything." Reporter mode didn't work, she closed her eyes and clenched her jaw. "I prayed to God for his help. I got no help. It went on for what seemed like a lifetime, but it was only a couple of hours, I think. Memory is fuzzy still or perhaps suppressed. I remember getting to my feet, I couldn't find all my clothes. I ran out without my shoes."

"Jackie, I'm so sorry. I don't need to hear more. You can stop now if you wish."

"I'm not done yet. The rape resulted in a pregnancy. Lucky me. I was no virgin by then but refused to carry the child of a rapist. I just got this beautiful body, I wasn't going to lose it like that. I aborted the child," she said, venom in her voice. She dropped her head wiping her eyes with her fingers.

José reached out his hand to her. She wouldn't take it.

"Where was God in that? But no, there's even more. I worked through most of that after a few months, I could date again. After graduation, I got married to a wonderful man. I didn't tell him this until after. I thought it was behind me and life would move on. Michael Hyatt was all I longed for. Handsome, appreciated me, a great lover, a good provider. But he wasn't patient and wanted things when he wanted things. We all have our shortcomings. After two years of marriage, our careers were taking off, but he wanted a family too. We tried over and over. I miscarried over and over. I went to church. I prayed for forgiveness. I prayed for a child to call our own. All Michael wanted was a baby. I couldn't produce one. I, the protector, was too defective to protect the child in my own womb. I was hormonal and depressed. A joy to be around, I'm sure. He lost interest in me and took up with another. I hear they have three children now." The last part trailed off to a whisper as she bowed her head and patted her eyes with a napkin. She sniffed back tears.

José reached out for her once more, but she wouldn't accept comfort.

"Abby, Robbie, Isabel, Samuel, Edward. Do you know who they are, wise man of God?"

José shook his head.

"I named them all. They were my children, who died inside me. Oh, God." Tears flowed down her face now as she wrung her hands in front of her. "I named the aborted one after my third miscarriage. God was punishing me for my sins. I vowed that if he didn't help, I would leave and not come back. Do you see any children here? No, neither do I." At that she bent forward sobbing with complete abandon.

José could watch no longer. He got up and knelt by her chair stroking her hair gently with one hand and laying the other on her clasped hands while she cried rocking back and forth. He wept with her. She pushed him away, struggling to her feet, but he grabbed her shoulders and held her tight. She tried to twist away, and then gave in to his embrace. She continued to sob, shoulders heaving. "Why? Why did you make me go there?" She asked through sighs and sniffs. "I never wanted to go back there. It's been years since . . . " Her breathing began to slow.

She pulled back to look in his eyes. "I think I got snot on your nice shirt."

"I wouldn't trade it for anything. I think I got tears in your hair."

She moved away and grabbed some tissues, blew her nose and wiped her eyes. "I must be a mess. Now you know why I can't follow this God of yours."

José wiped his eyes too. "Jackie, he didn't abandon you. Sometimes we suffer and don't know why. It's part of the fall of man. He is for you not against you." He struggled to speak a message of hope since he could feel the deep despair that overtook her. "Don't you see? He sent me to you to tell you, he loves you with amazing love, incredible love. Beyond any a man could give you. You are not defective, you are his remarkable creation. The very image of God, the Imago Dei. You're even more since you are in Christ. You're the Imago Christi. He wanted me to tell you, please come back to him. His burdens are light. He can heal you of this pain and give you peace and joy, if you will accept it. You did once when you were ten, come back to the Master, he beckons you."

"I'm not sure how. Not sure I want to."

"May I pray with you?" He pulled her close once more. "Loving Heavenly Father, please heal and bring comfort to this tormented soul. Show her your love. Free her of her guilt. Bring her back to her first love. Plant her on solid ground. Restore your Spirit. Help her to know, for sure, you died for her sins, and they're washed away. She has suffered so, Lord. Please Father, if you've ever done a miracle through me, heal this amazing sister in Christ. In the name of our risen savior Jesus, I pray. Amen."

They both let out an exhale at the same time and tried to smile at each other although tears came again, they were no longer sorrowful. "Thank you, José. I feel a burden lifting. It's going to take some time, but I think I can come back now. I had very different plans for you and me tonight. I was going to tell you 'I'm still not sure how to reconcile all this miracle nonsense.' But now I feel like I'm one of those miracles. As much as I hated you at the time for it, I feel like you've healed a very fractured soul. I don't know what happens next."

"I should go now. You need to spend time with the Father and I have an early morning."

"Shall we do this again next week?" She asked as he tucked a lock of hair behind her ear. "The dinner I mean, but let's leave out the sobbing part please."

"Agreed, it will be a time of rejoicing. May I join you at a church of your choice that morning?"

"You may be rushing things señor. I'll let you know."

"I'll call a ride share and do the dishes, while I wait."

"I'm going to get cleaned up and get the tears out of my hair." She smiled.

When the driver arrived, José headed to the door. She raced to meet him there and kissed him intensely. "You've taken me to a place I never thought I would go back to. I feared it. I buried it. I hated it. I wanted to hurt you for bringing me there. But somehow, there is freedom and peace now on this side. Please continue to show me this way. Be patient with me."

"I think before long you'll show me a new path. Good night sweet protector, my Jacqueline."

ARISE

Arise my spirit from the darkness
Seek the light once more
Darkness surrounds
It is chased away by the light

Arise oh tormented soul
Listen to the lies no more
He calls you to life
He calls you to forgive and be forgiven

Arise for a new day dawns
There is hope anew
He brings love
He brings peace

He brings joy at the dawning
      arisE
      ariSe
      arIse
      aRise
      Arise

AUGUST

CHAPTER 25

Monday brought back the rains. The rainwater seeped into the exposed soil at the top of the hill in Summit Spires for weeks now. It united with the natural underground springs and gradually eroded the surrounding soil.

The erosion started to show earlier in the summer with significant potholes up the hill that were moving downhill via the underground water. It was hard to trace, and no one put together the fact that these potholes were related. Most people thought they were just because of the rain. The land began to slump in a few areas. It happened in the woods several hundred feet from the road and the nearest house so only some local kids noticed it. There were plenty of social media posts of trees toppled over, uprooted. The kids thought it was cool and could play king of the hill and paintball combat games with their friends. Lots of folks got muddy but no one had serious injuries.

The next big slump came between two houses of one of the older neighborhoods up the hill in Berkshire. The houses were large and well kept. Many prominent citizens lived nearby. The homes got bigger and more expensive the higher you went uphill. Pastor Rich was just a few blocks down the hill.

✣✣✣

Jackie enjoyed her oatmeal with cinnamon, raisins and blueberries while she watched the rival station's morning news report. She couldn't stop thinking about what happened last night. She ruminated on it when she woke during the night. She felt different. Peaceful but not. *Can't understand it at all.* She snapped back to reality as . . .

"Steve Gaskin reporting. I'm coming to you from Robben Street in the Berkshire neighborhood where two houses were damaged by what appears to be sinking soil. Geologists call this a land slump. It happens when land is saturated by rain and the ground water begins to wash away the soil underneath." *Gaskin's a good reporter. Not great but good. What's he out doing a land report for?*

"As you can see the foundations of both homes are now cracked. The driveway and garage in between them are significantly damaged. A nearby tree uprooted, landing on the garage and the car inside. Thankfully no one was injured, and city containment crews are on the scene to keep onlookers away and stabilize the area. Clearly this is a result of all the rain in the area. We'll have more news later this morning."

Jackie smelled a story and called Karl to see if there was any more to this. *It's early, hope he picks up.*

"Well hello Ms. Hyatt. Haven't heard from you for a while." She could tell he was yawning. "What can I do for you Jackie?"

"Are we going to see more of this *land slumping*?"

"That's all I get. All business, huh? It's been a busy morning already and can't answer lots of questions right now. According to my team on the site, we're lucky no one got hurt. Lucky, it didn't happen in the dark or under someone's house. This can happen anywhere there is subterranean water flow. The water table is very high and washing the soil away from underneath. We're speaking to the US Geological Survey, as we begin looking into this. I don't want to start a panic, but all this rain is beginning to take a toll on the soil up the hill. I'm hopeful, it'll all stop soon."

"When will the USGS get back to us?"

"I'll let the media know when we get a report from those guys. You'll know right after I do," Karl said curtly. "Sorry, it's early Jackie. We haven't been out since that frustrating wedding fiasco. How about we get together this weekend and move the earth on our own."

With a hint of sarcasm, she said, "Karl, as inviting as that is, I have plans for this weekend. Perhaps another time."

"What's his name? No wait, are you still chasing that Latino chef around?

"Karl, you know I don't chase men, they chase me. And his name is José."

"That's the crazy religious guy from VM right. Didn't take you for a *salsa* lover. But hey you're my fun-loving Jackie. Never know where you'll get your kicks. But we can still have fun."

"Karl let's not go there right now. It sounds like we have a pretty major issue developing."

"Crises pass. I suspect this is overblown. Don't know for sure yet. If I wrung my hands for every crisis my job faces, I'd have no hair left. Hard to believe you're chasing a destitute Latino. Didn't you tell me, he lives in a boarding house. He must be wonderful in other places."

"I'm not having this conversation with you, Karl."

"Oh wow, you don't know yet, do you? How can he resist your charms? You aren't losing your touch, are you honey? Hey, he's been to some bad places. You said he was tortured. Maybe he's missing something?"

"Karl, you're horrible and I had no idea you were so jealous and mean hearted. He's more of a man than you in so many ways. I don't measure people by their net worth but by what's in the heart. He has more heart than you ever will. Did you bring peace to the city?"

"Ouch. Look Ms. Hyatt, you and I both know we help each other often and we both enjoy those benefits. So, I'm going to credit this conversation to us both being up too early to be civil. Let's not say things we'll regret. I'll leave you with this. I'll let the media know when we get a report from the USGS. You'll know right after I do. Good day."

"Thank you, I think." Jackie hung up the phone. *Things must be more of an issue than he's letting on. Can't believe I let him get to me. I'm way off my game. C'mon lady get it together.*

Her mind moved back to the land slumps. *This is very disturbing. 'It could happen anywhere.' Don't start a panic Hyatt.* She decided to look up the geology professor at Carlisle State and get his thoughts.

※ ※ ※

As she drove to meet him, the horrible things Karl said came back to her. Not just about José but about her. *What kind of a reputation have I developed? I don't . . .*

"Lord, I'm sorry for what I've become. I know better. I was taught better. What can you do with such a broken thing? I wanted you to fix everything to please me. I see now that's not your way. You're chasing me. I see that now. I have no idea why except what the man you sent has already told me. You love me with a crazy love."

She swallowed hard at that last comment as a wave of conviction and sorrow rolled over her. She looked for a place to pull off the road and found it in a small church parking lot. The gravel crunched under her tires as she pulled in. She leaned forward on the steering wheel and wept. Again. It wasn't for her children now, but for herself. Out loud she prayed, "You love me. Thank you. I can't believe it, but I know it's true. I just need to accept the forgiveness I've pleaded for. I accept it, Lord. Bring me back. Show me the way forward. I want to live for you again." A calm came over her. She cleaned herself up again. *I've got to stop this.* Checking her face out in the rearview mirror she said, "Feeling good, Jackie but you've looked better, dear."

※ ※ ※

It took Jackie a couple of hours to track down and catch up with Dr. Marcus Rizner, the head of the geology department at Carlisle State. They met in his small, beige office overlooking the campus early Monday afternoon. Geology wasn't the money subject at CSU, so he was on a lower floor. Old wooden desk and chairs. Lots of musty smelling books and a few rocks. Faded pictures of volcanoes and hillsides. Photos of the Dr. in various stages of life. When he was thin and had hair. Before the thick hornrims he now sported.

She wore a form fitting canary yellow sleeveless blouse with black pencil skirt. Yellow heels. She noticed him look her over when she came in and for the first time in a long time, didn't like it. *'Are you losing your touch?' Karl asked. Is that what I do? Distract men with my looks, to get what I want? Yes, Hyatt that's what you do.*

"Have a seat Ms. Hyatt," Dr. Rizner said.

"Call me Jackie, please." She sat in a wooden chair that had one leg shorter than the others.

"What can I do for you?"

"Thanks for seeing me today. I guess you're busy getting ready for the new term."

"Yes, that's true, but I'm happy to make time for my friends in the media."

That's nice, no one else seems to be these days. Gotta love the academics.

"I want to speak with you about these land shifts that are happening around town."

"I've been away most of the last month on vacation, I heard about them this morning," he said.

"Do you mind if I take some notes or record this on my phone?"

"Not at all."

She pulled out her phone and stylus, turned it to record and crossed her legs. He was staring at her legs, so she pulled her skirt over her knee as much as possible. His eyes moved back to her face.

"I need to study these slumps. Where they are on the map? Where the underground creeks are? That kind of research. Quick glance this AM, I noticed they appear to follow a pattern of getting larger going downhill from the Summit development."

"You mean Bald Head Hill? Many say Paul Stanley is trying to put his face on the hillside kind of like Mt. Rushmore, in mud."

Dr. Rizner laughed and leaned back in his creaking old wooden chair. "This is a result of too much water flowing underground. Having that clear-cut area at the top of the hill isn't helping. We've lost a natural buffer. Even with that buffer in place, with all the rain we've had, I'm not sure it matters. I've not reviewed the real estate development geological studies at this point but know it can't be good."

"What can we do about it?"

"Pray for the rain to stop. We need to call some shaman over to get the rain gods to turn off the spigot. We need an un-rain dance." He must've thought he was clever. Jackie didn't think so, but kept it to herself.

"If the rain continues, what happens?"

"Have we seen any reports of large cracks across the hillside?"

"Not that I know of, I'll check with the City Manager's office to see."

"I don't want to be the harbinger of doom, but landslides are the next thing to happen in this sequence. The issue there is, they're without warning and hard to predict. They happen all over the world, not much in the south, but with all this rain, it's the next step."

She decided to change the questions to something more hopeful. "If the rain stops, will we see any consequences for drying out too quick?"

"When it stops, depending on the saturation of the groundwater, we'll see improvement in yards and vegetation for weeks to come, while they enjoy the abundance. We'll also see root rot and a number of trees will die or fall at the next big wind or winter storm. I hope we don't get any of those this year. We need this to dry out over a long period.

"Unless you're in politics, landslides sound bad. What does that look like?"

He pulled out a large book with photos from South America. It hit the desk with a thump as a plume of dust kicked up on the impact. Flipping through the pages he landed on a before and after photo of an area in Brazil then twisted the book around to her. She could see buildings in the before and nothing but mud in the after shot. "This is what landslides do," he said.

"That's tremendous devastation. What's the scale of this photo?"

"This was a major slide it covers about twenty city blocks. I can show you more." He reached for another book.

"You can see from this illustration, the whole side of the hill just moves downhill, it's bad for those on the area that moves but it's devastating for those downhill. Anything in the path is wiped away. It's like an avalanche with mud and debris. The land liquefies and takes the entire area between the rock below the ground and the surface downhill."

"How soon will we see that?"

"I'm an alarmist, I suspect. I've been away, I need to review some data before I can even venture a prediction but with the amount of rain and the land slumps, I've got to believe it's feasible within just a few weeks. We just need some dry weather."

"When will you get your research done, doctor?"

"It'll take me a week more like two to be thorough, I'll get one of my grad students to help."

"Sounds like we need to move quicker than that professor."

"We'll have something by next Monday. It won't be definitive, but it should be reasonable."

"What can we do while we wait?"

He stroked his chin with thumb and forefinger. "Well, there is laser-based technology out there that can help detect slides before they happen. I can call the USGS. If there were cracks, you can measure them over time to see if they widen. That is the type of data we need, to attempt predictions."

"Are you in contact with the City Manager's office on this, doctor?"

"No one has reached out to me. But like I said, I've been away. I'll call the City Manager and see if he can connect me with whoever is working on this. I'm sure they're doing something, I just haven't heard what."

She shut off the recorder on her phone and scrolled her way through her contacts. She jotted Karl's number on her business card handing it to Dr. Rizner. "Here's his number, please make that call today. Tell him you and I've been talking, if he tries to put you off. We need to get this issue front and center. Dr. Rizner, thank you. If you come to any conclusion before Monday let me know. You now have my card with my cell phone. Call, day or night. The news never sleeps." She smiled.

As she left his office a shiver came over her. *This could be a disaster brewing. But nothing to report yet.* She called Mitch to give him a status and get her next assignment.

She drove back to the station thinking about life and what comes next. Remembering Karl's stinging comments, and how painful last night was. Remembering how kind José was even though, he's the one who pulled the old wound open. She recalled her ex-husband Michael and how painful all this was for both of them. There were no tears this time. She processed the memories and prayed for guidance through them, not fully believing she would receive it.

I need some 'self-time'.

Just then, Mitch called with a new story on some smaller detail of the Bank of the New South deal.

"Mitch, get someone else to cover that one for a while. I need some time off. I'm going to take the rest of the week. I'll work the land slump story from home. I need a break."

"Whoa Jackie, not heard that from you before. What's up? Give a story to someone else? Really?"

"Okay, I'll tie up the details on the BNS deal this afternoon, but I'm gone at five today. Got to clear my head and come to terms with some issues from the past."

"Jackie, you've worked nonstop for years. This makes you sound human. Good for you! Perhaps José is having a positive impact on you. Take the time you need. I'll take you off the roster for now."

"You've no idea how human I am Mitch, and yes, José reminded me of that recently. I'm in a good place just need some time."

AUGUST

CHAPTER 26

The rains continued with such persistence that locals started calling Carlisle the Seattle of the South. Bass Lake was swelling to unusual heights and the Lumber River was being watched for flooding. Creeks upstream and up the hill were at great depths. The daily deluge would bring new torrents of water downstream. The creek beds were eroding but the city wanted to wait until an extended dry spell to repair, for fear it would all just wash away. Best they could do was sandbag around the more hazardous zones.

Paul Stanley and his SMT, Senior Management Team, met to discuss status of their various projects around town in the ornate conference room adjoining Paul's office. None of the projects were dearer to him than the Summit Spires project excavated in June but now stuck in a perpetual state of slow progress. *We cut corners on the erosion control and managed to get it past the inspectors. It pays to be connected in Carlisle and I know just what to do. Besides that, the erosion controls were all cooked up by some bureaucrat. They just slowed down a project. If I can get this done fast, no one'll notice or care.* "Money saved is money earned!" He blurted out to the SMT as his mind came back to the meeting. The managers stared back at him since the comment had nothing to do with the conversation going on.

Paul let his mind wander in these meetings when one of the team droned on about their projects. This morning was no different. Several

Project Managers were going on about issues and costs with slowdowns caused by the weather.

Paul saw himself not as dishonest, but aspirational. He spoke as if his aspirations already occurred. So, he'd tell people how he wanted things to be, whether they were that way yet or not. He thought this allowed him license to adjust his language to add clarity without coming off as untruthful. Such talk made it easy to dodge questions when people turned his words against him. It also let him sound like a man of vision. Sometimes he even believed his own pontificating and would lose his temper when reality challenged him.

Over the years when competition in Carlisle got tougher in the real estate world, Paul's aspirations caused him to deceive himself and others more often. His ego encouraged him to surround himself with those who seldom challenged him. The delusions got larger with greater implication after his business grew.

He cut corners on most of his developments now letting prior reputation carry them. Any manager who challenged him didn't stay around long.

Interrupting the meeting again with random thoughts, "Summit Spires will be a great community. Perched right on the top of the hill. No one could build anything higher in the area. Unless they could get the national park to part with the land on the tallest hill across the river. Not likely but wouldn't that be something." He said to the stares of his managers.

"Back to reality. The meeting isn't going well, gents, all these issues and no solutions but to spend more of my money. Let's hear Mark's update on Summit Spires."

Mark Norris reported on the Spires project and how all the rain delayed them far too long.

"As y'all know we clear cut the land weeks ago. That was good to start on a bunch of lots at once't. It 'lowed for the roads to get graded and loads o' traffic to start. People could commence to dream of their house at the Summit. We got good press to start. Now we're an eyesore, a *bald head* on the top of the Summit as the fake news likes to report. The mud's running down the hillside into the streams and creeks not to mention into the backyards of the neighborhoods below. We got oodles of complaints. The 'nspectors haven't come out for a bit but sooner than later, we're gonna get cited if'n we don't increase the erosion control. We can't continue work until rain stops for a week or so. You just can't dig holes in mud."

Paul looked at him over his bright blue rimmed reading glasses. "So, you want us to spend more on a project that's already months behind schedule. The way it is now, we won't generate any income for months more while we rack up interest on construction loans. You know better than that Mark. It's not going to happen."

"We're losing topsoil now, sir, it's got to be replaced or Summit Spires'll look like a prairie, once't it's complete."

"Will we not sod all the homes there?"

"Yes, but it needs good dirt underneath to grow right . . . "

Paul cut him off. "This is a ludicrous argument; the rains'll stop soon, and this will no longer matter. If we get cited, we can appeal it and tie things up for months while we get some revenue going on this deal. In the meantime, did you report that there was bad soil on the site?"

"Yessir. We found a large area with what ya call *'bull tallow'*, ya know that's bad news. We got a big swath of it on the side of the hill near Carlisle. We can't build on it or the houses won't perk, ya' know, they'll not settle right. We need to dig up and truck it out once't we get dry."

"Move it to the edge and let it wash down steam with the rains. Might as well save ourselves some money and time when it does dry. Rain's good for something."

"Sir, you want us to push this to the top of the hill? It's truckloads of dirt!"

"It must go somewhere, what better place for bad soil to get washed away and dispersed across the whole area. Much better than dumping it in one place for someone else to have to dig up. You can do that in the rain, right?"

"Yessir, we can use dozers to do that. It'll further grade the land on the overlook too."

"Make it happen . . . and get me some houses up! Soon! We need the money."

❈ ❈ ❈

For several days now, the dozers moved the bad dirt toward the edge of the hill and the natural streams. They didn't push it in but wanted to be sure they could get it near. The operators didn't understand the instructions which made no sense to them. Seemed like a strange idea, but this project had been anything but normal due to the rains. So, they pushed the mounds over some cracks that were forming at the top of the hill.

As the rains continued, the loose soil and the runoff began to become a major source of complaint by those downhill from the Summit. He heard enough complaints, so Karl Shuford sent someone up to inspect.

On Friday, inspector Harold Henderson arrived at the Summit Spires site. He'd lived in Carlisle his whole life. He graduated from the University just a few years ago and was a Red Eagle through and through. When he drove onto the site, he noticed all the standing water and couldn't understand the mounds of dirt toward the edge of the hill. He met Mark Norris to review the progress.

Mark wore his safety vest, hard hat and Summit Spires work shirt. He was all smiles. "Hey Harold, how ya doin'?" while he shook his hand with vigor.

Harold smiled in return. "I'm great, 'cept for the rain."

"Yes, the rain's a real problem. What can I do ya for, friend?"

"I'm here to deal with the complaints downstream. Lots of mud and debris coming from up here over the past few weeks. Last couple of days been real bad."

"Ya know how water flows right."

"Yeah, I know, but you know that too. Looks like you're pushing soil to the hill crest and letting it run down based on my drive through here."

"Why the heck would I do that? I need all the topsoil I can get."

"Telling you what it looks like. How about you telling me what you're doing. I need to report back to those voters below you and we all know the City Manager and the Mayor love those voters."

"Do ya got tickets to the Red Eagles football opener next week, Harold?"

"No, but don't change the subject on me."

"Not changing the subject, I just 'membered we got seats available for the big game in October too. Conference opener. They're in the suite. You can bring your kids or not, whatever ya like. Lots of beer and good food."

"Really? I got some alumni buddies who'd love that. How many can I get?"

"The suite only holds sixteen so less'n that. How many ya need?"

"Six, I think. Do the cheerleaders come up to the box?"

"Oh yeah man, they make pictures and dance around anything y'all like. Ya like the cheerleaders, don't ya?"

"Let's just say my buddies do. Anyway, let's get back to the inspection. I need you to deal with this runoff."

"Ya got to give me some time, looks like my guys cleared the bull tallow out of that area and piled it up on t'other side. Ya know how hard it is to get good operators these days. These Mexicans don't know what they's doing. They just want tacos. And a siesta. I'll get them to move it, once't we get some dry days. Please don't cite me on this, I don't want to go back to Paul Stanley and deal with him on a citation. Ya know he'll tie it up with appeals anyway. Gimme a couple of dry days and we'll get it moved pronto. In the meantime, get your buds together and let's plan on a great season opener and then later for the conference opener with all them cheerleaders."

"I'll be back in a couple of days to see that you're doing what ya say. In the meantime, it's late and I can delay my report until next week. I need it addressed though."

"Don't worry, it'll get done."

Harold drove back down the hill.

There would not be an inspection next week.

✥ ✥ ✥

Late that afternoon, Mike Winter walked into Paul's art deco office unannounced as Paul loaded his briefcase standing by his desk.

"What do you want Mike? I got to head home and then out for a wonderful dinner at the club."

"You need to sit down, Paul. Cancel your dinner. The IRS has assessed Stanley Builders and its subsidiaries millions in taxes. I got the letter right here. They figured out we didn't do legit like kind exchanges. They figured interest and penalties. This letter isn't from the agent. It's from the supervisor. They're no doubt seeking a criminal indictment for you and me." He took a deep breath and exhaled.

"I don't know how they got wind of it, but right after the letter from the IRS came, Eric Reynolds called to tell me the bank is cancelling all lines of credit. They're tired of waiting for financials. He said it was out of his hands. We can't pay them back. We must declare bankruptcy. Once the receiver takes over, they'll find that we've been moving investors' money around between projects illegally. Paul, we're done."

Paul was looking out the window at the rain. "Nah, it's just a setback. We can get out of this. The rains are gonna stop and we can get Summit Spires back on track . . . " His voice trailed off.

"Paul, you're not listening. We're done. I'm calling my attorney. I'm making a deal. I got lots of records off site. I can't take this anymore. I'm only comforted by the fact that you'll get more time than me. You're a crook and you turned me into one," Mike said.

"You can't quit Mike. You're fired! You're spineless! Get out of my office and out of my sight. Any decent finance man would've come in here with solutions not problems."

"You still don't get it. You won't until they take you away in shiny silver bracelets. Then you'll show up pleading before a judge in one of those nice orange outfits! Investor fraud, tax fraud, code violations. It'll be bad for me, but worse for you."

Mike threw the letter on Paul's desk and left.

Paul glanced it over.

✥ ✥ ✥

As he arrived home he told his wife, Ally to cancel the club dinner. "Tell people I don't feel well. We'll make it up to them another time."

"You can't do this to me the night of. These are my friends. I'm going. I'll make your lame excuses. I may be out late. I'll just stay at the club tonight. No need to wait for me." She went back to getting ready. Paul went downstairs to the wet bar in the study.

He grabbed a bottle of fine bourbon and sat at the covered bar by his pool. Gazing out at all he'd built. He looked at the house, then up the hill and could still see the mud-covered area where he planned to build Summit Spires. As he drank, he got more sullen.

"Orange jumpsuits?" he muttered to himself. He could just see that Jackie Hyatt reporting from the Hart Building. A major indictment . . .

I just wanted to create jobs make some money . . . How'd it come to this? That moron Winter is the one that got me into this. Can't believe how stupid he is . . . Hey, wait a minute, I can make him the fall guy. I can come clean. I can do this before the news breaks next week. I'm the victim here. Winter took all those shortcuts and tried to pin it on me.

He stood up to get his cell phone and almost fell over. Once he found it, he tried to call Bill Shire, his attorney. He flicked past the S's and went to the T's. Pastor Richard Taylor's name came up. He licked his lips and thought about dialing. *Pastor Rich's been trying to get in touch with me. Might be good to talk to a pastor now. I'm in a bad place. Need all the help I can get. I bet he probably wants to gloat about what happened when we tried to take him out. He was preaching about how we need to help the blacks and the Mayans. Even those terrorists. Put them in my neighborhoods. Everyone knows only white people've built anything great in this country. Now he wants us to help those people. Just dilutes the race. We need to be focused on the pure Americans. If they can't cut it here, they should go back where they came from.*

He flipped back to the S's and found Bill Shire's name. With slurred speech he said, "Stanley here Bill. We got major issues, IRS, the bank. Big news breaking next week. Meet me at the office tomorrow. I know it's Saturday. We have to plan. No not early, I'm too drunk now to meet you early. We need a meeting with that news babe Hilton. I met her a while back. She's not too bright. Nice body though. Too bad she's not blond. Have her wear something tight and short. She can be our unwitting spokeswoman. Winter's the problem not me. See you at noon tomorrow."

He hung up and lumbered back to the pool chair where he toasted himself for being so smart. Then finished the bottle.

AUGUST

CHAPTER 27

Jackie reflected on her long but productive week off. There was time for a long hike in the park across the river on the one afternoon it didn't pour rain. This week helped her make peace with God and with herself. After downloading a Bible App, she started just reading at random whenever she could. José directed her to the book of John on the phone one night. She spent each morning in study, even skipping the gym, which never happened before. Then a mid-afternoon study as she craved to read the Word. Some answers to her life questions came fast but she realized others would come in time. There were no visits to Restaurant Tapas this week. She wanted to go, but felt solitude, alone time with God, was better than the distractions of time with man. Even a very special man. They spoke on the phone in the evenings, reflecting on their day. She longed to see him again. His words were wise and gentle.

Her outlook changed. The sarcasm didn't flow naturally anymore. She saw people with fresh eyes and less judgment. Up to now she looked at people only for the next story, how to get information out of them they didn't want to divulge. The new viewpoint wasn't formed completely, but she was different now.

Not going to church this week. Not ready to go mainstream, yet. She did watch the Carlisle service online this morning. She needed to do her research before she just showed up somewhere. *The music is much better than I remembered.* Pastor Rich spoke the same way José did about the love of God and how he pursues us.

Sunday afternoon she got a call from Paul Stanley's attorney requesting an interview, 10 am, tomorrow at Paul's house. *Big news* he said. He had the gall to request wardrobe. Instead of reading him the riot act like old Jackie would, she told him, her on-screen appearance was hers alone to dictate. "If he wants me to interview him, he agrees to my terms."

Nervous and excited looking forward to their dinner, she spent the bulk of the day getting her apartment just right. She changed clothes several times to make sure she gave the right message of 'how crazy I am for you but don't want to be too obvious.' Doubt crept in with waves of insecurity. *Why would a miracle worker want me? Was I just another person to him or am I something more? Is he as attracted to me as I am to him? We've been together for almost three months, and he's not made a move on me after this much time. Maybe Karl is right, perhaps he can't. Stop it lady, you're not in middle school.*

Then the waves of confidence came too, *you're a woman to be reckoned with. He likes to kiss my neck. He likes to hold me. We talk in such depth even more now that I'm back in the fold, over the backslide. How much do I really know about him? I'll know more later when I show him what I found out.*

"Dear Lord help me to know what to do. He's so remarkable. So firm in his belief and so gentle in his way. I'm not sure I can help myself around him. Not sure I want to. We're not school kids but consenting adults. There's got to be room for that. You made him perfect for me. Please let this go even deeper."

Just like last week, she selected her lingerie with care. *That turned out so much different than I planned.* At last, she settled on a red faux-wrapped surplice halter top with a deep V-neck, not too revealing. She paired that with white skinny jeans and low-heeled shoes. A single white pearl necklace adorned her neck with matching earrings to complete the look. After fighting with a cowlick for a few minutes, she pulled her hair to one side to expose her neck giving José an open target. She assessed herself in the big mirror, still insecure about her looks. *Looking good Jackie. He doesn't stand a chance of resisting you lady.*

José would arrive soon. He said someone would drop him off. *Must be meeting at Pastor Rich's house again.*

The doorbell rang and her heart jumped. One last look in the mirror smoothing out her pants along with checking her lipstick and hair for that troublesome cowlick. *I hope he likes what he sees. It's the best I got.*

She greeted him with a hug and kiss on the cheek, but he wouldn't let her go so fast, lingering over the hug. *Such strong arms and hands.*

"You look sensational this evening, señorita."

With her exaggerated southern belle accent she said, "Thank you kindly, sir. May I take your jacket?"

As José took off his rain jacket, she said, "I see you dressed up for me again. Same shirt?"

"Si, you liked it so much last week, I didn't want to risk a change."

"You did wash it right?" She smiled.

"Si, señorita. It was very dirty."

As she hung up his jacket in the foyer closet, she looked him over. "It does look good on you. Come on in, I'll get things started."

"Telephone?'

"Already off, Señor Chef."

"What am I making for you tonight?"

"Nothing Señor Chef. I am making it all."

"You no like my cooking now señorita?" She could see the false look of surprise.

"You know I love your cooking, but I didn't want you to have to do this again. My house, my rules. Sit while I prepare our first plate. May I get you a beer?"

"Yes Jackie, that would be wonderful."

"No more Spanish accent, eh?"

"I don't want to pretend in front of you. I want to be real now."

"OK but I enjoy that Latin accent. I think it's sexy."

"Gracious señorita. Anything for you. Por favor, what're we having?"

She pulled a variety of cheeses and salted meats from her fridge. All needing to be sliced and arranged. "We'll start with some cheese and crackers. I also have some honey and dates. Once we have our fill of that, we'll move to some olives, melon and Iberico Jamon. You won't believe how much trouble I had to go through for that. Ramone helped. If he told you, I'm gonna get him." She said as she brandished the cheese knife and laughed.

"He said nothing to me. This is very sweet of you. But please let me work too. I like doing things with you."

"OK but you do what I say. I have this all planned out. First you have to get me some pinot gris."

"Si, señorita." He hopped off his barstool and went to the fridge.

"I like the sound of that. You do what I say tonight," she grinned.

"I'm game as long as you go easy on me." He said as he made a big production of opening the wine. Jackie paused to watch. It was so over the top he almost missed the glass as he poured.

"That was graceful." She sipped her glass of pale white wine while José washed his hands.

"Ready now?"

"Si."

"You can drop the Spanish, if you wish. The crackers are in the pantry, second shelf. That French accent you did a couple weeks back could be exciting too." She wrinkled her nose and winked.

"Oui señorita. Oh, sorry, Oui, Mademoiselle Jacqueline. I think I'm distracted." He smiled and just looked at her.

"Here they are filled with different herbs and seasonings, just the way I like it. Shall I plate them? I don't want to overstep since it's your meal Mademoiselle Chef."

"Oui Monsieur, merci beaucoup."

She continued to slice the Wisconsin Cheddar into bite size morsels. Then moved to a salty Manchego. There were bleu cheese crumbles and Smoked Gouda to round out the cheese collection. It was difficult knife work due to the thick cheeses.

José came up behind her, reached around her to give her some extra leverage. She waited for the kiss on her neck. Which came next. She felt it shiver all the way down her back.

"I think that's enough cheese, don't you, mi amour?"

"Oui Mademoiselle Jacqueline, that should be trés beaucoup." He laughed.

He finished his beer while she arranged the pieces along with the dates and honey. She washed her hands as he poured them both a some of the pinot gris and joined her at the bar.

"I don't remember anymore high school French, so I'm switching back to English," She laughed.

"To life."

"To us."

She leaned over and kissed him.

"Wait, we need to bless it. And oh, I know you like this."

She grabbed a remote nearby and tuned the music app to jazz.

After the blessing, they enjoyed the saltiness of the cheese along with the sweetness of the company.

"Now, that we're appetized, let's talk some. I need to tell you more about my week. I also have some questions. I've been doing some research on you. I need you to fill in the holes."

"Alright. Tell me about your journey, I suspect that will be far more interesting than me."

"I spent the early part of the week trying to come to grips with what happened last Sunday. You got way past my wall and kicked it down from the inside out. I didn't expect that and to be honest, I had loads of venom for you. I hated you for bringing this up after so many years of suppression. I learned to live with it as it was and preferred it stay that way. No one has ever gotten that close to me. I realized how much you were risking in this, and I want to thank you, not just in a polite way, but in a deep and heartfelt way. That's why I made dinner tonight. I wanted you to feel special. Because you are special . . . to me. I know what you did was out of love for a hurting lady. Thank you, José." Her lip quivered as she spoke.

He reached across and touched her shoulder.

"You are very, very welcome. I never wanted to hurt you or see you suffer. I didn't know what was going to happen. I'm not sure I would've done it, if I had. I'm brave for the Lord but not sure I could've put you through that last week, if I'd known in advance the raw nerve I exposed. It was His wisdom not mine."

"I was weepy over and over when the week started. I wept for the children, my lost marriage but then I went deeper. I found myself weeping for a lost relationship with God. When you told me, he was for me not against me. How you said what a crazy love he has for me. Those words just kept coming back. I found the verse in Jeremiah about how he has *plans to prosper you and not to harm you.*"

José finished the verse, *"Plans to give you a hope and a future."*

"Yes, that's the one. It was one of my favorites growing up. I forgot about it after the darkness came. I began questioning my life, what I've been doing. What I've become. I started feeling condemned and broken. I asked for his forgiveness and to lead me back. So, the week went on and he began to show me, I was his beautiful creation. He loved me with an amazing love. He could use me to work in his kingdom, but I must grow more. I'm a child of God and an image bearer of his Son." She took another sip of wine to wet her dry mouth.

"On Thursday I went to hike in the muddy, messy park across the river. It was wonderful to be in nature. I stopped to smell the forest, watch the deer and chipmunks. It was cool. I'm happy to report, there were no snakes. I haven't taken time for that in ages. I knew I needed to let go and forgive others. I called my ex that night. Surprised he answered. He thought I was calling to put him on a guilt trip. I've been known to do that. I told him I'd renewed my faith and that I needed to forgive him for what happened in our marriage. I asked for his forgiveness. I didn't cry. After he realized I was serious, he did though.

There was peace between us at last. I know that chapter is over, he has a new family. I told him I'd pray for them."

She took another long sip of wine and popped a piece of gouda in her mouth.

"Jackie that's remarkable. He is working in you. 'I knew I needed to let go and forgive . . . ' That's the Kol Yahweh. He's speaking to you."

Her eyes brightened. "You're right. I didn't know it then, but I know it now that you say so. With that success, I reached out to my rapist."

"Oh no Jackie, that's very dangerous. We should talk long and deep before that happens."

"I had to follow the Kol Yahweh as you say. Just as you do. I was willing to forgive. I searched the internet for hours to try to find him. After all that, I confirmed that he died of a drug overdose five years ago. I was willing to forgive. I think that's what God was trying to show me. Funny I wanted Briscoe to die spitting up blood but now I just have pity for him and his family.

"I called my mom and spoke to her about faith and renewal. She still lives near Charlotte but isn't getting along so well these days. I made plans to go see her over Labor Day weekend. I've not done that in years. I usually just go for Christmas. She gets on my nerves something awful at times. I may get mad at you all over again if that doesn't go well."

"I'll take that punishment if it's needed. I see you're different now. I could tell on our phone calls as the week went on, your insights have changed. He was moving and I was praying for you and praising him. Thank you for sharing this with me. It touches my very soul."

Their eyes met and they sat gazing at each other for a long time without saying a word. "You know, from this angle I can see myself in your eyes, Señor Chef. They are so bright. José, I owe this to you." She swallowed hard. "I would never, ever have gone there without you. God does use you in mighty ways. I see that now in a very personal way. How can I be more like you?"

"We must seek to be more like the Master. Is that what you mean?"

"Yes, you got it."

"I'll continue to help you learn more. I enjoy being around you like no other."

"Back in the hospital you said I was a special case for you. I like being special."

"You're truly special to me, Jackie."

"I told you that you were a mystery to me as well and I needed to study you too, remember?"

"Yes, I do. I hope I've kept you interested."

"You've no idea how interested, mi amour." She leaned in and kissed him once more this time longer than the last.

Coming up for air José said, "I think we need more wine, and we have a second course as well."

As he got up and turned his back to get the wine, she dropped her head and tried to understand this man. *Why does he change the subject the moment we start to get heated up? Is he just not interested or is something else wrong? You said you made a vow but c'mon man. What's a girl got to do?* She decided to go with the flow. "That Jamon won't eat itself. I hope. You can help me make some cantaloupe melon balls, while I work on the ham. Get the olives out too, please. We'll need some red wine next. I got some Rioja from Spain to go with the Jamon and melon."

"It's been a long time since I've had Rioja. That area of Spain is an amazing part of creation. It has dear memories."

She smiled at his comment trying to figure out her next move.

After they plated the Jamon, they moved to the dining table for the next course. José brought the fresh glasses of red wine, while she delivered the tray with panache to the table. He came up behind her again and kissed her on the neck which led to several kisses in different spots. She smiled with delight and closed her eyes.

"OK, you sit there, señor."

"Gracious, señorita."

"Here's a napkin. I've a few final comments while we eat."

She fed him a bite of Jamon with melon. He reciprocated. And they both took a drink of wine. She placed her hand on his and tilted her head to one side.

"I've not known a man like you before. I've said that to you, I know several times, but each time we're together I feel so much closer to you than the time before. I know what it is, and I just have to say it. I'm hopelessly, madly, deeply even scarily in love with you José. I know that's a lot of adverbs. You do this to me. I'm so crazy I can't be objective about you. I can think of little else. I got it real bad. I don't want this feeling to stop. I want to see how much deeper this feeling can go."

José wet his lips. He looked at her with those wonderful eyes and smiled that amazing smile. "Jackie, you know my life is dedicated to following the Master. I've been sent here to love and to show his love. I've done that for many and not felt it returned as often as it was given. But with you, I'm helpless. I dream of you at night. My heart jumps when I see your name come on my phone. You're a comfort when I'm troubled. You're a constant stimulating surprise. I can give lots of silly examples. I've got it worse than you. I'm afraid of this feeling for you. It's not happened to me for a long time. I don't ever remember it this deep or rich. I have the gift of prophecy but I've no idea what happens next."

What's he waiting for? Is he too blind to see what happens next? No, he's waiting for me to ask for it.

"José, kiss me."

He leaned across and kissed her. They stood and he pulled her into his arms. His lips moving to her neck. His hands moving along her back. She ran her fingers through his hair and just enjoyed the bliss of his touch in so many places at once.

"My house, my rules. Make love to me, José. Please."

He picked her up and carried her to the bedroom.

⁂

Afterward, once they rested for a time, she put on a short white waffle weave robe.

"Time for dessert. I think we worked up an appetite again." She saw him about to put on his t-shirt and asked him not to.

"Tell me about the scars."

He sat on the side of the bed. "They came from scourging. It's an old but effective form of torture. Outlawed today in civilized societies, but those rules aren't enforced everywhere. It happened because I spoke for the Master in enemy territory."

She went over and traced them with her forefinger, then her whole hand. "That's horrible. Why do we do such things to each other?"

"A good question. One I ask often. Always the same answer. We're corrupted by the fall."

"This one must be the scar from the gunshot wound."

"Yes, how does it look?"

"Like a scar." She snickered and kissed it. "All better now."

She stood and looked in the bedroom mirror while she tied her hair back in a ponytail. "I've got some ice cream and chocolate sauce. We have one more thing to discuss. I tried to get to it over the Jamon, but other things developed first. Besides I was so desiring you at that point, not sure I would've listened like I should."

She took his hand as they went into the open living space again. He ate more of the Jamon while she started to dish out dessert. He fed her the last morsel of Jamon and moved to clean the dish.

"Give us more of that Spanish red please. It'll go well with chocolate."

He obliged and sat back at the dining table.

She took her first bite of ice cream and licked the spoon, smacking her lips then said, "Now, I need to know who you really are."

He grinned with a confused look on his face. "I don't understand your question. I've not deceived you in anything I've told you."

"Don't get defensive my lover, I meant every word I said earlier. I'm wild about you. You must know that now. It's not what you've told me, but what you've left out that I want to know now."

They both took another bite and a drink of Rioja. She could see him getting nervous.

"You tell me you're in your mid-thirties. That seems right. You have the body of a man in his thirties. I know that now. Very nice body. But you don't act like a man in his thirties. I told you, I did some research, while I've been going through this renewal you helped bring on, I decided to put what I know about you on a timeline. May I show you?"

"That's a little creepy, but OK."

She went to the far side of the kitchen counter and produced a large notebook. On her way back she asked, "How many languages did you say you speak?"

"Fifteen. If you count the dialects, it would be closer to thirty."

"Okay, how long does it take you to master a language?"

He shrugged his shoulders "Six months to two years depending on the language."

"So, if all you did was learn a new language every two years you must be in your fifties. But you know much more than just languages. You know whole cultures, trades."

"OK, I'll play along."

"No need to play, my sweet. You said you went to the University of Paris. It hasn't been called that for decades. To be specific, you said you studied theology at the Sorbonne. It hasn't been called that since the French Revolution. There haven't been Christian libraries in North Africa for centuries."

She pointed to various spots on the rough handwritten timeline. "I can't reconcile this. You told me before that you have your flaws but that you always tell the truth. So, if you're telling the truth, you're hundreds of years old if you're a day."

He looked at the page, then at her, then back at the timeline and laughed. "You're a remarkable woman. Few ever get close enough to me to piece these things together. Fewer still confront me with it. Carlisle is special indeed. The meetings with the other three pastors these past two weeks have been on this very topic. I'll share this with you, but I'm not sure you're ready to hear it."

She leaned forward in her chair in anticipation. "I'm a big girl, señor. You should know that by now. Tell me, I can take the truth."

He paused and looked around, then he looked back at her. "Jackie, I am thirty-five years old. I didn't lie to you about that. I've been thirty-five for almost two thousand years."

She gasped and looked at him like he was crazy. "Please don't take advantage of one who loves you so she can't think straight. José, I just want truth now." Her eyes were beginning to well up.

He reached across the table and took her hand to steady her. "This is too much for you to take in. I had no intention of burdening you with this. Please breathe deep a couple of times."

She closed her eyes and breathed. She began to withdraw her hand, but he wouldn't turn it loose.

"Jackie, have you finished reading John's Gospel as I suggested."

"Yes, three times so far this week."

"Where is your Bible?"

"If you'll you let my hand go, I'll get it."

"Sorry, Jackie, you asked for this, I would've done this another time or perhaps not at all. This is a burden but once shared it becomes yours also. Please stay with me."

She was torn between being terrified and fascinated. She retrieved her Bible from the same location as the notebook. Her hands shook.

"Go to John, the last chapter and read what Jesus said in verses twenty-two and twenty-three."

"Okay, so you're John the Apostle. It says here not to take that literally. Jesus was using a crazy example to illustrate a point."

"Yes, you're right in this case. Please stay with me Jackie. Now flip just a couple of pages over to Acts 1, where they're selecting a replacement for Judas the Betrayer."

Her fingers fumbled with the pages. "Okay, I'm there."

"Read verses 12 and following. Stop when you get to 23." She read, the Scripture coming alive to her. She could almost see Peter speaking. Then looked up when she got to verse twenty-three. "So?"

"Read the next four verses with great care, they're about to change your life again."

She mouthed the names when she came to them, sounding them out in her mind. Joseph called Barsabbas also known as Justus. "What does this mean?"

"He was passed over from being an apostle because the Master had a different plan for him. I'm Joseph. I move throughout the world doing his work. I go where he sends me. I help to remind the Church of what he intended. I'm to live until he comes again in the clouds."

Her breath came fast and shallow as she began to hyperventilate. She backed up her chair. "This can't be. I'm afraid of you now. I think you're delusional."

"Jackie, I know this defies the senses. I cannot explain it. I've tried for several lifetimes. Look at your timeline. You did this, not me. I didn't volunteer this. You asked me, remember? Please pray with me."

She tried to control her breathing and held out her hand to Joseph. "It can't be but here you are. This is crazy. I don't understand. How is it possible? Now I'm babbling. Joseph help me. Hold me." Now she was tearing up again. When he stood to hold her, she almost slammed into him, she grabbed him so hard, shaking all over.

They prayed together and her heart calmed. "What does this mean for us?"

"It means you know who I am, and I know who you are and that we are still scarily and wonderfully in love. I don't know what the Master has in store for us next, but I do know few have found me out before. I'm glad you did. I never wanted to deceive anyone but between this and the miracles, you can see my dilemma with being too forthright about it."

Memories flashed in her mind. *He works with troubled youth, helped to reconcile racial gangs, cooks like a cordon bleu chef, works in a dive and lives in a boarding house, he doesn't drive, dresses modestly, claims to hear the voice of God. Even in all this humility, he's well known in almost every community in this city. On top of that he has me, a crack TV reporter babbling about him. That's something I swore I'd never do for a man again. Since he's been in town, we've had purported miracles and many disasters including him getting shot. Yet he's calm through it all.* "I'm beginning to understand."

She pulled back and looked into his eyes. She wasn't crying but smiling. "Your burden is much heavier than mine. You seem to bear it well. How can I help you, my sweet two-thousand-year-old Bible man? I want to help."

He kissed her again and she melted against him.

She felt closer to him than ever now. They were somehow joined in this knowledge now. *Was he amazing? Was he insane? Perhaps both?* The rush of the adventure overtook her...

AUGUST

CHAPTER 28

José woke up with a jolt at 3:00 am. He saw Jackie sleeping beside him illuminated by the glow from the window. He began having wonderful and horrible thoughts all at once. A wave of guilt overtook him. Swinging himself to the side of the bed he sat up hoping not to wake her. He knew he had to get to work by 5:30 before the breakfast rush. His usual routine would have him up soon for a time of prayer and meditation. Today he woke with the guilt that he fell short of the mark again. *No one's trust was betrayed. We're consenting adults.* He tried to rationalize. It was still wrong outside of marriage. He knew it. *This complicates things in so many ways.*

He stood and gazed out the window at the rain in the nearby streetlight, a thousand thoughts racing through his mind. Looking at her sleeping, the wonderful part of last night came to the fore. She was a remarkable lady. Beautiful, witty and fun. *I didn't take advantage of her. She wanted this too. What would've happened if I turned her down? Who am I kidding, there was no turning her down. I wanted this. At least I held out until we confessed our love for each other. I stand ashamed. I didn't run 'cause I didn't want to.* He turned back to the window lost in thought. Now he had to decide to wake her or leave and make his way to work. *She'll need more time than me to get ready and I have a change of clothes at work.*

After a few moments his mind turned to coffee. Then, he felt her hand on his back as she nuzzled up next to him at the window. She was warm and soft as she kissed the scars on his back and reached around and held him from behind. He enjoyed the feeling of her hair on his back that sweet subtle smell of jasmine, enraptured in her embrace.

Then he turned and held her so he could taste her once more and see her eyes. He remembered her smile.

"This is wonderful but wrong, Jackie."

"I know this was hard for you. I felt your struggle during dinner. Realized you wanted this but had to be true your calling. I tried to make it easy for you because, I've never felt this connected. I've never been this close to anyone. I didn't know it could be like this and I've been in love many times, Joseph. Please don't tell me this is wrong. It just can't be."

"Jackie, I'm defenseless in your arms, absorbed in you. I don't ever want to leave this room. I just want to make time stand still and stay here with you."

"Can you do that? I mean, have you done that before?" He could tell she was only half joking. Then she tucked her head into his chest. "The romantic in me says *yes*, there's no place I'd rather spend a long, long time than here in your arms. I'll stay with you."

"We both know we can't." He signed, "but it's a marvelous fantasy. Jackie as amazing as last night was, you know we've created incredible complications. I told you I'm in love with you too. That scares me. I can't remember ever feeling this way. That goes back thirty lifetimes."

She pulled back enough to look up at his face. "You do know how to get a girl all hot and bothered," as she brought back her old southern belle routine. "Speaking of scared, let's call in scared today. You know, *I'm afraid I can't make it*. We could play house all day long."

"Jackie, when I sin on a mission, there are often horrific consequences. I've already tried to rationalize this, we're not married but we're very much in love. We aren't the first ones to do this. Maybe this isn't a sin? I've tried to rationalize this, but I can't shake the guilt."

"So, are you going to try and marry me? Make an honest woman out of me?"

She's toying with me now. This isn't as large a moral dilemma for her as it is for me.

"I need to open the restaurant for breakfast in an hour or so. Would you take me?"

"But I don't want you to go. I like your idea of staying frozen in time in this place. I'm not sure I can be any happier than I am with you right now." She took a deep breath and exhaled slow. "But life goes on, I have an interview at 10:00. I guess we should get ready. I'll drop you off and head to the gym. Not many folks there this time of day. Cuts down on the oglers. However, before we go, I must confess, there is one moment I'd really like to be frozen in time with you." She kissed him and backed away so that her silhouette was highlighted by light from the window…

While she took a shower and got ready, he made coffee. He found eggs and turkey sausage and made a quick omelet for two. She came out in her workout gear; form fitting high waist steel blue leggings with matching sleeveless tank.

"You can close your mouth now, hate to see a grown man drool."

"You go out in that?"

"Don't start sounding like my dad. I wear a jacket."

Over breakfast they talked about the other big revelation of last night.

"You now know who I am. Do you believe me?"

"That's a lot to accept for a small-town, country girl."

"But you're not a small-town, country girl anymore, you're a well-educated news lady from a growing new south city. You're a skeptic by training and by nature. You're also a renewed follower of the Master. Do you believe me?"

"You won't let me wiggle out of an answer, so I'll be honest. The skeptic in me says you must be crazy. The believer in me says, it's possible. I read it in John, Jesus did more than was written down. Old Testament people lived long lives. So yes, I do believe you. I'm just not sure

I'm rational around you. You get my logic askew, when I look or even think of you right now. So yes, I believe, but help me to believe more."

"That's up to the Master, but I'll do whatever I can to prove myself to you and to prove worthy of the trust you've now put in me. So, how do we deal with this? Jackie, my life isn't like those of the men you've known. I go where I'm called, often to very bad places. I live a simple life and am dedicated to the Way. That's how he's made me."

"So, in all this time you've never been married? Never been with a woman?"

"I didn't say that. I wasn't that out of practice, was I? I measure my life in lifetimes, not in years. In my thirty lifetimes, I've been married in almost half of them. It's hard on my wife though. In five years, I still look the same. In ten years, the same. I can disguise it with facial hair, but while this goes forward, you're the one who changes. We can't stay for more than a few years in one place or people notice. They begin wondering why you're with this much younger man. That's what you sign up for with me. I don't have the heart to ask it of you, but unlike any time before, I don't know how I'll live without you either." The sight of her in workout clothes took his mind to other places and he lost his train of thought. "I can't do this with you so close, especially in that outfit." He got up to take some dishes to the sink. She slipped on her jacket.

"Joseph, we'll work this out. We don't have to do it all this morning. We need to be getting on the road or there'll be bunches of hungry Mayans shortly."

They were out of the house by five fifteen.

En route, she said, "Joseph, you're over thinking this. What we have is a blessing, maybe we got things out of sequence, but that can be fixed. I love you with a depth, I didn't even know was possible. Maybe it's the power of the Spirit, the maturity I have in life now, or both? It's not teenage romanticism. I see the reality you describe and look at it as an incredible adventure. He brought us together. He brought me back to himself through you. I have to believe he has a plan to prosper us. To give us a hope and a future. Let's see where this goes together. Perhaps we should take a day or two apart and pray about this. That'll allow us both to be clear headed. If it's the same Spirit in us, we'll come to the same place in time."

"You do have quite an insight for a renewed believer. I think there is strong wisdom in what you say. I'll call on Wednesday. Can you come by the restaurant that night? Less temptation there." He gave her a long kiss good-bye, lots of loving caresses, then opened the door to get out, but paused, "I'll remember you in that outfit until I die. You continue to bewilder me Mademoiselle Jacqueline."

He watched her drive away in the rain, then he went inside and changed.

❦ ❦ ❦

As Jackie drove back up the hill, the groans began. The mounds at the top of the hill, all the water underground and all the development on the hill over the years caused a shift in the surface of the soil. It showed up in slumps and cracks over the past few weeks. Now the earth moved. Suddenly, the soil on the top of the hill came sliding into the neighborhood just below. It bulldozed trees, houses, cars, and swamped a shopping center and elementary school. The power went out, which cut down on the fires. Natural gas lines ruptured and created sporadic explosions. Thankfully, the gas lines were sealed tight by the mud flow. The force of hundreds of trees descended the hillside like battering rams.

The water, soil and debris were inescapable. The earth moved at forty miles per hour. The percussive sound waves knocked cars off the road. The sound was like a fleet of tractor trailers or fighter jets going by all at once. It all happened in less than two minutes. A whole neighborhood was under ten to thirty feet of mud.

❦ ❦ ❦

Pastor Rich awakened by the sirens and to the distant thunder of the gas explosions. He wiped the sleep from his eyes and moved to the living room, closing the bedroom door to keep from waking Maryanne. Turning on the news to see the reports and watched the aftermath of the of the mudslide up the hill in horror. *It's only about a mile away from here.* It took out twenty homes. Helicopter footage with spotlights showed places the homes used to be. You could see houses broken and buried up to their windows. Some houses crashed into others like cars on a freeway in the fog. The spotlight kept jumping with the throbbing of the helicopter from one horrible sight to another. The voice over reporter in the chopper kept trying to describe what he saw, but the geography changed so and with the rain and darkness due to the power outage, it was hard to tell. There was a steady strobe on the ground from all the emergency vehicles now on the scene.

The anchor at the news desk kept repeating, "We are seeing a very large mudslide from Summit Spires down to the neighborhoods below. It's several blocks long and at least three blocks wide. Many are presumed killed. We'll have more news when it comes in. We are sending crews now."

Jackie realized that her phone was still off. She pulled it from her purse, hit the on button and laid it in the cupholder on the console. *Mademoiselle Jacqueline, I could get used to that.* Warming all over a slight quiver came over her as she continued to process and remember last night, at times smiling, and at times sober minded. When all the connections were made, her phone went crazy. She got calls, voice mails and texts all at once. She decided to answer Mitch's call.

"Are you alive?" Mitch asked.

"More than ever, Mitch. What's up?

"You're okay?"

"Yeah, you're starting to scare me. What's going on?"

"There was a landslide up the hill about twenty minutes ago. Houses, people. It's real bad."

"Where'd it hit?"

"I think it hit your neighborhood and others further up?"

Now she was scared. "I'm heading home to see."

Jackie got as close to her home as the emergency crews allowed. With the dawn's illumination of the scene, she got a first-hand look at the extent of the disaster. It overwhelmed her.

She called Mitch back. Still in her workout gear, but she did have her station raincoat to cover during the report. "I'm on the scene but need a cameraman. Where's Bradley? Oh my God, this is horrible. I think my house is gone too."

"He's with Swain at Hillcrest and McDowell. I feared the worst when I couldn't reach you. Didn't think you ever turned off that phone. 'The news never sleeps.'"

"Forget the rookie, get Bradley to Wilmont Avenue and Kelley Road. I can do this report."

She walked around the site perimeter until Bradley arrived and got set up. Even in her running shoes she slipped a couple of times. Mud was everywhere. "Get a shot up the hill and then come back to me," she told Bradley.

"Jacqueline Hyatt, WWNS News reporting. I'm on the site of this morning's landslide. You can see the footage from our Sky Chopper, the neighborhood of Berkshire has been devastated. There are no trees standing, all the homes have been pushed into each other and are in a pile at the distal end of the flow.

"The rescue workers appear to be using thermal imaging to search for survivors. The police are advising anyone who can hear this and may be in the slide area to please move to the top of the debris. They're also advising others to stay out of the area. The mud is like quicksand or cake batter. Anything you drop in will be swallowed up. That includes emergency crews. Please, if you're a volunteer, follow instructions carefully or you'll be in danger too. The whole neighborhood is under twenty feet of mud.

"As you can see from this footage, the emergency crews have rescued a couple of people found in the debris field. They also rescued some family pets.

"It appears that at least twenty houses are impacted. There are many unaccounted for. They've found four bodies in one house already. The death toll is going to rise. Most people were at home asleep."

Pastor Rich walked up the hill from his home to the slide zone. He was there to speak with and comfort survivors, and to encourage the emergency crews on break. He felt drawn to the site. Noticing the big light and then Jackie finishing her broadcast, he went over to see if she could give him more information. That way, he could determine the best ways for the church to help.

José watched while Jackie reported and dropped his head to pray and lament. He knew she was safe, but he wept for those buried alive in this muddy pudding. He was going to go to the site, but somehow, he knew they already found all the survivors. He was lost in a sea of remorse for his sin. He was convinced their blood was on him. He knew something awful was coming. A great downfall. Now he knew it was his and all these people suffered for it.

After an hour or so, Jackie took a break to try to get to her house to assess the damage and collect some belongings, if anything was left. She and Bradley made their way on foot through the outside edge of the mud, to get close to her home. It wasn't taken off its foundations and appeared to be intact from the front. When she got closer, she noticed the privacy fence was knocked down. The foyer and kitchen were intact, as they continued to survey. She entered the master suite with its unmade bed next to a shattered window. The spot where she and Joseph stood a couple hours ago. Debris spewed inside on the bed linens and her dresser. The stench surprised her. But it looked like she was lucky, no blessed. Her home was a near miss. The memory of what Joseph said flooded in, *when I sin on mission, horrific things happen.*

After sending Bradley out back to do some damage control, she closed her walk-in closet door and changed out of her workout clothes, tossing them in the hamper right on top of the red halter and white jeans. Memories of last night rushed back to her mind again and now filled her with trepidation. *What have I done? Did I corrupt a man of God? Did I, for my own selfish pleasure, do this? Are these lives on me? Dear God forgive me. Lighten up, Hyatt. Lighten up. You're a disaster victim in your damaged home. Ask the questions, don't jump to the answers.*

She grabbed a suitcase and packed a few days' worth of clothes, toiletries and her more expensive jewelry. She and Bradley could only carry so much on foot back to the car, which was blocks away.

While she packed a gym bag, Bradley, outside near the patio, was able to pull some of the fencing from the mud despite the pelting rains. He took one piece around to the side where the window was broken, and he propped it against the side of the house so that it more than covered the open space. He crammed the patio loveseat up against it to hold it in place. "Not much more we can do without power tools. Any other damage we can mitigate?"

They completed the survey inside. She saw the breakfast dishes in the sink. Bradley noticed two coffee cups and plates and looked at her with a smile.

"Not a word."

"Who was the lucky houseguest? Looks like you got out just in time."

"Not going there."

"Any other damage?"

"None to the house but I'm shaken to the core. Let's get to the station, I've got to get cleaned up and then we're off to hold Mr. Stanley accountable for this catastrophe."

They struggled back to the car in the rain with two drag bags and a gym bag. Bumping along the uneven terrain almost slipping into the goo several times. The smell from the morass nauseated her.

DEAR FATHER, FORGIVE ME, PART 1

I stand before Holy God
I am filthy with sin
He cannot look upon me
How can I even be here, now

Again, the enemy won
I am undone
I should not go on
But give up and succumb

How can you bear my presence, Lord
After what I've done so often before
I don't want to do evil, but I do it
I desire to please you, but I don't

I don't deserve your grace
I abuse it so often
Slay me and send me away
It is what holiness requires

I cannot go on without you
Yet I choose to disobey not just once
As long as I have been with you
I should know better

I've fallen short of the mark too many times
Have I used up your grace
Is there any hope left for me
Will you even hear my plea . . .

AUGUST

CHAPTER 29

Jackie and Bradley arrived at Paul Stanley's house at 9:45. A lone, luxury SUV was parked in front of the courtyard leading to the front door. They parked the van near the ornate oversized fountain in the center of the circular drive. Bradley went to unload the equipment and she went to the door and rang the bell. No answer. She waited another few moments, since they were early. While standing in front of the double front doors, she made sure her appearance was just right in the reflective windows on each side. Crisp, high-collared, white blouse and a turquoise double-breasted pants suit. Still had her news jacket on top. She was as far away from the requested wardrobe as she could get.

They lingered till 10:05 and went back to the door. Still no answer. *Did I get it wrong?*

A sports car pulled up after a few minutes. Alexandra Stanley got out with a small overnight bag and glared at the news crew in her drive.

"What do you want?"

"Paul Stanley requested an interview at 10:00 this morning but we can't get anyone to answer the door."

"Why would he request an interview? You're that lady on the news, right?"

"Yes ma'am, Jacqueline Hyatt, WWNS." She extended her hand. It wasn't taken.

"No idea where he is, I've been gone all weekend. Come inside, the least I can do is get you out of the rain."

Alexandra unlocked the door and went inside, tossing her keys in a bowl near the door. She heard the TV on and asked that they wait in the foyer while she figured out where Paul was. When she entered the study, she screamed.

Jackie and Bradley ran to her and found her in shock next to Paul's lifeless body. A gunshot wound to the head. Handgun on the floor nearby. Brains and tissue still glistening while it dried. Jackie thought she was going to be sick. Bradley went to cover the body, but Jackie reached out a hand and stopped him. In between deep breaths she said, "Get her out of here. Don't mess with a crime scene."

She turned and took in more oxygen trying to calm herself with more deep breathing. She breathed through her mouth. The stench of death was rancid. She pulled out her phone and dialed 911 to let them know and to get officers here pronto. She knew that would take time considering the other big story today. She then called Bill Shire, Paul's attorney. He said he'd be right there. She could feel the sweat breaking out across her brow. She left the room to clear her head.

She called Mitch and told him. "Should we do a report on this. Next of kin is aware. We scoop everyone in town. Okay, got it."

Alexandra was calming in the living room. Bradley got her some brandy from a decanter on a table nearby and she was drinking the second snifter full slower than the first.

Within thirty minutes the attorney arrived just ahead of a squad car.

Bill Shire was short, balding and clean shaved. *He should spend more time in the gym*, Jackie thought. He wore a charcoal gray suit with white shirt and no tie.

As he entered, Jackie greeted him. "Don't go in there if you don't have a strong stomach. Looks like it just happened. He was watching the WWNS news still reporting on the landslide. We pre-empted normal schedules to stay on the air until noon."

"Thank you, Ms. Hyatt, I'll take a look before the police take over."

He went as far as the door and peered inside the study then returned to the foyer with Jackie while she let the police in.

As the police began their investigation, Bill gave her the statement Paul was going to give in the interview. He handwrote an official statement about Paul's death on the back.

She scanned the front page quickly, 'Wrongly accused. The real villain was his chief financial officer, Mike Winter. He did many illegal things and didn't tell Paul until it was too late. He was fired on Friday night. Paul wasn't a micro manager, not involved in the details. He was going to fight the charges.'

She looked at Bill who then said, "Apparently, he was overcome by the emotions and became suicidal. We see the result. He's a victim here. His good name and all he worked for was going down the drain. Surely you can see that."

She took the paper copy of the statement and folded it up. She put it in her jacket pocket.

"Do you believe this?"

"Ma'am, not sure I understand. That is our statement."

"Not what I asked."

"That's the answer to your question."

"Okay, let me ask it another way. Do you really expect anyone not on the payroll to believe this?"

"Ms. Hyatt, I'm going to have to ask you to leave. You have our statement and there is no interview to be done. The family is grieving."

"May I quote your handwritten statement on air."

"That's why I gave it to you. Don't go off script or there'll be trouble."

"I'll decide what to do with this. But suffice it to say, I've no intention on being an advocate for Paul Stanley. You should attend to your client's grieving spouse."

She motioned for Bradley to join her, and they went out front for her report. Mitch told her to wait until the police arrived, so it wouldn't look like she was there alone.

They set up in front of the fountain, so there was a shot of the opulent house and the fountain in the background for irony. Always thrilled to scoop the other news outlets, she reported.

"This is Jacqueline Hyatt WWNS News, reporting from the home of prominent businessman Paul Stanley, President of Stanley Builders and President of the Carlisle Chamber of Commerce. His wife Alexandra came home today to find his body inside. An apparent victim of a self-inflicted gunshot wound. Details are still developing. The body was found around ten this morning. His attorney told me that Stanley Builders released the following statement." She read from the handwritten side of the page he gave her. "While we don't know the exact circumstances surrounding Paul Stanley's death, we ask that you respect the family's privacy. Business will carry on as usual at Stanley Builders while the Senior Management Team determines a path forward."

Then she went off script, "Back in May the IRS seized assets of Stanley Builders, but those matters were reportedly resolved. We don't know if they are related to Paul Stanley's apparent suicide. However, there is a major scandal brewing around Mr. Stanley and his firm Stanley Builders. They were also the developer of the site that is the epicenter of today's mudslide. Coincidence? We'll continue to investigate this until all is brought to light. Jacqueline Hyatt WWNS News."

As she went off camera, Mr. Shire stormed out of the house and came straight for them.

"How could you do such a thing? The body isn't even cold yet. You accuse him of causing a landslide that killed all these people. We'll have you up on charges."

"Check your law books counselor. You can't defame the dead. You know as well as I, his construction site is the epicenter of this slide. You can see how much responsibility he took for this by the brains on the wall behind him. I have no patience for crooks who profit at the expense of those less fortunate. He got what he deserved. I'm just sorry we didn't get a chance to see him in court in one of those attractive orange suits. This is the coward's way out. Perhaps you'll be there instead.

Good luck sorting this out and staying clean. He went down and no doubt will take those near him down too. Good day counselor. Bradley, we're outta here."

"I think you should leave these premises now!"

"Nothing could keep me here, sir."

She was trembling when she got back into the van. The adrenaline rush that surged through her a few moments earlier subsided and her body shifted back to normal. They headed back to the slide zone. A terrible evil had been perpetrated on her city and she was determined to bring any responsible for it into the light.

✤ ✤ ✤

She also had an insurance claim on her hands and needed a place to live. *Wonder if Maria has a room? No, I'm a B&B kind of lady, there's one close to the station. It's going to be busy for a while.* She spoke to her claims agent to be sure all was covered. As the busyness of the day calmed down, she thought of Joseph and wondered if he was tormenting himself over this. *I doubt he wants to speak with me right now. God, please help him and me too as we sort this out. Please have mercy on all these poor souls that were victims today.*

✤ ✤ ✤

Mayor Hamilton held a news conference in the early afternoon. Sherriff Ward, the fire chief and other officials flanked him.

"I'm grieved to report that at five thirty-four this morning, there was a massive landslide that started at the top of the hill in the construction area of Summit Spires. It moved down the hill with great force and wiped away nineteen homes damaging two dozen others. People were asleep in their homes. This slide started and finished within two minutes. Whole families are dead or missing. There was no time to get out. We rescued two people. A child age five and a youth, age seventeen. We recovered eight bodies from areas at the edges of the slide. While rescue efforts are continuing, we fear we're now in a recovery mode. There are forty-seven people still missing.

"Please pray for these families and for our teams while they work tirelessly to wrestle with this horrible, horrible tragedy," he paused to compose himself.

"I must now address those in the area neighboring the slide. I'm told by the US Geological Survey, whose experts are on-site now, that slides often come in pairs or even clusters. We must not endanger any more of our citizens. I'm, therefore, ordering an evacuation before sunset of all the area between Hillside Drive and Creighton Avenue. We'll have these areas under lockdown tonight beginning at sunset. Police and National Guard troops will keep everyone away after dark. This includes seven neighborhoods and homes that may be in stand-alone areas. The evacuation zone includes my neighborhood. We'll open a shelter in the University Coliseum to house those who need emergency shelter and can't find it in local hotels."

Several people in the affected area didn't heed the mayor's call being like so many who decide to ride out a hurricane on the coast. They were warned but didn't want to leave their homes to looters who knew all the homes would be empty and undefended.

However, most found their ways to local hotels. Still there were over 300 people in the coliseum before nightfall. People were scared. Many panicked and left with next to nothing. Others were much more well equipped for this *campout*.

The Church rose to meet the needs of the displaced. Ms. Roberta, Reverend Tony, Reggie and others from the AME Church were on hand to help. Father Menendez was there with a group from Villa Maya. Pastor Rich and over one hundred volunteers from Carlisle Church were on-site both supporting the emergency crews in the slide zone and in the coliseum to minister with hot food and blankets. Amena and several of the ladies from New Rojava were there, giving medical aid to the women and children where it was needed. All the locals rallied to help . . . except for one.

※ ※ ※

Joseph sat alone in his room at Maria's paralyzed by his grief and guilt. He'd fasted since he heard the news. He kept begging the Master for forgiveness and lamenting the loss of so many. The waves of guilt washed over him in a sickening rhythm.

"I was right there. I could've stopped it. I know why you didn't speak. I was too guilty to hear you, our relationship fractured by sin. I'm so sorry to let you down. To let others down. I'm bewitched by your creation. You made her so perfect. You brought us together. I'm unable to reason this out. Please forgive me! Please help me! Please help those who mourn! Please don't turn away from me! I don't seek my comfort Lord, but comfort those in such distress. Dear God, stop the rains. I was too preoccupied with my own love affair to realize, I hadn't even asked this of you. I didn't realize the danger. Rebuke this storm system. Please . . . Please . . . Please . . . "

He could no longer speak, he just sat there on the side of the bed rocking back and forth weeping bitterly.

The hours passed into the early morning. He became convicted that he must leave now. The single greatest miracle was missed due to his fallibility. Evil won on this front. He didn't even see it coming. The Spirit reveled to him that he would leave soon, but he didn't realize it would be in disgrace. It seemed appropriate now. He was prideful when it came to his encounters with Jackie. He remembered telling Father Menendez he had it under control. *Some control. She has complete power of me. Great job weak man. I can't face these men again. I'm too ashamed. I owe Jackie a call. Not sure I should do that either. None of them will understand. I saw the downfall but couldn't stop it, because the Enemy took me out of the fight just when I was needed most.*

Exhausted from the agony, he drifted off to sleep for a few hours with those unpleasant thoughts tormenting his dreams.

✠ ✠ ✠

It was early afternoon on Tuesday and the shelter was now open for almost twenty-four hours. During a pause in the action, the three friends, Tony, Father M and Rich noticed Joseph was missing.

"He'd be so proud of how the city came together to help. It was such a move of God to have the wealthy ministered to by the poor. Joseph should see this, it'd do his heart good," Tony said.

Father Menendez had a terrible thought. "I dropped him at Jackie's that night, do you think he got swept up in the slide. He may be buried under all this. Her house was in the zone," then he chuckled, "No, wait a minute, that means he would've been there all night. He wouldn't have done that. He must be safe somewhere."

"I saw Jackie on-site after the slide yesterday morning. She's fine. It must not have hit her house. But where is Joseph? I'll give him a call," Rich said and tried his cell but there was no answer.

Tony called Ramone's and reported back to the team. "Ramone said he turned in his notice today and asked to leave after breakfast. He took what pay he was due and left. He did give Ramone a letter for Jackie. He said she would come by Wednesday and asked him to please give it to her. Then he prayed a blessing over Ramone and the staff before he left."

The Father dialed Maria who gave a similar account. The Father recounted the story to Tony and Rich. "He'd paid through the end of the month, but that was only a few days away. He seemed depressed. She couldn't talk sense to him. He prayed over her, and the house then took a small gym bag of belongings and left, headed toward the Wharf."

Rich called Jackie but got her voice mail. *Maybe he and Jackie were leaving together, called on another mission. The one in Carlisle was so successful. A shame he didn't get a chance to see how successful.* "I'll have to wait for her call back," he told Tony and Father M.

The demands of those in the coliseum re-emerged and they were all overcome by the workload. Chasing down Joseph would have to wait.

He disappeared in a whisper just as he arrived. But Carlisle was a much different place because the Master brought him there.

SEPTEMBER

YEAR 2
CHAPTER 30

At long last, the rain stopped. Not before Bass Lake was over full pond. The rains over the past many weeks were so relentless that the lake flowed well over its banks along its coastline. It funneled toward the Lumber River Dam putting pressure on the structure, but even more on the people running it.

There were debates on how much water could be released without flooding the valley below and Carlisle itself was just a few miles downstream. They succeeded in managing it up to now. They'd increased the flow for almost a month. Despite releasing so much over the spillway the water level was getting very close to the emergency spillway. The river basin could handle the current flow plus another twenty five percent without major flooding. However, if the emergency spillway was activated, it was all over.

Such flooding hadn't happened in almost fifty years. The engineers created new models, befuddled about what to do next. They needed relief from the water upstream. Perhaps the dry weather would be the break they needed at last.

Carlisle was still far enough away from all the issues at the dam, that this was a story for the weather slot of the news but didn't merit headlines. The weather news concentrated on the sunshine at last until . . .

Hurricane Mercedes became the big story. It formed off the Atlantic coast over several days in early September. More unpredictable than usual, the various models had it going in many directions, but the majority view said it would spin ashore well north of any direct impact on Carlisle. Much of the state's emergency resources including the National Guard and highway patrol were gearing up to deal with the storm. The federal agencies were busy trying to determine where it would hit and kept their emergency resources mobile since it could well make landfall in different states.

Carlisle wasn't high on either of the priority lists at this point. Since the dam release was working, most thought all was under control.

After the Labor Day visit to her mom, a devastated Jackie poured herself into her work. She recalled how proud her mother was to show her off at the same old Baptist church on Labor Day Sunday. Her heart sank as she realized how small it became. Many seniors but few young people. She thought about how it would be good to be closer to her mother in these later years. But duty called. It was the only thing she could rely on.

How could he just leave? Don't go there again Jackie. What a selfish fool he is. I knew fleeing was his MO from back in April, but I went for the whole thirty lifetimes thing and fell crazy in love. I guess, I was the fool. He got what he wanted and left. It was amazing for those few weeks since the shooting. I wouldn't trade it. And, if he was who he said . . . Don't be a fool for another man Jackie. You got work to do lady.

Today, she got the fun job of flying over the dam reporting from the Sky Chopper. She rolled her eyes at the assignment but relished the thought of being in a copter. She didn't want Mitch to know he was giving her an assignment she wanted. She hated owing men favors now.

As they flew over the dam with the sun setting, she could see the water levels and the great plume at the end of the waterfall as the volume of water released dropped to the river below. The deafening roar caused her to film the story and then do a voice over.

Wow, the power of nature is awesome. Do we think we're in control of this? Who are we kidding?

Then the level-headed Jackie took over and she remembered the power company spokesman, Don Arnold, saying 'all of these scenarios are planned for and we're working the plan. Nothing for the public to worry about.'

Then the skeptic kicked in comparing the calm spokesman to the raging water. Out loud, she said, "Right."

As they made one last fly over, she noticed the emergency spillway was now wet all the way down the center section. "Was it coming over the top?"

She told the pilot to take another fly by.

Then she signaled to Bradley to get a shot of the spillway. "No question. The emergency spillway was in use by nature, not the power company. I need to call Don. No one told us about the emergency spillway."

The nearby parking lot was evacuated, so she told the pilot to land there. He complained about trees and power lines, but Jackie always hard to deter when she was on a story, insisted.

He cut the engine and all they could hear was the roar at the end of the spillway.

"This is Jackie Hyatt with WWNS News, I want to speak with press liaison Arnold immediately."

"Ma'am, he's very busy right now and we already issued our statement today. Shall I connect you to his assistant, she can email that to you?" said the receptionist.

"Get me to whoever can connect me with Don Arnold, this is Jacqueline Hyatt. I'm at the Lumber River Dam right now and need to inform Mr. Arnold about something. He'll want this call."

"One moment please."

After thirty seconds Don Arnold clicked on the line. "Jackie, how nice to hear from you. What can I do for you?"

"Are you aware the emergency spillway is in use?"

"Jackie, that's just not so. I checked it on our cameras within the hour. All was bone dry."

"Don, I'm right next to the emergency spillway now and I assure you it's in use. Cut the PR blather and tell me what you're doing about it!"

"Jackie, I'm unaware of this. Let me speak with my engineers and get back to you. I'll call back when I know something more. Is this the best number for you?"

"Don don't put me off. I have a story to do at six and this is going to be the lead with or without your statement. It'd be better for you and the people of Carlisle, if you have a better response than *I didn't know*! I've got about twenty minutes until this story is ready to air. I'd like an official position before that."

"I'll get the team together and respond back to you post haste."

She decided to do the voiceover using sound deadening equipment while she was on-site. She got back in the chopper anyway since it was a nice element to have in the background. Bradley was ready to make her look good.

Her phone rang. It was Don.

She finished up her commentary and answered.

"Jackie here."

"Jackie, we're sending our on-site crew to inspect things now. They're coming your way. We plan for this eventuality, and while it's concerning, it's not beyond our control. We're going to increase the volume through the main spillway to alleviate the pressure. Now that the rains have stopped, it appears this is just a temporary issue."

"That's the official statement?" she asked.

"Best we have until we get our team's report in an hour or so."

"I see your team now, thanks for coming back so fast. I'll include part of it in my report at six."

She transmitted the report to the station and decided to stick around to see the inspectors do their work.

After the team of engineers inspected the spillway, they could see that the increase of output down the main spillway seemed to have fixed the issue although the water level wasn't changing much. They told her off the record that these things happen at this point in the cycle and, while the optics didn't look good, it wasn't a major concern. "Nothing we can't handle," the supervisor said.

She got word her story was moved back since water dribbling over an emergency spillway wasn't very entertaining. It was getting dark. So, with Mitch's agreement, she decided to head back to Carlisle in the chopper.

In the light of the setting sun, she could see the river moving in torrents toward the city with *nothing we can't handle* echoing in her mind.

SEPTEMBER

YEAR 2
CHAPTER 31

Earlier that same day, as life returned to normal post landslide, Tony and a team from the church resumed the jail ministry they'd done for years, giving hope to the troubled at this critical juncture in their life. Success came in small, encouraging ways.

Today, he and the team led a Bible study in the dingy rec room with its mismatched tables and chairs. Toward the end of the session, he could tell the prisoners were anxious to leave to get their lunch first. "I didn't know jail food was worth rushing to. What's the attraction?" Tony said.

One inmate, Spider Louis said, "Sheriff Ward got hisself a new pris'ner to hep with the cookin' a couple of weeks back. The food went from awful to good. The Sheriff liked it, 'cause the inmates don't cause so much trouble when they's well fed. One less thing for them to complain 'bout."

It didn't take Tony long to figure out, Joseph was the new cook. *Now ministering to the souls in prison. That's where he went.*

Because of his jail connections, he arranged a pastoral visit with the prisoner Jesus Sabio.

Tony waited in the pastoral visiting area. A room with two doors one for him to come and go and one made of steel that only opened from the other side. The wooden table and chairs were not designed for comfort but convenience. The strong smell of body odor and disinfectant was distracting. The overhead lights buzzed with only one blub working. The prisoner door clanked open, and Joseph came in. He saw Tony and quickly turned to leave.

"No wait! Don't go. We wondered what happened to you. Tell me the story my brother. I didn't know you had yet another name."

He slumped down into the wooden chair opposite Tony. "The name's a mistake, I'll explain. My story is a familiar one Tony. I fell. I betrayed the Master and dozens of people died in a landslide that I could've stopped."

"Whoa, wait my friend, I need to get caught up here. Tell me more."

"I left you all on Sunday night and went to Jackie's for a late dinner. She was a renewed believer, thanks to all your prayers for her. While dinner went on, one thing led to another. We confessed our love. Perhaps we had too much wine. We made love." He looked down and shook his head.

"Oh no. That was the night before the slide."

Joseph looked up at Tony. "Terrible things happen when I sin on a mission Tony. I was right there, I could've stopped it, but I couldn't hear the Master's voice. Our relationship was broken by my sin. Those people died, because I wanted carnal delights. I had to go. I couldn't face any of you. I'm so weak when it comes to her." He hung his head low.

"Tell me about your charges. Drug trafficking? That sure doesn't sound like you."

Joseph recalled his meeting with Deion at the Excelsior club two weeks ago.

"Hello, El Diablo de Villa Maya." Several in his entourage backed away at that greeting. "You look much better than the last time we met. Glad you got over the shooting in VM. Hated to see you taken out that way. What brings you to this fine establishment? Want a job? I could use a man of your talents."

"Deion, I want to leave Carlisle and head back to South America. There's nothing for me here anymore. I'd like to book a passage on one of your barges down to the seaport. I can catch an ocean freighter to Panama from there. I can get lost in the jungles of South America once more."

"What happened to you? Why not get one of your church friends to help? You and Lady News ever get together?"

Joseph didn't respond to that. "I'm just ready to go. Let's say my immigration status may complicate other means of travel."

Chuckling under his breath, "You got lady trouble I can tell. Broken heart. It's all over your face. That's so sweet. They ain't worth it my friend. No need to leave town. Just go for a change in scenery. See anything you like here? I could use someone like you. You got wisdom my team lacks. Stay with me, I'll make you rich. It comes with other benefits too." He spread his hands open wide.

"Da Wyz made me such an offer once. I turned him down before preaching the Gospel to him. Is that what you seek now?"

"I'm not the Gospel type. Might be best if you wait for the barge leaving tomorrow."

"No, I want to go now."

"Suit yourself. No one rides for free."

"I can be a deck hand or a cook."

"I'll make sure Captain Hazard knows you're coming on board. With all your experience in VM, I'm sure you a better cook than what they got. You can sleep with the crew in the berths. Happy Travels."

"Before you go, how was Lady News? Her fruit had to be sweet. That's got to be what this is about."

Joseph, again, didn't respond.

"Not the kind to talk about it, I see. How noble. Well, now that she's back on the market, maybe I'll go find out myself. Be nice to have a news lady in my stable. She could be the cream in my coffee."

It was all he could do to constrain himself from pronouncing curses on the place. With a calm and firm voice close to boiling over, he said.

"Please don't do this. I came to you for help offering to pay my way. We're not the best of friends, but you're alive today because of me. All I need is your word to get me aboard the ship. Then you'll be rid of me. But it sounds like you'll still have to deal with El Diablo."

"Wow, she messed you up good bro'. She's too old for me." Deion laughed. "I'll get you on the barge."

※ ※ ※

He arrived at the dock before three and asked for Captain Hazard.

Near the entrance, a grizzled older man with teeth missing laughed and said, "Don't call him that. It's Captain Howard. He got that nickname when he hit the bridge back in July. What's your name?"

"They call me José Sabio."

"You the new cook, right? Old cook didn't like getting demoted to deck hand. Doubt you guys are gonna get along now. But get aboard." He yelled up the gangway, "Jimmy show the new guy around. Name's Jesus."

The name stuck and for their brief encounter, he just let it be.

They cast off at five o'clock, about thirty minutes behind schedule.

Captain Howard addressed the crew. He was drunk or high. José couldn't tell which. Speech slurring, he said, "Just sail her straight with the current boys. This is the easiest job we got. I'll be on the bridge."

José went below deck to start dinner. When he got all the pans clean enough to cook with, he felt the barge lurch to one side and then right itself. They hit something.

He scurried above deck to see the hands all scrambling to control the damage to the barge. They passed the Lumber River Bridge. José could see a chunk of concrete missing at the base of the bridge support. They hit it again. He heard the captain saying, "We're not stopping. No major damage to it or us."

As they moved further away, José looked back and could see the repair shroud around the other side of the support they hit in July.

"Father, please get me out of this place."

Further downriver when José was about to serve dinner, the barge stopped. They were boarded by the Port Authority Law Enforcement Division for hitting the bridge and not stopping. With probable cause, they searched the cargo and found a substantial shipment of heroin. They impounded the barge and arrested the crew.

✠ ✠ ✠

"My status as an illegal makes me a flight risk. Which is accurate. The name mishap was due to the way they wrote me down on the manifest. I didn't try to correct it. I'm awaiting deportation to Guatemala. Accused of drug smuggling. Perhaps, the Master will use me again someday, and I can do some good there."

"Wow, the enemy has really messed with your head Joseph. I don't think God wanted you to stop the landslide or he would've used you to do it. That would've been quite a miracle indeed, but I doubt he would have you change the course of nature. You said a great downfall was coming. It was the landslide and maybe even Paul Stanley but not you. You know better than I how sometimes we must suffer to be purified. The aftermath of the slide, while grievous, was also a rebirth of sorts for the city. You weren't there the first night of the evacuation. The city came together in a beautiful way. The underprivileged ministered to the wealthy. The poor helping the 'newly' poor. It was a sight to behold brother. The Church showed up in his love. You missed that. Father M, Rich and I were there. We talked about what a wonderful gift you'd brought to us from our Lord."

Joseph looked hopeful. "Really? You were all together?" He hung his head again shaking it from side to side, "What a fool I am."

"You're not a fool my friend, but you've been fooled. The enemy got in your head. Once you committed the act, he convinced you how despicable you were. Having the landslide, I'll give you, that was a good tool for him to use on you. Have you repented my brother?"

"I've been repenting for weeks now."

"Okay, let me speak truth over you now." In his best African American Preacher voice, he said, "YOU ARE FORGIVEN! Stop listening to the Enemy! Listen to the Master! You know he died for you!" Then he toned it down. "You know better than any alive today, he rose again. Why won't you accept his forgiveness? Why won't you forgive yourself? Let's pray together."

While he prayed, Joseph felt the Spirit awaken in him. He felt remorse now for not sharing his burden with those who love him. But the time for remorse was passed.

"Thank you, Tony. I needed this more than you know. I feel his power alive in me again. You're a powerful believer and I wish his blessings on you and all you love. I just wish I could get out of here. There seems to be only one way out now."

"You know he can make a way. Look, let me see if I can get the drug charge dropped. The illegal thing may not be so bad if there's no other charges. Should I tell the others?"

"Not Jackie. Not yet. She deserves more than this. Tony, I can't trust myself near her. She is that deep in my soul. She is special in God's eyes. I know her part now. I just wish there was more time. I've been alive for thirty lifetimes and now I want more time."

"I need to leave you. But before I do, know He loves you and we love you. Don't let the enemy tell you different. I don't know how it plays out from here, but you're back in relationship with the Master. I do know, he's in control."

They embraced as brothers and Tony left. Joseph smiled as he realized in his weakness, the Master strengthened him. He rejoiced over the wonderful news of God's forgiveness.

DEAR FATHER FORGIVE ME, CONCLUSION

I see now, it is not me who deserves
It is you who love so deep that you will not let me go
The sacrifice I saw all those years ago still holds
For a believer who still falls

You proved it when you raised him
Thank you for loving me so much
Thank you for lifting my burden yet again
Thank you for restoring my soul

It is mercy you give
By the grace of my Lord
I still grieve for the pain I have caused you
Please let me help make this right
Use me anew
Be glorified in my weakness
That is on display for many to see
You are strong not me

Thank you
Praise you
Hallelujah
Gloria, in excelsis Deo

SEPTEMBER

YEAR 2

CHAPTER 32

Once they landed, Jackie settled into the cloth passenger seat of the news van. The older van came with a dark gray interior supplemented by the smell of all the electronics emanating from the back. Bradley drove to the evacuation camp by the river. On the way, she watched the trees go by while she contemplated the letter from José after the landslide. She had it chiseled in her mind. Whenever her mind was quiet, parts just came to the fore.

> 'Jackie, what we did should not have been. I led you on. I committed a sin against the Master and a sin against you. I can't get over it. I can't get over the feeling that those people died because of what I did.'

In her mind, she argued with his letter. It was the only way to work through the hurt.

José it's what we did. I was there, remember. I was a willing participant. I feel like I seduced you. If anyone has those people's blood on them it should be me, not you.

If you didn't insist on going to work, I could've been one of the fifty-five who died. You saved me. That should mean something. Even if you don't like me anymore. You still saved someone. That's what you do. You make people better by being near you.

I can't bear to see you like this. I feel like I've defrocked a great man of God. I never intended that. We both had strong, deep, crazy feelings for each other, unless I missed my read. People in this culture act on those feelings. We expressed them and it was beautiful. The timing stinks but the feelings were and remain very deep and very real.

The letter continued, 'Jackie, I think we should stay apart now. I fear what may happen next. I don't trust myself near you. I must go on a journey and get far away from here. I let you down and I let the Master down. I must go.'

"What's on your mind news lady?" Bradley asked while he drove.

"Was it that obvious?"

"I've not seen you like this in the time I've known you. You're changed yet you're still the same."

"Thanks for your concern. Just remembering an old friend."

"I think you remember him all the time. He did a number on you, didn't he?"

"You have no idea. I think, we did a number on each other. Wish I could've seen him again. Talked it through. Now it's just a raw wound that doesn't heal."

They arrived at Camp Mercedes as it became known. Mayor Hamilton issued a new evacuation order with the hurricane threat. The land, still not stabilized since the landslide, could crumble again if the hurricane turned toward them. He didn't want another fifty plus deaths on his watch. Ward and Karl agreed with his logic. The evacuees gathered at the University Coliseum near the riverfront next to Hart Park, just as they did the first nights after the landslide a couple of weeks earlier.

The rain stopped almost two weeks ago, and things began drying out and the whole city's spirit seemed to be lifted with the sunshine. Tonight's weather was good, a crisp fall evening. The looming storm didn't manifest itself yet.

People had more practice at evacuating now so while there was no panic, people moved to the evac center ready for the night. Most were inside the coliseum, but some were camping outside in the parking lot near the river. This created a festival atmosphere. The coliseum located at a bend in the river just up from Hart Park, such that they were forty feet above the water which is why it was used as the evacuation site.

Jackie saw Ms. Roberta working one of the water stations. She stopped by to get some water and say hello.

"Good to see you, Jackie."

She likes greeting people like that, especially the ones who knew Joseph. Her memory flashed of the first time they met— 'she used to be blind, ya know.'

"It's good to see you too, Ms. Roberta. How are things down here?"

"People seem nervous but comforted by others' company. Never thought I'd live to see this. All the colors of Carlisle together. Praise our Lord for his love."

"Praise him indeed. It couldn't have happened any other way. I know that now. Thanks for the water."

She stopped by the outdoor grill set up by Ramone and manned by Carlos and Hamsa.

Fried peppers, onions and spices filled the air around them as smoke billowed away, driven by the breeze. "Give me a chicken taco. With some rice and chips."

Ramone came over and gave her a hug and a kiss on the cheek. He turned to the cashier and said, "This señorita's money is no good here."

"No, I want to pay."

"My gift to a wonderful lady, who I know must be hurting. We miss him too."

She bit her lip and turned her head to one side so he wouldn't see her welling tears.

She regained her composure and turned back to him. "Thank you for dinner. I'll come back by the restaurant, once this is all over."

She took her dinner inside the building and decided she didn't want to talk to anyone else right now. So, she found a dining area, sat down at an empty picnic table and enjoyed her taco dinner. *I remember all those experimental dishes he tried on me.* She dabbed her eye with her napkin.

Some locals recognized her and waved as they went to sit at another table carrying more of Ramone's delicacies from the grill.

After her meal, she moved into the main coliseum floor now alive with activity. Amena and a group from University Hospital checked on people near the door. They exchanged waves from a distance. *The older and less mobile folks are going to have a more difficult night with the evacuation than others.*

In the distance, Pastor Rich, Tony and Father M, along with other clergy walked through the crowd encouraging folks, passing out blankets and toiletries. Church volunteers seemed everywhere. *The city was coming together in a crisis. This is so amazing to see. I wish he could see it.*

Reverend Tony noticed her and went out of his way to chat. He gave her a side hug in greeting.

"How are you, my sister?"

"Tony, to be honest, I feel like my guts got kicked out. But I'm getting over it. Wish Joseph could see this. Any idea where he went?"

"He wouldn't like me to say. He confessed a few things to me about his sin and his guilt. Said he felt responsible for all the loss of life. I told him the Lord doesn't work like that. He knew it, just needed a brother to remind him. He's restored now."

"I'm glad one of us is better. At least he's talking to you. How'd you find him?"

"God led me to him."

She looked at him, bewildered. "When did you speak with him? Where is he? Oh wait, he's here, isn't he? That little . . . "

He laid a hand on her shoulder.

"Jackie, he's in jail. The police arrested him for drug trafficking the day he went missing. Since he's illegal, he can't get out. His phone is in an evidence lock up. No way to contact us. They got his name wrong, so he didn't show up on any searches. He's going to be deported."

She stood with her mouth open. Unable to speak. She licked her lips and cocked her head to the side. She moved her mouth trying to speak but nothing came out.

Tony pulled her close and she leaned into his powerful side. She clinched her jaw. "He was too ashamed to speak with any of us. He didn't want you to see him like this. He tried to run, but the Master wouldn't let him."

She steeled herself and wiped a tear away from her eye then exhaled slowly. Shook her head and said "Unbelievable. I'm going to him. No more letters. No more arguments with the man who isn't there."

"It's not visiting hours, my child."

"Tony, they'll let me in. Or I'll rip the gates open!"

※ ※ ※

She headed to the jail and remembered what she wanted to say. She played it out in her head, "I won't follow a God who plays on our guilt and our fear. I don't believe he struck down those people because we slept together. If that's who he is, I'm glad I walked away from the church." She knew that was intended to hurt him and she didn't want to do that now. She also knew how false that theology was. The Spirit in her witnessed to the heresy of her thinking. He is God and we are not.

Maybe we had to sacrifice ourselves for the city to survive. Not sure I buy that either. It seemed to work though. At least for a couple of weeks. Now I'm not so sure.

Her phone lit up with Mitch's smiling face. *He always calls at the worst moments.* "What's up boss."

"Do your report on the camp and get back to City Hall. The storm has changed directions again."

"That's just where I was heading boss." *He didn't need to know the reason.*

SEPTEMBER

YEAR 2
CHAPTER 33

Hurricane Mercedes shifted one more time daunting the meteorologists again. It moved straight inland, instead of moving up the coastline. It savaged that area with all the fury of a category four storm. Massive storm surge; wind roaring through like a great angry beast. The rain coming in sheets, while the ocean overwhelmed the shore and all attempts to hold it at bay. The storm moved inland. The wind and rain seemed to accelerate.

The people of Carlisle watched the news breaks on the jumbotron in the coliseum while the storm assailed the northern part of the state. The bulk of it missed them, although some clouds gathered overhead. A drizzle began as a cloud band at the edge of the storm passed over.

✣ ✣ ✣

Sheriff Ward, in his office listening to the news of the storm, awaited a call to help the most impacted areas of the state. He looked over his staffing levels to see if he could send a team to help, once the storm finished its assault. *At least that one missed us. Poor souls up north. Best we can do is help them when it's over. Maybe we can get some good publicity.* He instructed his assistant to get some officers working on pulling together emergency supplies to take with them, if called on.

The slumps and cracks that preceded the landslide in Carlisle two weeks earlier also developed at the far end of Bass Lake. Since the area was mostly uninhabited and few visited due to all the rain, no one noticed. The high lake levels also kept the water from normal run off, this further weakened the substrate. With the flow of water from upriver caused by the storm, the land gave way much as it did in Carlisle with just as devastating an effect. No homes or businesses to wash away but the massive amount of soil and debris hit the lake with force of an earthquake. Just as ice dropped into a full pitcher of water causes an overflow the massive wave caused by the slide launched down the lake headed straight for the Lumber River Dam. It swamped the spillway, passed over the top of the dam, spillway and emergency spillway as tens of thousands of gallons of water cascaded down the front of the dam and then on toward Carlisle through the narrow channel.

With all that water and all that pressure behind, it crashed into the lower Lumber River with more force than tons of TNT. The sound was deafening. When it hit the bottom of the valley, the foam and clouds it created displayed the awesome power of the living God. The rampant water damaged power poles and lines causing a large swath of Carlisle to go dark.

The leading edge of the deluge flashed downstream inundating bridges that were twenty feet above the river at normal levels. It careened through the channel with such force, it took out trees and everything in its path. The increased flow in advance of the massive wave surged past the Lumber River Bridge and the damaged abutment furthest from Carlisle buckled, sending concrete and asphalt into the river with great bursting displays. Twisting guardrails like taffy more than halfway down the bridge.

People on the riverbank, who could see that far, were terrified by the sound, like rushing water chasing a freight train, as much as the sight of what was coming.

As the torrent came blasting by, the river rose out of its banks with swift rushing water moving downstream. River levels were now several feet over the top of flood walls on the Carlisle side. People at the river side panicked as they fled the flood waters. Once the deluge passed, the flood walls could restrain the flow as the initial swell drained away down river.

Don Arnold got called to the Carlisle Power and Light Storm War Room, a conference room with massive monitors and all the modern tech a successful utility could afford. Many in the war room worked for days now with little sleep. Don knew it was bad news by the grim look on everyone's face. Morgan Robinson, the chief engineer and Edward Calhoun, the company president, were the highest-ranking officials present. Morgan was seated at one end of the large conference table with Ed looking over his shoulder at a laptop while the news played on a large monitor on the far side of the room.

"Wh . . . what's happening?" Don asked.

Morgan looked up and said, "We got swamped by what appears to be a tsunami from the far end of Bass Lake. There was no seismic activity, so it must've been a landslide like the one that hit the city last month. It displaced too much water, and we lost containment. It came crashing over all our efforts to contain it. Our team at the river tells us its staying just inside the flood walls along Riverside Drive. Good for now." Then he shook his head.

"With all the churn from the waves washing back and forth, there is another wave coming. Mercedes dumped so much rain upstream. We couldn't expect this. There's no plan. We don't know how much damage the swamping caused, we must release thousands of gallons more to take the pressure off or we could lose the whole structure. We just have to open the spigots so to speak and let it run until the lake drains twenty or thirty feet. We can't control it. We don't have much time. We must evacuate the waterfront. There's only a short time before we open those valves and the flood arrives. People must find high ground."

Don didn't hear it all. The shock of the flood comment knocked him off his feet. He slumped into a chair at the table and got a sinking feeling in the pit of his stomach. He had no idea even what to ask next. He muttered to himself. "We planned for everything. Our team is the best. We can't be outdone by this."

Ed handed him a statement they crafted that needed review. He got in Don's face and said, "Breathe Don. Deep in and out. We need your help to get the word out and avoid panic. Review and adjust this statement. We won't release the flood until we've had time to inform city officials and notify the press. With the swamping, if we don't drop water levels fast, the dam could crumble. Then over one hundred feet of lake comes crashing down all at once. This is going to be a very bad night. May God have mercy on us all."

Don snapped out of it. "I'll call Sheriff Ward, the Mayor and the City Manager." He took in another deep breath and let it out slow. "Shall we have them come or just a phone call?"

"Just a phone call. Finish the statement and then get them on the line pronto!"

"Right here?"

"Yes, right here, ASAP!"

Don reviewed and adjusted the statement by hand then returned it to Ed. Then Don pulled out his cell phone to get the phone numbers and set up the conference call on the nearby speaker phone. His hands were shaking as he dialed. In addition, he called the fire chief, the Port Authority captain and the Governor's office.

The Governor, unavailable due to the storm in the other part of the state, had her spokesperson on the line.

Ed Calhoun took the audience through what was about to happen next.

"Ladies and Gents, our situation is dire. There appears to have been a landslide into Bass Lake that created a tsunami like wave that washed over the top of the dam, down the spillway and the emergency spillway all at once. We couldn't stop it due to lake levels and due to the speed it moved. You see the result of the first wave. We also know the storm dumped too much water upstream and it's heading our way. The dam was already releasing as much as possible without causing major flooding. With the swamping from the tsunami, and since we're about to be overwhelmed by another massive rush of water we have to open all valves and let the water flow to reduce lake levels now or we could lose the whole structure. I know the hill area evacuated to the riverfront yesterday due to the mudslide threat. The bridges across the Lumber River can't be used due to recent damage from the barge accidents and the raging waters. The only way in or out of town now is the main highway and a handful of sideroads. We've got to get as many people as possible up and over the ridge, before we open the spillway, and another wall of water hits the riverfront. Best guess to impact is sixty to ninety minutes. Anything past that puts the whole dam at risk and then the flood won't be tens of thousands but hundreds of thousands of gallons."

A brief discussion ensued. "Who should notify the public?" the mayor asked.

The group agreed, it would be a combination of the Mayor Hamilton, Sheriff Ward and Ed. They needed time to set this up and craft the right message. Everyone else had to prepare for the evacuation. The announcement would come in thirty minutes to allow time to get emergency crews in place working to direct traffic up the hill while the mayor's team got the press conference setup.

Ed hit the call end button then told everyone in the war room, "Get your families out before the order comes down. All of us need to stay with the ship."

The room cleared as everyone made emergency calls. The comments were all the same—"Pack what you can, find the kids and the pets, head up the roads out of town. What you can't get ready in twenty minutes should stay behind."

After calling his wife, Sheriff Ward made his way back to Karl in the meeting room. The mayor and his wife Susan joined them.

Motioning at Susan, "I told her to go, but she insists on staying with us. She may be able to help. We need all the heads we can muster right now," Marcus said.

Wade informed them of the emergency procedures. "It doesn't look good. Much of our city may be destroyed tonight. Many will die. We can't get everyone out fast enough. But we must try to save who we can."

"Let's get the press in here pronto," the mayor told his assistant, who lingered just outside the door.

"Should I be scared?"

"Yes, but only after you call the press."

"I saw Jackie Hyatt in the building a few minutes ago. I don't know if anyone else is around. I'll make some calls," the mayor's assistant replied.

"What's she doing here?"

"Said she got a tip. Wants to speak with Wade."

"Get her in here, if you can find her. Make the other calls, to the paper, the radio, etc. Then you better get out of town. This is bad."

She pulled out her cell phone calling Jackie as fast as her nervous hand could. "Come to the Mayor's conference room now!"

"What for?"

"NOW!" and she hung up. Then she called her husband and told him to get the kids, the grandkids and the pets out. They needed to head over the hill in twenty minutes. Finally, she called her contacts at the paper and the local radio news and said they need to have reporters at City Hall or on the phone, ASAP. In her haste, she didn't call the local Spanish speaking station. She told the mayor she was done and headed out.

"Drive fast," he said.

"What's going on Mayor?" Jackie arrived in the conference room just as the mayor's assistant blew past her out the door.

"We need to inform the public the best we can without a panic. The dam was swamped by a tsunami on the lake. They have to release enough water to get the lake down twenty or thirty feet. They have to open the spillway completely. A flood is coming. We have less than an hour."

"What're we going to do?" she asked.

"Evacuate the waterfront. Get people to higher ground. They need to get over the ridge if they can. The Lumber River Bridge is washed out thanks to our barge captains," he paused, "What we really need is a miracle." He paused again his voice trailing off and swallowing hard. "Otherwise, Carlisle dies tonight."

"Lady and gentlemen, we may have one." They looked at her with skepticism mixed with hope. "Is José Sabio, the former chef at Restaurant Tapas, still in jail here? I don't know what he can do, but I've seen amazing things happen near him. He claims to have the power of God. At least he did. If we ever needed that, this is the time."

"Are you're out of your mind, Jackie?" Karl said.

"You want to evacuate, and you should, but for those who can't get out, they at least need a rallying call. They need a hero, even if it's for their last moments on earth. Let's use him for that, even if you don't believe he can do anything. He helped unite the city, brought peace to the Wharf. I just walked the camp, I've seen it."

"Many say he helped to destroy our city," Ward chimed in. "For crying out loud, he is an illegal and a drug runner. Probably a gang leader, too. Who knows what he's done. We can't trust him."

"No, he's not those things. José is a gentle and kind spirit who loves people and his God. We have nothing to fear from him," Susan said.

The mayor paused and looked at Susan and nodded his head. "What do we have to lose? If he can't stop it at least we've given people something to occupy their time instead of panicking. If he can, why wouldn't we let him?"

"I'm against it, but I can live with the rallying cry idea. Who's going to talk to him?" Karl said.

Jackie started to speak but Ward cut her off.

"I'll do it," he said.

"I'll handle the press conference about the announcement alone. You guys go below and see if this José can help us. It's our most desperate moment," the mayor said.

As she headed out the door, the mayor said, "Jackie, aren't you going to stay for the press briefing?"

"I have your news, sir. The real news is happening in a cell below us, that's where I'm headed. You have the others coming. I'll have my cameraman here to broadcast. I'll join as soon as I can."

Ward, Jackie and Karl all headed downstairs. Ward called ahead to have José put in an interrogation room. On the way, Ward said, "You two wait in the observation room. I want your opinion, based on my interview, if we should let him do this or not."

She grabbed her phone and told Bradley, "Get to City Hall in the next ten minutes and go to the mayor's conference room. Big news. I won't be there. Just broadcast."

SEPTEMBER

YEAR 2

CHAPTER 34

Sheriff Ward entered the interrogation room with José seated and cuffed to the table. He towered over him.

"Comfortable?"

"No."

"Who are you?"

"Who do you think I am?"

"Don't be cagey with me buddy! I don't have time for this! We have a city in crisis and much of it points at you. I have people all over town that say you go by lots of names. I speak to my team in the New Rojava, they say you're Yosef. I speak to my guys in Villa Maya, you're called José Sabio. The guys in Broken Wharf think you're a troublemaker named Joseph. The guys up the hill call you Justus. Your record here shows you as Jesus. Anyone with that many aliases must be a crook. I have news reports that call you some kind of miracle worker." He leaned on the desk and got in José's face. "So, tell me, who are you? What do you want here?"

Looking up at Sheriff Roman Ward, José said, "I try to be all things to all people. My names help me blend in better with each group I minister to. I came here with a group from Mexico last year. I've been a part of this city for many months. I came just after the riots and before the gang wars. I've tried to help those in this city, who are poor and downtrodden, by speaking words of kindness and doing acts of mercy. I challenged those up the hill to be more conscience of the under privileged and the mission field in their backyard."

Ward moved to the chair and sat down. "You're an illegal by your own admission. You seem to be near trouble too often. I'm not sure if you create it, or it follows you around, but I can't have you causing any more trouble in my city. I don't have to prove much of anything. We're getting you on the next plane back to Mexico or Guatemala or whatever it says here." He held up the file he brought with him.

Leaning forward in his chair, the handcuff chain rattling as he moved, José asked, "Why did you come in here Sheriff? My case doesn't warrant such an important interrogator at a time of crisis. What're you looking for?"

The Sheriff looked at the prisoner and wondered if his internal panic was so easy to read. He was at the end of his rope. Carlisle was about to be destroyed. The mudslides, the river rising, the dam overflowing. He didn't know what to do but felt drawn to seek answers from this prisoner. He came in to be the interrogator with bluster, but now felt tentative. *Has all this trouble made me lose my touch? Is the prisoner that perceptive? Is he a miracle worker? Lord knows we could use one. Lots of people are about to die. The city will be devastated by flood.* The Sheriff knew. Not everyone else did, at least not yet.

No, my poker face is still good. This guy's fishing . . . We may all be fish food if something good doesn't happen quick.

After a long pause the Sheriff responded, "The stories about you. The healings, the reconciliations no one thought possible . . . I don't believe it all, but many folks out there do. They need hope right now. You seem to be the only one who can cross all the groups. I need order, so I could use your help. People consider you a holy man. I won't lie, our situation is dire. Can you do anything to stop what's coming?" He paused again.

"But before I let you help, I need to know who you are and what you want. I need to know quick, or you'll die with all of the rest of us."

"Sheriff, I can't stop what's coming. I serve the Master and have for over two thousand years. You'll find me in the book of Acts. I'm Joseph Barsabbas also known as Justus. I was the one passed over to be an Apostle. My mission is to wander the earth and speak on behalf of my Master until he returns, as he said he would. To bring people back to his teachings that seem to get distorted over time. Anything I do is by his power, not mine. I can assure you he doesn't want to see many lives in this city lost today. Take me to the river, where it leads into the city. Have the city repent and pray. And ask God to have mercy on us. If this is our last hope, we must have faith that he can deliver us from the destruction that's coming. I perceive there's not much time. If this is my time to go, may I do so saving others, for his glory."

"I need to step out for a moment."

He got up and signaled the officer on the other side to let him out.

✤ ✤ ✤

In the observation room, Ward went to Jackie and Karl. "What do ya think?"

"He's delusional, out of his mind. We can't let this guy out and put our support behind him. We'll be a laughingstock. Who knows what he'll say or do?" Karl said.

"Roman, you know I'm a skeptic when it comes to this stuff, and this is one of the most outlandish statements I've ever heard. But I've researched his work here trying to overturn it. I've spent time with him. He's not insane. His story is consistent. I can't reconcile all he says, but he knows a whole lot more than your run of the mill illegal. He speaks thirty languages. He knows how to bring people together, like I've never seen before. It's possible he has something we don't understand. It sounds crazy, but I believe him. He has never volunteered this two-thousand-year-old story. He responds honestly when asked. He doesn't seek notoriety. What other options are there now? If nothing else, perhaps he'll help to keep people calm. They just need to feel like we're doing something to help. They're looking for leadership in time of crisis. When all else is lost, prayer is the only option we have left. I now know, it's a wonderful last resort."

"She's as crazy as he is. I'm getting out of town the best way I know. You can stay here and die if you wish, with your lunatic prophet. Jackie, you're welcome to join me," Karl said extending a hand her way.

Sherriff Ward looked at both of them. There was no decision to make. Karl was running. He couldn't leave the people of Carlisle on their own. "Jackie, are you leaving with Karl?"

"No Roman, I'm with Joseph, to the end."

"Are you cool enough to get him on TV, for those with power left, for a brief interview? We'll get him to the bridge by boat or car whichever can get there now."

Turning to Karl he said, "Karl, I took an oath when I got this job to protect the people here. You can run if you must, but I can't leave them without a leader or a fight. I may not have done it well so far, but I'll finish it now." He repeated, "Run if you must."

Karl motioned his hands at them in a good riddance gesture and left.

Jackie texted Bradley to meet her in front of the building then looked back at Ward, "I can be professional in this storm. I'll get my cameraman. Let's do this fast. We'll do it on the steps of City Hall to add some authority to it."

The Sheriff went into see Joseph with Jackie in tow and un-cuffed him. "Sorry to be hard on you earlier, but I had to know quick."

"Not to worry Sherriff, it's not the first time I've been persecuted by a Roman." Joseph rubbed his wrist.

"Cute." Looking at Jackie he asked, "is he always this funny?"

Looking back at Joseph, he said, "If you are who you say or even part of who you say, we need your help now. Jackie will give you an open mic and then, we'll take you to the bridge. May God have mercy on us!"

"He's a God of Justice and Mercy. If we humble ourselves, he will do amazing things." He reached out and touched Roman on the shoulder. "Take heart Sheriff, all is not lost. He's bigger than the flood," Joseph said.

"Ward, get him a jacket. He doesn't need to be in orange out there," Jackie said.

Ward produced a police jacket fast then was called away by another officer, Joseph removed the orange shirt revealing his white t-shirt. As he put the jacket on, he prepared for the onslaught.

"We need to talk señor, before we appear on camera together. I need some answers."

"I'll go first."

"You'd better." She had the familiar cynicism in her voice laced with venom.

"Jackie, nothing I can say will repair what's happened between us. I can't say how deeply I apologize for taking advantage of you that night. I thought the landslide was the result of my fall. Tony helped to show me the err of my thinking. I ran and got caught. The Master wouldn't let me leave. I had to face the thing I feared the most. My brothers . . . and you. He has kept me here these past few weeks. I couldn't reach out. Lost in depression, a defeated man. But that's no longer the case. Tony helped to restore me to God and the thing I feared was what healed me. I trust you got my letter."

"Oh yes. I got that one. It was a gut punch. You've no idea the names I've called you. They weren't the ones Ward mentioned earlier. You took my heart and left with it. I couldn't breathe for days. I just want to beat you with something. I may yet."

"I understand."

"No! You don't. You're not that good a prophet. You can't possibly understand." She shook her head.

Joseph looked down and swallowed. "What I mean is, I don't blame you for feeling this way."

"You gave me no credit at all. I understand you're a man of God and I sure can't compete with that. But I do care for you more than anyone I've known."

"That's just it, Jackie, you do compete with that. I promised to follow a long time ago and I remain a loyal follower, but if you ask me to leave with you now and not come back, I'll do it. That's what scared me so. No one has ever rivaled him in my life. You stand alone as the one."

Her tone softened. "How do you do that? You hurt me deeper than anyone ever, and I've been hurt a lot, bub. Yet you stand there telling me, you love no one more than me. The acts don't match the words, but how can I be angry at that? I hate you for the hurt you inflict but I love you more. You got me babbling again. I don't know what happens next."

He reached for her, and they embraced. They kissed face, neck, lips.

"Freeze time now. Freeze it right now, Joseph. Don't ever leave me again."

"Are you sure that's what you want?"

"I just want you with me. He brought us together. What about those plans for a future?"

"Jackie if you ask, I'll stay with you here and now."

She pulled away. "I think I got snot on your jacket."

"Tell me what you want." He emphasized the you.

"Well okay, go save the city." She was defeated.

Ward reentered the room and said, "they're going to open the valves and flood the spillway in fifteen minutes, the city will be flooded within twenty. You better do whatever you're going to now."

Joseph turned to Jackie, "Before I go, I now know your part in this. It became clear to me here. You must tell the story. This story. His Story. You've been planning a documentary on the city since the riot. It's been delayed by all the events up to now, but it was his hand holding it off for the perfect time. Now is that time. Tell it. Write it. Record it. Present it to those who'll listen. Don't leave out God's hand moving. Show the alternatives, people need to make their own decisions, but present the truth as well as the facts."

"You trust me to do that."

"It's not me who does. It's him. Listen, you know what I say is true."

"Do I tell about you, too? The whole two-thousand-year-old thing? Won't you be hounded? Chased for miracles? A sideshow? What about the Church's work?"

"Yes, tell it all, but most won't believe that part. They'll think it an artistic device."

She took in a deep breath and looked at him. "You're leaving me again, aren't you? I won't ever see you again, will I?"

"I'll only leave your side now, if you tell me to go."

She started to turn away and then looked back at him. "This sucks. I find the man of my dreams, who gives me the assignment of a lifetime, and I must choose, the job or the man. Oh, on top, if I pick the man, thousands die. No way I can live with that."

"I don't make the rules, Jackie."

"Go, of course, go, Joseph. But take me with you."

"It's too dangerous, you must tell the story. I don't know what happens next to me, but I do know there's more for you. That will become apparent soon."

Joseph looked at her, longing for her. Her glistening hazel eyes shined green and reminded him of the trip to the lake when he first kissed her. She was scared and he couldn't turn away. He longed to comfort her.

"Save the city from this mess," she said. "Come back to me Joseph Barsabbas. Find me!"

"Find another, Jackie. Settle down after all this."

She scoffed at the thought. "Not likely, Joseph. Let's face it, you're a tough act to follow."

"I'll miss you, Jackie. I feel incomplete without you. But since you believe, we can see each other again if nowhere else than on the other side. Shalom, Jackie . . . My protector . . . My Jacqueline."

She knew a calm she had not for several weeks.

✥ ✥ ✥

Ward guided them to the front stairs of City Hall via a back route only his officers could access. Bradley was ready.

The interview had to be brief. Time was critical now. *Dear God, save us now. So many lives at stake, including mine. How can I be calm now? Come on Jackie you're a professional, get it together.*

"Jacqueline Hyatt, WWNS News, reporting live from City Hall. Many of you have heard, there's a flood heading toward Carlisle. We haven't seen one of these for decades. The spillway will release completely causing a massive flow of water. A torrent is coming. Please seek higher ground. All who can, please evacuate the city per the order of Mayor Hamilton. Time is short. The main bridges across the river are damaged or will be swamped, don't go that way. If you can't get out, please seek higher ground in your home and in your neighborhood.

"I have Joseph Barsabbas here with me. Some of you know him better as José, Yosef or Justus. He'll give some further instruction." She moved the mic toward him.

"Many of you know me. I've been in your homes or cooked for you, spoken to your church leaders. We've been a city under siege this past many months, but we've grown together. We no longer see our neighbors only as those who are like us. We see them as people, who may have different color skin, that may live in a different part of the city, that have different habits but who're just as human as we are. All created in God's image. We're all the Imago Dei. For that I thank the Master, whom I serve. We've risen to the challenges of our city so far, but now we face our most dire moment. We can't fill enough sandbags in time. We can't stop this coming flood with the power of men. We must seek our deliverance from El Shaddai, God Almighty. We know the stories of old. He has the power to help us now. I'll go to what's left of the Lumber River Bridge and pray for God to avert these flood waters. I need you all to do what the mayor and Ms. Hyatt instructed. Seek high ground, love your neighbor as yourself and bring them into your home or your office buildings take care of each other as I've been told, you do so well lately. Repent and ask the Master to spare us all from the coming torrent.

"Remember what God requires of you . . . do justice, love mercy and walk humbly with God. We're all in this together one city . . . one people . . . love God with all that you are . . . love one another. As you seek safety pray to God, that he'll have mercy on us. We are sinners, but he is merciful. Once you survive this, seek God with all your heart, soul, mind and strength. May Jesus, our Risen Lord, be glorified. Listen or don't."

He repeated the last part in Spanish and in Arabic.

※ ※ ※

Morgan Robinson got the order from Ed. "There's no time left, open the spillway completely." The next wave would be much larger than the first.

※ ※ ※

Joseph turned to go. Jackie made a signal for Bradley to cut the feed. She reached out to hold Joseph one last time. She kissed him knowing he was going, but hoping he'd stay. "Bring Joseph Barsabbas back to me, please."

"It's not up to me, Jackie."

"I know. I wasn't talking to you."

She watched the officer take Joseph to his cruiser. She prayed again this wouldn't be their last meeting. Then she heard Mitch in her ear saying "they've opened the spillway! And we got dead air. What's going on Hyatt!?" She looked back in the camera and gave Bradley the signal to go live again. While the rain started to pelt her, she realized she was crying. She managed a strong voice over her emotion, took a deep breath and said, "Carlisle, the spillway's been opened. We face our darkest moment but make it a time that we will proudly tell our children and grandchildren about. God is going to do something amazing tonight."

The camera clicked off and she thought, *God is going to do something amazing. Is that the best I could do? It's not about you, Jackie.*

Bradley stepped from behind the camera wiping away his own tears and said, "That was amazing. I loved the tears at the end. Wow."

·

She lingered on the stairs looking in the direction of the cruiser barreling away into the night.

"Ah, Jackie, we need to follow your advice and seek higher ground." He tugged at her arm. They proceeded back into City Hall and headed up to the highest floor toward the roof.

⁂

Officer Jim drove the cruiser.

"I didn't expect to see you, my friend," Joseph said.

"I volunteered. I couldn't miss this." The car was screaming up Riverside Drive, with lights flashing and siren wailing, as fast as it could go, toward the bridge. Rain hit the car hard, due to the speed. Windshield wipers thumped with a frantic rhythm. While they traveled Joseph prayed. Shalom came upon him.

He smiled a crooked smile and said, "It's good to see a friend. Thank you for being here. Once you drop me off, you must go quick. Seek high ground."

"How will you get back?"

"I'm not coming back. I'll miss you my friend. I'll miss them all."

"What if, I won't leave you?"

"You must go. It's not safe to be on the bridge near me."

Jim opened his mouth to argue, but then said nothing.

Jim pulled onto the bridge as far as he could and dropped him off. With the head lights, they could see the washed-out section on the other side now. Jagged steel guardrails and concrete with rebar showing through on both sides. The river raged only a few feet below. "See you on the other side, my friend," Joseph said as he got out.

He walked onto the bridge. In the darkness, he could hear the torrent all around. As his eyes adjusted to what little light there was, he could see it. He stood in the middle and prayed.

"Dear Lord of Justice and Mercy, I pray now for mercy on these people, whom you love. They've come so far from a year ago. They're not perfect, but they've seen you move in their midst. Make them a shining example for your glory. I pray now that you will stop this flood, as only you know how. Spare these many lives, as only you can. Giver of light and life, may you receive the glory. In the name of my Master, the Risen Lord Jesus I pray. Amen."

The wall of water hit the bridge with such force as to bend the steel further. The ground shook under him. He didn't brace himself well enough and he was driven back hard. The force impaled him on the twisted guardrail behind, fracturing his back in several places. He felt the Spirit empower him and raised his left hand. Due to his wounds, he couldn't move his right arm. The water stopped in place and built up, higher and higher. He held his hand high for as long as his strength held out as the water and pressure built. He waved hard to the left as he dropped his arm. The water released up the national park side of the river. It blasted over one hundred feet up the hillside, washing away the trees and rocks and soil, all that was in its path. It flattened the area, like a massive bomb blast. It moved downstream well past Carlisle and other populated areas then washed back into the river basin and out to sea.

Justus knowing the crisis passed peeled himself from the debris that impaled him, leaving behind the entire right side of his police jacket. He staggered a few steps and fell into the abyss in the bridge, into the rushing water below, unable to resist its flow. He hoped he'd open his eyes and see the Master again.

✠ ✠ ✠

From the other side of the river, people couldn't make out what happened. Some had their cameras going, but the light was bad, and the rain didn't help visibility. Jackie and Bradley got to the roof of City Hall, but not in time to set the camera. Bradley got some footage but not what he wanted.

Hurricane Mercedes calmed immediately. The winds died and the rain stopped. The stars came out revealing a partial moon. The flood and the storm now rebuked.

✠ ✠ ✠

No one could explain the water flow or the speed with which the storm passed. Some called it a thermal inversion that caused the storm to dissipate. Some said a new air pressure system entered unwatched, due to everyone's eyes being on the storm. The reality was, no one understood or could explain it. The epicenter seemed to be a washed-out bridge in Carlisle.

Everyone had to acknowledge that this was something beyond the science of the day. Another miracle by the Spirit through Joseph.

Most would call it God's hand moving among us.

Others say it was just human knowledge being too small to explain it.

LISTEN OR DON'T

Whatever it was, the city was spared an epic flood and the rest of the state, a massive storm. For that, all rejoiced. There were many questions to answer but for now it was a time of thanksgiving.

The city now cleansed. A new era for Carlisle began.

A PSALM OF THANKSGIVING ON THE DELIVERY OF THE CITY FROM FLOOD

Your great might saved us this day
Your love and power are eternal

You redirected the mighty waters
Your love and power are eternal

You did it in ways that mystify the learned
Your love and power are eternal

You move among us but we do not see
Your love and power are eternal

We sinned before you by mistreating our neighbors
Your love and power are eternal

We ignored the need that was obvious to see
Your love and power are eternal

We repented after much tribulation
Your love and power are eternal

We received mercy from your mighty hand
Your love and power are eternal

We were in danger of death
Your love and power are eternal

We sought you when nothing else was left
Your love and power are eternal

We watched as you transformed our disaster
Your love and power are eternal

We must seek you now to know even more
Your love and power are eternal

Today we must love you and love one another
Your love and power are eternal

Today we have new life and a new chance to show
Your love and power are eternal

Today we must decide to seek wisdom and follow
Your love and power are eternal

Today we must seek justice but give mercy
Your love and power are eternal

SEPTEMBER

YEAR 2

CHAPTER 35

Officer Jim returned to City Hall to report what he saw. Jackie was there when he got out of the car.

Jim looked at her, then at Ward and the others gathered. "He stopped it. I don't know how, but he stopped it. I drove up a side road to get to high ground and be close by after it hit. I saw the water hit the bridge and then move as if on command. I don't know if my body cam got it, but it stood at attention and then left like a stampede of horses diverted. When I drove back down to the bridge, he was gone. I checked it out. I found a big piece of the police jacket he wore, impaled on debris from the twisted collapse of the bridge. It was covered in water-soaked blood. I brought it back in an evidence bag. He got hurt bad based on all the blood. We should check the river but . . ." He shook his head now, unable to speak.

Jackie's knees buckled and she fell against Bradley. Staring at the group. Bradley tried to comfort and stabilize her. She was limp and shaking. Jim came to her.

"May I have the jacket?" she asked quietly.

"Not now, I'm afraid it's evidence ma'am."

"It's okay." She said in a whisper to herself, out loud. "He's okay. He's lived for two thousand years. It'll take more than a flood to take him out. He's okay. He's okay." She was going to break down. She could feel it. Her head was spinning, she found Bradley's face in the group and said, "take me home, please. Now!"

He supported her as they walked to the news van. Pastor Rich came out of the gathering crowd. He wrapped an arm around her, to help her walk.

He prayed peace over her. "Comfort her, Lord of those who mourn. Bring shalom to this hurting soul."

Bradley and Rich got her to the van. When she got in, the prayer for peace took effect. She didn't understand it all, but she looked at Pastor Rich and said, "It's okay. I'm gonna be alright. Rejoice in what God has done today. Please forgive me, if I don't join you now. He saved the city at the cost of one so dear, but that doesn't change the salvation he brings. Thank you, Pastor."

"We have a counseling ministry to help you through this, if you need us. Call me. It's discrete. Please call."

He closed her door and they drove away. It was a bittersweet moment, but he had to go back to Tony and Father M with the news. The celebration now moved to Hart Park from the coliseum nearby. Rich, Tony and Father M as well as other pastors and church leaders knelt in the middle of the night, in the park, to thank God for his miraculous provision. People fanned out in a circle around the central group. Carlos, Hamsa, Ramone, and Roberta, as well as Officer Jim were there. Susan and Marcus Hamilton stood nearby amazed by what they saw. Even Roman Ward broke a smile at this sight.

As they prayed, they remembered their dear brother Joseph wherever he was and commended him to his Master's care. They prayed he knew how many he saved.

Some of the festival atmosphere returned as music began to play in different parts of the park.

A time to mourn and a time to dance.

EPILOGUE

Jackie did what God led her to do. She preferred hard work to grieving, and decided she'd done enough of that when he left the first time. She completed the documentary. It showed the footage of the various phases of the city—riot, parade, dogs killed, Da Wyz redeemed, bombing, affordable housing at last, gang wars, peace, shootings, success, landslide, death of Paul Stanley and a flood averted by an act of God. All the time speaking of this mysterious man of God who was here to unite the city behind the only power on the planet made to transform the human heart. A God who loves us and changes lives.

The documentary made quite a splash and is still shown in various church settings to encourage. The intent was to give hope in uncertain times. It can still be found on social media posts and re-posts. The one that got the most views was the seven-minute version. The full story lasted almost sixty minutes.

After a few months she moved back to the Charlotte suburb, with her mother, to care for her in her last months. They needed each other now. She stopped doing the news but started reporting weather again at a local cable station. She needed a regular schedule now that was less physically demanding.

Months after these events the city built a monument to St. Joseph of Carlisle on the hilltop where the slide occurred and around it, they placed multifamily housing including affordable housing. Sponsored by many of the Church, with all its diverse manifestations, in the city.

He wasn't beatified by the Catholic Church with sainthood, but Carlisle didn't bother to wait. They regarded him as their saint.

The mayor would announce a run for Governor.

Ward abandoned his political dreams and stayed on as Sheriff, then became the first police chief of Carlisle, now that the city was growing again.

Ramone never did start the catering business, but thanks to all of Carlos' great work as head chef, they founded a very successful restaurant business with several sprinkled around the city.

Deion was forced to close and sell the river barge business and concentrate on the less legal activities of the Wharf in a much smaller Biz.

Officer Jim turned down many promotions to stay in the Wharf. He liked being on the front lines of the fight. He constantly found ways to thwart Deion, until he died on the job several years later. He inspired many in the Wharf to go into law enforcement.

The gangs of Villa Maya continued in place despite all the progress, but they were much smaller and more confined.

Hamsa, after he founded a Youth for Jesus movement in New Rojava, went to seminary and then to work on the mission field in the middle east, working with those who suffered under injustice there. He married Renata Vega who could speak so vividly of the presence of Christ.

Amena went on to marry one of the newcomers to New Rojava who wanted her to stay at home. She told him 'no' and went on to be the head nurse in the ED at University Hospital. She didn't have any other children.

Sami died of a stroke a couple of years after these events.

Dijlin went to CSU on scholarship to study information technology. She stayed in New Rojava despite making enough to move out. She joined the leadership of the village.

Rima became the prominent leader of the village and was a great interface to the rest of Carlisle. She became a believer thanks to Hamsa, but kept it secret for many years.

With the ongoing success of Carafe Homes, Reggie went on to run for Mayor of Carlisle after Marcus left. Reggie paid for D'Andre to take auto mechanics courses at the community college and D launched a great career with a luxury car dealership.

Father M decided to follow the rigors of the Society of Jesus and left for the mission field in South America.

Pastor Rich stayed in Carlisle and continued to lead efforts to unite the Church there.

Reverend Tony received a promotion within the AME Zion Church and became an honored member of the Board of Bishops. He was asked to speak all over the country about church unity and what happened in Carlisle.

Roberta continued to meet with the ladies outside her home, ministering there and keeping gang activity at bay. It became a model in many cities all over the country.

✣ ✣ ✣

A cook with no tattoos and a knack for making everything taste better watched on the local cable station while a very pregnant Jackie did the weather. He was on break after the breakfast rush sitting in a booth at the café where he worked. She wore a white flowered dress that turned light gray at the shoulder. He remembered the steel blue workout gear from the last ride they took together. The promise of seeing her again is what got him through all the rigorous treatment and physical therapy he'd endured over these months. He thought of how excited Adam must've been to see Eve for the first time. At last, he found her.

Though the memories didn't all come back, he remembered that a Norwegian freighter, on its way to ports in the Caribbean, found him floating on debris in the shipping lane along the coast several days after the flood. He was in a coma for weeks. From what others told him, they dropped him at a hospital in San Juan. After several surgeries and weeks of physical therapy, he learned to walk again but still needed a cane to get around.

After lunch he gave his notice to the café owner and resolved to go to the station. The time had come for their next adventure to begin. Time to let Jackie know the other reason she was so special.

⁂

He came into the station's reception area and asked for her. Officer Freeman at front desk security tried to deter him thinking him a misguided fan. Despite her obvious maternity, Jackie still had many male fans that wanted to meet her in person.

He continued to press. "She's an old friend. I just want to say hello. Let her know Joseph is here. If she declines to meet me, I'll leave."

With an I'm-going-to-get-in-trouble look on her face, the officer dialed the phone, "Yes Ms. Hyatt, there's a gentleman here at reception. He claims to be an old friend of yours from Carlisle. Says his name is Joseph . . . Ms. Hyatt, are you there? Hello . . . ?"

She burst through the security door and almost overwhelmed him, unaware he wasn't stable on his feet. They embraced and kissed. Then she caught herself and said, "I'm very glad to see you."

"I was afraid you wouldn't want to see me after all this time."

She composed herself and said, "Wait, this isn't the place. Wait here for a few minutes. I'll take the rest of the day off. Get my things, we can go for a walk or a ride."

Nodding to the cane he said, "A ride would be better for me. But I'll go wherever you like."

"Meet me out front in ten minutes. Joseph, there's so much to tell."

As she left and while Joseph waited, Officer Freeman pulled up Jackie's documentary on social media. She was a young black girl in a crisp white security blouse. She fast forwarded through some and when she finished, she said. "Are you the Joseph in her documentary? I thought he died at the end."

"No Helen, I'm not dead. It could be me. But, if you have to ask, you weren't watching what just happened." He smiled wide.

"How did you know my name was Helen."

"I serve the Master who knows all things. He knows your name too. Your father, Hector, gave it to you. The Spirit just told me."

"My father passed away not long ago. He was a believer. Said I was the most beautiful thing he'd ever seen so he named me after Helen of Troy," she smiled.

"Now he sees the Master face to face. Miss him but mourn him no more. Rejoice with him, he is with the Father."

She looked away and paused. "Thank you, Joseph. I believe too."

"May you be blessed and know peace. Helen of the freed men."

Jackie drove up and took him to local coffee shop. She recounted her journey since the flood. "I got counseling with Carlisle Church. That wasn't easy for me, but they helped me through the post abortive process which I suppressed for so many years. I have healing at last. They helped me deal with the loss of you, the father of my children." She rubbed her belly gently.

"Rich wasn't sure if you survived. But I realized why it had to end with you leaving when I finished the documentary. There must be doubt so no one would come seeking you after the story came out. They needed to seek the Master, not the student."

"The Kol Yahweh revealed that to you, I see."

"So, where have you been?"

"The force of the wave broke my back in several places and punctured my right lung. Now I have matching scars from Carlisle on each side." He laughed. "I fell into the river and was taken out to sea. Not sure how but I ended up floating on debris into the shipping lanes. I seem to remember gentle hands guiding me to the debris, but it could've been a dream. I convalesced in San Juan. I left the Carlisle jail so quickly, I had no ID, no phone. It was a long, hard road back. Much worse than being shot. It drew me closer to the Master, but it was also the thought of you that got me through. I had to get better as fast as I could to seek you out. Before you found someone else."

He leaned across the table and kissed her. They stood and embraced. "We should go home," she said.

"Not yet, take me the church where you were saved. I have a wonderful idea, so we don't get in trouble again."

They went to the little Baptist church and visited her mother's grave in the cemetery nearby while the minister prepared. They were married that very day.

"When I was a little girl, I always saw myself getting married in this church. You have a way of making my dreams come true," she said, rubbing her belly again.

"Good thing you wore that white dress today."

"White and gray, pure white might've been a touch hypocritical in my condition."

He laughed outload.

"You can't leave me now. You're stuck with me. I go where you go and stay where you stay. Besides you made an honest woman out of me and I, an honest man out of you. You're legal now. Married to a US citizen."

As they drove up to her new patio home, Joseph looked at her and just stared. He could admire her legs now with abandon. "It was a long journey back, Jackie. I want to believe you're not a dream. But then again, you are a dream."

"You want me to get snot on your shirt again? I can do it. Believe me."

"No, I want you to be as happy as I am. Aren't you glad we didn't freeze time?"

They got out of the car with their respective struggles.

"I would sweep you off your feet again and carry you across the threshold, but things being the way they are, best if we just hold hands while we enter. Thank you for waiting for me. The thought of spending a lifetime with you brought me back from the brink."

"I knew you would come back to me. He told me so. Thank you, Lord, for this man and his love, for bringing him home."

❊❊❊

As they lay in bed that night. Jackie asleep with her head on his chest. He could smell the jasmine in her hair. He felt a gentle kick on his side. Then another. She adjusted in her sleep. He remembered the Psalm. *For you formed my inward parts; you knitted me together in my mother's womb. I praise you for I am fearfully and wonderfully made.*

He remembered the vision from two years ago: The dark-haired lady—Jackie; the three partial men all of a different color—Tony, Rich and Father Menendez; the well-dressed black man—Jeremiah Michaels; the strangers—Amena, Sami, Dijlin, Rima, Hamsa; the blood—all the gang wars; the river—flood; the rain and the hills—landslides. He also remembered the promise—*I know the plans I have for you . . . plans to give you a hope and a future.* Words Jackie repeated that ministered to both of them before the most difficult part of their story. He praised God for his provision. For the impact on his life of these the Master loved so. For the souls of so many of the lifetimes he was blessed to touch and be touched by. He was content now to be in the arms of his love with his unborn children resting inside her. He went to sleep praising the Master.

A few weeks later Jacqueline Barsabbas welcomed her twins into the world. They went full term. A boy and a girl. She and Joseph named them Justus and Mercedes.

JUSTICE AND MERCY

They decided to move to a small rural area of an island nation to raise their children until they were of age. They needed to ready the children for their calling. The children of Joseph have very long-life spans. Before they were done, they would play a major role in the nation of Israel during the end time. *Perhaps this will be my last lifetime.*

ACKNOWLEDGMENTS

As I stated in my Acknowledgement section of *Carlisle Divided*, this journey started in 2016 as I found myself asking God what to do from here. A man in his fifties looking for a new challenge. Looking for where God wanted to use me over the next many years. A word of warning to us all. Don't ask God that question unless you want to be challenged way outside of your own self-reliance.

After many hours spent in prayer over weeks and months, listening for the Spirit to guide, the message finally came. It sounded crazy to an independent man with no formal writing training and little fiction writing experience.

"Write a Story." That was all He gave me to start with. I always enjoyed reading and did a lot of non-fiction writing for my business career. There is power in story to explain tough concepts to others. However, I wasn't qualified to write fiction. The Justus and Mercy journey began there.

I must repeat hearty thanks to those who helped in those early days: Angela Haigler taught me creative writing in her classes at our local community college. Maureen Ryan Griffin, who reviewed my early work and gave me hard but much needed advice. Her review and critique of the poetry in this novel was invaluable. The ministry team at my home church of Carmel Baptist. The challenges issued by Pastor Alex Kennedy, help along the way from Jeremy Amick and David Bass. The many gifted writers and speakers I've met and been guided by through the Blue Ridge Mountain Christian Writers' Conference over the years. Various consultants like missionary Jackson Landham who give wonderful insight into the Syrian Kurds section of the novel. An old friend who happened to be a power company engineer, Ed Haack also gave me great ideas on the dam issues and flood section of the book.

My brothers Ray Russell and Richard Russell also helped and encouraged me as well. Without Ray, I doubt this would have made it to publication.

My lovely bride of 40 years, Janie, agreed to read the story and give me her thoughts. She has a great copy editor's eye and did her best to get through some very rough drafts not to mention a temperamental writer.

Using connections and content from the Blue Ridge Conference and at Janie's continued encouragement, I found an editor, Karen Saari whose insights changed the story and made it a book. She challenged in ways no one had to that point and made the story so much better throughout 2020. She also showed me that this story was two novels, not one.

During the years leading up to the novels, the Lord led me to spend a lot of time reading Christian non-fiction as well. Dating back to the early church writings of St. Augustine, St. Francis of Assisi, Brother Lawrence and St. John of the Cross. He continued to guide me through the Protestant writing of the early church by Martin Luther, John Calvin, John Wesley. The writings of modern-day authors are equally insightful, the wisdom shared by CS Lewis, Dietrich Bonhoeffer, RC Sproul, Richard Foster, Timothy Keller, Gregory Boyle and Richard Stearns. I hope that you see their influence throughout the story. I owe a special debt to Lewis, Bonhoeffer, Foster, and Boyle for the impact they had.

Finally, after many rejected book proposals during 2021, it was time to look at partnership publishing. There were many options, but I felt led to EA BooksPublishing, having enjoyed the lectures of Cheri Cowell from the Blue Ridge Conference. I appreciate Rebecca Ford who shepherded and encouraged me throughout the EA process and was blessed by the cover design and other work of Robin Black.

In the end, it was God's prompting that led me to write this. If you enjoyed it give Him the honor; if not, it's all my fault.

> To God, the Father
> Jesus, the Son
> and the Holy Spirit
> three in one
> be the glory for this.

He asked that I write a story and between these two novels, the story is now complete. Or is it? Perhaps he will lead me to write another adventure for Joseph Barsabbas in the future.

Made in the USA
Monee, IL
12 June 2023

35558881R00173